"Survival of the fittest," Mildred stated

"What do you mean?" Ryan asked.

"There's something called the principle of natural selection that says the strongest survive, and that a species continues to evolve through natural and sexual selection. The baron's contest will ensure that the strongest male survives to breed with the strongest female."

Ryan nodded, then got up from the table to sign up for the contest. Brody stood, as well.

"Where are you going?" the one-eyed man asked.

Brody put a hand on Ryan's shoulder. "There'll be at least a dozen men in that ring, all wanting to chill you. If you're going to make a break out of here, you're going to have to be alive to do it. You'll need someone to watch your back, and that's going to be me."

"Thanks, Brody. You're a good man."

"You're a good man, too, Ryan. Let's just hope for the sake of your woman that you're also the best."

**Other titles in the
Deathlands saga:**

JAMES AXLER

DEATH LANDS®

Skydark Spawn

A GOLD EAGLE BOOK FROM

WORLDWIDE®

TORONTO • NEW YORK • LONDON
AMSTERDAM • PARIS • SYDNEY • HAMBURG
STOCKHOLM • ATHENS • TOKYO • MILAN
MADRID • WARSAW • BUDAPEST • AUCKLAND

First edition March 2003

ISBN 0-373-62571-5

SKYDARK SPAWN

It seems most strange that men should fear;
Seeing that death, a necessary end
Will come when it will come.
　　　　　　—William Shakespeare
　　　　　　Julius Caesar

THE DEATHLANDS SAGA

This world is their legacy, a world born in the violent nuclear spasm of 2001 that was the bitter outcome of a struggle for global dominance.

There is no real escape from this shockscape where life always hangs in the balance, vulnerable to newly demonic nature, barbarism, lawlessness.

But they are the warrior survivalists, and they endure—in the way of the lion, the hawk and the tiger, true to nature's heart despite its ruination.

Ryan Cawdor: The privileged son of an East Coast baron. Acquainted with betrayal from a tender age, he is a master of the hard realities.

Krysty Wroth: Harmony ville's own Titian-haired beauty, a woman with the strength of tempered steel. Her premonitions and Gaia powers have been fostered by her Mother Sonja.

J. B. Dix, the Armorer: Weapons master and Ryan's close ally, he, too, honed his skills traversing the Deathlands with the legendary Trader.

Doctor Theophilus Tanner: Torn from his family and a gentler life in 1896, Doc has been thrown into a future he couldn't have imagined.

Dr. Mildred Wyeth: Her father was killed by the Ku Klux Klan, but her fate is not much lighter. Restored from predark cryogenic suspension, she brings twentieth-century healing skills to a nightmare.

Jak Lauren: A true child of the wastelands, reared on adversity, loss and danger, the albino teenager is a fierce fighter and loyal friend.

Dean Cawdor: Ryan's young son by Sharona accepts the only world he knows, and yet he is the seedling bearing the promise of tomorrow.

In a world where all was lost, they are humanity's last hope....

Chapter One

Ryan Cawdor opened his eye, then closed it quickly as a blinding jolt of pain lanced through his skull. He half rose to his feet, then sank back to the floor, dizzy. Bastard jumps always took a toll.

The mat-trans jump was over, and, as usual, he and his companions lay on the floor of the chamber, trying to gather their wits and keep the remnants of their last meal in their stomachs.

After a few minutes, Ryan tried opening his eye again. The pain was still there, but had now settled into a dull throb that he could handle.

"My word," Doc Tanner said, removing his swallow's-eye kerchief from a pocket of his frock coat and wiping away a trickle of blood that had seeped from his nose, "it never ceases to amaze me how utterly incapacitating these jaunts of ours can be."

"Still able talk," Jak Lauren commented, lifting his right hand and moving his fingers in a motion meant to simulate Doc's flapping gums. Jak hadn't fared as well. The front of the young albino's tan T-shirt was stained with vomit that had leaked out the corners of his mouth. He tried to clean himself up with a few wipes of his sleeve, but all that did was spread the mess around.

Ryan's son, Dean, had fared better than the others. He looked a bit dizzy, but was already able to stand. J. B. Dix sat with his back against one of the chamber's walls. He'd lifted his head and had his eyes tightly closed as if he were in pain. He was struggling to catch his breath.

"You all right, J.B.?" asked Ryan.

The Armorer shook his head as he removed his wire-rimmed glasses from his shirt pocket and put them on. "Had a nightmare. I was alone in a forest somewhere. As I walked along a path, I was confronted by a huge mutie."

"Chill it?" Jak asked.

"No, that's the thing. It approached me and I leveled my blaster and squeezed the trigger...but the scattergun didn't fire. I tried it again and again, but nothing. The creature kept coming, but the blaster wouldn't fire. Dark night! Didn't know what was wrong with it because I'd just finished stripping and cleaning it in my dream. So there I was, pointing a dead blaster at a mutie just itching to chill me."

"And did it?" Mildred Wyeth asked.

"Tore me to pieces with a set of talons as long and sharp as my Tekna. And I couldn't even wake up. Hurt like hell."

Ryan looked at Mildred, wondering if the dream meant anything.

"Performance anxiety," Mildred stated.

"What? I don't have any problems with that."

"No, I don't mean sexual performance, John," Mildred chided. "Our lives often depend on your knowledge. My guess is that lurking somewhere in your subconscious you have a fear that at some point, when it matters most, you'll let one of us down.''

''But I was the one who was chilled.''

''Yeah, and that's probably the way you'd want it to happen if it ever did.''

''Not worry,'' Jak said, putting a hand on J.B.'s shoulder. ''Not let us down.''

''Thanks.''

The few moments Mildred had spent analyzing J.B.'s dream had done wonders to revitalize the group. Krysty Wroth was showing signs of coming around, and the rest of the companions were on their feet but still pretty groggy.

''I suspect,'' Doc said, tapping the silver lion's-head handle of his swordstick against the walls of the chamber, ''that this mat-trans is not constructed of armaglass as is customary.''

Ryan raised his arm and pounded the butt of his SIG-Sauer against one of the dark charcoal-gray walls. Instead of the familiar tink of reinforced glass, his ears were met with the sound of a dull, hard thud. ''Concrete,'' he stated.

''Not only that, but look at the LD button,'' J.B. suggested.

Ryan scanned the walls, realizing that this chamber wasn't equipped with a Last Destination button. ''There is no button,'' he said.

''What does that mean?'' Mildred asked.

''Not sure,'' Ryan replied.

''Maybe it's a one-way chamber,'' J.B. opined.

"What would you need one of those for?" Mildred asked.

"Who knows?" J.B. answered. "It's just a thought."

"The motivations of your predark government have baffled me at the best of times," Doc stated. "Add another puzzle to the file for future reference."

Ryan agreed with Doc. Whatever the reason behind this installation's construction, it would be made clear to them soon enough.

"At least we're alive," Krysty stated.

Ryan turned and saw that Krysty was stirring. Her sentient hair had unfurled and was now stretching to its full length, falling over her shoulders like red waves. "How are you, lover?"

"I've had worse jumps," she answered. "Any idea where we might have ended up?"

Ryan shook his head. It was possible to get an idea of the chamber's location by the color of its armaglass walls, but they'd never been in this gateway before.

"I'll take a reading with my sextant when we get outside," J.B. said. "Hopefully the skies will be clear."

Ryan sat down with his back up against one of the room's six walls. Now that he knew his companions were all right, he decided to give himself some time to recover from the jump. This one had been easier than most, but he still had a fireblasted headache.

FIFTEEN MINUTES PASSED before the group had recovered and Ryan could risk opening the chamber door.

As they'd learned over time, the friends needed to be on triple alert when entering a redoubt, never knowing who or what lay beyond the door. Anyone or anything could have discovered a break in the solid concrete walls and found a way inside.

"Triple red, people," Ryan said, putting his hand on the door. He looked around the group, making sure that each of his friends was prepared for whatever might be out there. Krysty had her Smith & Wesson .38 at the ready, while Doc clutched his LeMat blaster. Mildred had her Czech-built target revolver in her right hand, bracing her right arm at the wrist with her left hand to steady it. J.B. had opted for his scattergun, despite its worrisome malfunction in his dream. Dean leveled his Browning Hi-Power and Jak brought up the rear with his Colt Python. Ryan had his SIG-Sauer ready, but since he was opening the door, it was unlikely he'd be the one taking the first shot in the event of trouble.

"Ready?" Ryan asked one last time.

Everyone nodded.

He opened the door to an empty room.

After a few moments of tension, the companions relaxed somewhat. The room was small and completely bare. The walls were made of cinder blocks, and the floor and ceiling had been constructed of poured concrete. When the door had opened, a single, naked bulb close to the high ceiling switched on, casting a dim light into the room. The room's main feature was a concrete staircase that led almost straight up thirty or more feet before terminating at a landing that was about four feet directly below a set of large doors. The doors appeared to serve as a hatchway.

"What do you make of that?" Ryan asked.

"Strange," Jak commented.

There was no arguing with Jak's logic. The entrance to the redoubt was like nothing Ryan had seen before.

"Hey, there isn't even a handle on the outside of the chamber," Krysty said.

Ryan turned to take another look at the chamber and saw that what Krysty had said was true. If they shut the door they wouldn't be able to use the chamber again.

"Looks like this really is a one-way chamber," J.B. said. "And that—" he gestured to the stairway "—looks like the only way out."

"Well, if that's the only way out, we should quit standing around and find out where it goes," Mildred suggested.

Without another word Ryan headed up the stairs toward the landing. When he reached it he had to crouch to avoid hitting his head on the doors above them. He signaled the others to join him.

"What now?" Krysty asked as the rest of the group reached the landing. Only Dean was able to stand up straight, but even he had to duck his head a bit to avoid hitting it against the heavy overhead doors.

Ryan pushed his right forearm against one of the doors. It didn't budge. For the second try he put away his SIG-Sauer and pushed against the door with both arms. This time the door moved slightly.

"J.B. and Jak, one on either side of me," Ryan said.

The Armorer and the albino took up positions to Ryan's left and right and got ready to push on the door. The rest of the group readied their blasters.

"On three," Ryan said. "One, two…"

On three they all pushed together. The door moved, and they could hear the metal hinges cracking, an understandable protest considering the hinges likely hadn't moved in close to a century.

"Again," Ryan urged.

Once more the three men pushed against the metal door. At last it began to move, allowing dirt, dust and daylight to spill down through the long crack that had opened up above them. They continued to push, but now Doc had joined them, giving just the little extra force they needed to get the door fully open.

The portal became lighter and lighter, then flopped over like a top hatch on a war wag. With the first door opened, they set to work on the second. It moved more easily than the first, and they soon found themselves standing at the edge of a long-abandoned farmer's field, with nothing around them but knee-high grass, high stands of rocks and clumps of weeds covering acres of rolling land in every direction.

Ryan and the others took a look around. A stand of trees grew some fifty yards to their left, but mostly they saw only wide-open spaces. Farther on, perhaps a mile or two away, there were more wooded areas, and then more farmland.

"Any idea where we are now?" Krysty asked.

J.B. lowered his glasses. "Middle of nowhere'd be my guess."

Ryan climbed up and out of the hole in the ground and onto the field. He immediately turned back to help lift out the others. In minutes they were all standing on firm ground.

"Close it up," the one-eyed man ordered, putting a hand under the edge of one of the doors. With J.B.'s help, he lifted the door and let it fall. He hadn't intended for it to make such a loud noise as it closed, but without anyone on the landing to ease the door into place, the noise couldn't be helped. Jak and Doc lifted the second door and let it down on top of the first. It closed with a slightly smaller bang, but still one loud enough to attract attention.

With the doors closed, the exit to the gateway was nearly invisible. The ground was disturbed slightly, but after a few sweeps of their feet and hands, there was no evidence of anything unusual lying just beneath the surface of the field.

"Well, it's definitely one-way," J.B. said.

"Mebbe for escape," Jak offered.

An escape hatch was definitely a possibility. That seemed to fit with the sparseness of the installation's construction and outfitting. Anyone coming through this gateway was on a one-way trip, but why would such an installation be needed, and why here? Both questions, like all the others, Ryan knew, would be answered in time.

"By the Three Kennedys!" Doc thundered.

Ryan turned in time to see Doc's feet being pulled out from under him by a strange mutie that had apparently crawled through the grass toward them. It was crouched low to the ground and seemed to move on all fours, like a spider. It was gnawing on Doc's leg, trying to tear away the material of his pants in order to get at the pale white flesh that lay beneath.

Before the other members of the group could raise their weapons, Ryan had leveled his blaster and squeezed off a single shot that caught the mutie in the shoulder. The impact of the blast rolled the mutie away from Doc's leg. As the one-eyed man prepared to get off a second shot at the mutie's skull, a blaster roared on his right.

A neat black hole appeared in the middle of the mutant's forehead, and a baseball-sized mass of gray matter and gore exploded out the back of the creature's skull, taking its miserable life along with it.

Ryan turned and saw Mildred lower her blaster.

A little embarrassed by being taken unawares, Doc got to his feet, unsheathed his sword and was about to run the mutie through when Jak's voice stopped him.

"More."

Ryan looked across the field toward the nearby stand of trees and could see that there were at least half a dozen more of the hungry muties ambling toward them. They were all bone thin, filthy dirty and naked except for a flap of material around their midsections. They moved low to the ground, like spiders, hidden by the grass, but betrayed by it as their bodies pushed the tall grass under and left a trail across the field that any scout could follow.

"Hold your fire!" Ryan ordered. He had his blaster leveled, but he wasn't sure that the muties were going to try what the first one had. And as he watched, his instincts turned out to be right. Instead of attacking the members of the group, the half-dozen muties crawled up to their dead brother and immediately set into its body with their teeth and hands. In minutes they were feeding wildly on the carcass, ripping into its flesh and muscles with all the savagery of a pack of starving wolves.

"Cannies," Ryan muttered.

"And crazed ones to boot," Mildred offered.

"Looks like they'll be busy for a while," Ryan said.

"So which way do we go?" J.B. asked.

"Feel anything, lover?" Ryan asked Krysty.

The fiery-headed woman closed her eyes and concentrated for a moment, trying to see if she could sense any nearby danger. "Can't feel anything at all."

"Okay, then, let's head up that rise to get the lay of the land. I'll take point, then Krysty, Jak, Dean, Doc and Mildred. J.B., you cover the rear. Okay, people, let's go."

Chapter Two

There was fear in her eyes, and Baron Franz Fox liked it. She was terrified of him, afraid of what he might do to her or what he might give others permission to do to her.

"It's been five months since your last," Baron Fox said softly. It was a statement, but both the baron and the woman knew it was intended more as a question. He placed his hands together, the fingertips pressing against each other. "Well, I'm waiting."

The woman was in her early forties. She was heavy-set, especially in her hips, and her breasts sagged, which was to be expected after giving birth to five children in the past forty-eight months. She was dressed in a thin white T-shirt that left her big dark nipples clearly visible through the worn cotton fabric. She also wore a pair of old denim shorts and pair of fairly new black Western boots, her reward for delivering a set of twins a couple of terms back. The outfit would have looked good on a woman half her age, but as it was, the clothes looked a lot like the woman wearing them—old, tired and worn-out.

"I don't know what's wrong," she said, her voice a little breathless and tinged with fear. "I've been rutting almost every night."

''With who?'' the baron asked, walking the length of his office before turning to pace back across the same track of plush red shag. His burgundy bedroom slippers had worn a path in the carpet from years of pacing. When she didn't answer his question, he came to a stop in front of her and put a hand under her chin. He lifted her head up so that she would have to look him in the eyes when she answered the question. ''With who?''

''Jon,'' she replied. ''Jonathan Wyndam.''

''The entire time?''

She tried to nod, but the baron held her head firmly in place.

''Has he sired with anyone else in the past five months?'' Fox asked his number-one man, Norman Bauer, who was standing quietly off to the side, observing. Bauer was an accountant by trade, and his ability to handle numbers and other statistics had made him invaluable in the successful operation of Fox Farm.

Bauer opened his ledger, leafed back and forth until he came to the page listing Jonathan Wyndam's breeding history. ''According to the ledger,'' Bauer said, ''Wyndam's sired fifteen in the past two years—all norms—but none in the past five months. Either Wyndam has gone sterile, or the bitch is barren.''

In a flash, Fox pulled the riding crop from a specially designed pocket of his bathrobe and slashed the kneeling woman across the face. ''You bitch!'' he screamed. ''When you knew you weren't conceiving, why didn't you turn Wyndam back to stud?''

An angry red welt appeared on the woman's left cheek, and beads of blood were beginning to well up through the reddened skin. "He didn't want—"

"Don't fuck with me!" the baron roared, striking her again with the crop, this time with a backhand stroke that put a matching red line on her right cheek.

She shook her head. Tears leaked from the corners of her eyes, similar tears of blood leaving red streaks down her cheeks. "He didn't want to go. He wanted to stay with me. He—"

Fox raised his hand again. "Don't even think of saying it."

"—loves me," she said, her face flush with anger. "He loves me and I love—"

Fox didn't let her finish. He struck her again and again with the riding crop about the head, neck and shoulders, much harder than before. Her T-shirt shredded and fell from her shoulders, exposing her breasts. Fox slashed at them, too, putting a series of X-like gashes across her chest.

"I don't want to hear talk like that...ever!" Fox bellowed. He was in the business of making and trading slaves, of selling babies and love wasn't allowed. Love destroyed everything, as evidenced by this over-the-hill bitch's romantic notion of living happily ever after. She'd figured that if she didn't get heavy she'd be able to spend more nights with Wyndam. She was right, of course, but the arrangement could never last long. At her age, five months without getting heavy and her days as a breeder were over. Same for Wyndam. Five months without siring a child, and he'd be on the next slave convoy out of Fox Farm. Then it would be six months to a year working in some mill or refinery and by then it would be time to board the last train west. And all for some triple-stupe notion like love.

The woman lay in a crumpled heap at the baron's feet. He turned to Bauer, who had stood by impassively while Fox had administered the beating. "Take her to the sec men's lounge. Tell them they can do what they like with her until the next convoy moves out."

Bauer nodded. "Any restrictions?"

Fox shook his head. "No, just that if anyone chills her they'll have to answer to me."

"And what about Wyndam?"

"Put him in the sec cell overlooking the lounge. Let him watch what happens to lovers on Fox Farm."

Bauer gave a little smile. "And after she moves out?"

"Give him a beating, then put him back in circulation. But keep an eye on him. He might get difficult."

Bauer went to the door and summoned a pair of sec men into the room. "Take her to the lounge. And don't chill her."

"All right."

"And while you're having fun with her, find Jon Wyndam and put him in a cell with a view of the lounge so he gets a good look of his sweetheart in action."

"Lovers?" the first sec man asked.

Bauer nodded.

"Stupe bastards," the sec man muttered as he dragged the former breeder out of the office.

When they'd left, Baron Fox adjusted his bathrobe, retied the sash around his waist and sat behind the large oak desk in the center of his office. To his right was a foot-high pile of predark hard-core skin mags that specialized in fetishes, everything from lingerie and leather to bondage and domination. He pulled a mag off the top of the pile and opened it to a familiar pictorial in which a dark-haired woman dressed in a black corselette and stockings had her wrists bound behind her back with a heavy-gauge rope. In some of the pictures she was being whipped by a cat-o'-nine-tails. But while Fox found that exciting enough on its own, it was the spread's final six photos that really aroused his curiosity. In each of the photos the woman was covered in blue-and-red wax, as if a burning candle had been held over her and allowed to leak hot wax onto her breasts, thighs and buttocks. Fox had wanted to duplicate the scene for months now, but quality candles were as difficult to find as working blasters, especially colored candles. He'd traded his human stock for a decent stockpile of weapons of all types, and was finally confident he had enough firepower to protect his operation from any outside attack. So maybe on the next trade mission to the east he might try to cut a deal for a few colored candles. If not, he could always use molten lead, which, as he thought about it, might even be more interesting than wax.

He replaced the magazine on top of the pile, then looked over at Norman Bauer, who was waiting patiently to be spoken to or dismissed. "What else do you have for me?"

Bauer turned the page of his ledger, but before he could speak, Grundwold, the sec chief, came in through the open door. The man was dressed in dark blue fatigues that were in good condition, and two rows of 12-gauge shells in bandoliers crisscrossed his chest. A Mossberg Persuader 500 shotgun rested in a holster belted to his thigh. It looked to be in remarkable condition.

"What is it?" Fox asked, knowing it would have to be urgent for Grundwold to walk in on him unannounced.

"A scout team spotted a group of seven outlanders approaching from the north, mebbe heading toward the falls," Grundwold reported.

"Are they armed?"

Grundwold nodded. "Each has a blaster, mebbe more." He paused a moment, then added, "They look like they know how to use them, too."

"Women?"

"Two. One black, one white."

Fox inhaled a deep breath and looked up at the ceiling as he wondered what the best course of action might be. From the sec chief's report, it sounded as if these outlanders might be better left alone. He'd learned from experience that there was a big difference between scooping up families riding in convoys headed to the eastern villes and taking on seasoned outlanders who had learned to chill attackers on sight. While he'd gained plenty of farmworkers ambushing wag trains, he'd also lost a lot of good sec men to outlanders who preferred death over enslavement.

"Have them followed," he said. "If there's an opportunity to take the women, do it." He waved his hand in the air. "Otherwise, let them go."

"Yes, sir!" Grundwold turned on his heel and left the office.

"Two new women," Bauer said, looking over his ledger and likely figuring out what that might do to the farm's monthly output of offspring.

"Yes," Fox said, picking up the mag once more and opening it up to his favorite spread. "They'll make a nice addition to our breeding stock."

Chapter Three

When they reached the top of the rise, Ryan used the ancient brass telescope he'd found a while back and spotted a ville some distance to the south. There were several tall buildings, and one strange structure looked as if a wag wheel cover had been impaled on a panga.

"Mildred," Ryan said, "do you recognize that?"

Mildred Wyeth stood by Ryan's side. "Looks familiar, but a lot of villes had towers like that."

"Okay. We'll head for it. Stay alert, people," Ryan said.

The companions moved on, and at the bottom of the rise they came across a predark road overgrown with weeds. It was still tough going, but easier than walking through dead forests and across weed-covered fields. After a half hour on the road, they came upon fields of flatland dotted with dead trees whose stumps were lined up in neat rows.

"Predark farmland?" Krysty queried as they approached the skeleton of a large glass house that had only a few panes, out of what were once hundreds and hundreds, still unbroken.

"That'd be my guess," Ryan agreed.

"Orchards," Doc said. "Apples and pears, it looks like."

"Acres and acres of prime farmland poisoned by rad dust, and chemical fallout, skydark, nuclear junk...." J.B. said.

"And who knows what else?" Mildred commented.

"The irony is rather precious, isn't it?" Doc said.

"How mean?" Jak asked.

"These were once magnificent farms, with fresh food as far as the eye could see...but now the muties here think my old and somewhat withered body is a gourmet meal."

Jak chuckled, but stopped abruptly when there was movement in the ruin of the glass house to their right. The friends stopped in their tracks, all eyes on the glass house looking for another glint of light or shift of shadows.

"J.B., Krysty and Doc, right side. Mildred, Dean and Jak with me. And mind the cross fire."

Without another word the companions neatly split into two groups and approached the glass house from each side. As Ryan neared, he was able to see through the jagged teeth of the broken panes to the inside of the glass house. Tall green vines grew inside, stretching from the ground to the ceiling, twisting and tangling about as if each vine were trying to choke off the other. Ryan decided that there was nothing else living inside the glass house and what he'd seen was simply the wind twisting its way through the vines. But then he noticed several leaves twitch as if something were slowly moving through the vegetation—close to the ground.

Ryan followed the movement of the vines with his

eye, waiting patiently for whatever it was to cross a small clearing to his left. Judging by the thing's speed, it would be in the open in about two seconds and would be exposed for about half that time. Ryan readied the SIG-Sauer and waited.

When the thing appeared, Ryan held his fire because he wasn't sure what it was. It looked like a gopher, but it was the size of a large dog. Its back was covered in glass shards embedded in its fur. The glass bits were sharp and jagged, and stuck out from its back at odd angles, making it look like a spike-covered war wag.

Glass or no, it was probably still good eating. Ryan raised the SIG-Sauer, but before he could fire he heard the sound of one of Jak's leaf-bladed knives slicing through the air and vines. A moment later the knife pierced the side of the animal. The creature gave a small yelp before falling onto its side, dead.

"Supper time!" Jak shouted.

"No," Ryan called, turning to see the albino already crawling through one of the glass house's empty frames. Ryan reached out with his hand to try to stop him, but was too late. As soon as Jak was inside the glass house, a vine wrapped itself around his leg, holding him in place long enough for other vines to entwine his legs, arms and neck. The vines were a species of tanglers, and vicious ones at that. They'd left the gopher alone because the sharp glass in its skin made the thing too tough to chill. Jak, on the other hand, was an easy meal. His vest, with its shards of glass and pieces of jagged metal, wouldn't protect him.

Jak was struggling to get at another of his knives, but the vines had already gotten hold of his arms. He opened his mouth to call for help, but a thick green vine slid between his lips, choking off his words.

Ryan holstered the SIG-Sauer and unsheathed his panga. After kicking in the metal framing in front of him, he stepped into the glass house and began hacking at the vines. They were tough, as thick as rope in places, each one requiring several hard chops with the big knife to cut through. When he reached the tangle of vines covering Jak, the albino was still struggling fiercely against the mutant vegetation. Wasting no time, Ryan began with the vines around Jak's head, but before he could cut through anything, a vine wrapped around Ryan's wrist, making his swings too weak to be effective.

He switched the panga to his left hand and used it to cut his right arm free of the vine. He had the panga back in his right hand and was again working on freeing Jak when another vine got hold of his right leg and pulled him off balance. The sudden movement changed the arc of Ryan's knife, and he came dangerously close to lopping off Jak's right ear. Luckily the panga cut through the vines wrapped around the albino's neck and mouth, allowing Jak to draw in a much needed breath.

But now there were vines around both Ryan's legs. He could cut himself free, but by the time he did that, Jak might be dead. He left the vines around his legs for the time being and concentrated on freeing Jak. Vines moved into place around his neck and head again, and Jak struggled for breath. Ryan cleared away the new vines from around his neck, but they now had him by the chest, as well, squeezing him hard and making it difficult for Jak to inhale.

"Ryan! Jak!" J.B. called.

"Over here," Ryan responded.

In moments Ryan heard the sound of J.B.'s Tekna and Doc's swordstick slashing through the vines.

Ryan doubled his efforts and began cutting and hacking at the vines around him. When he was free, he turned to Jak, who was now on the verge of losing consciousness. Ryan swung the panga over Jak's head in a wide arc, and the vines stretching from the ceiling fell away like rope. As he began working on Jak's left side, he could see J.B. and Doc approaching through the thinning wall of vines. They had cut a swath through the deadly vegetation and were now close enough to keep the vines away from Ryan as he continued working to free Jak.

It took a few moments, but Jak was finally free. His pale white skin was covered with dark red abrasions, but at least he wasn't bleeding. "Let's get out of here," Ryan growled.

"Sage advice," Doc said, slashing at a thin but persistent vine that was still trying to encircle the one-eyed man.

"Wait!" Jak took a few steps and picked up the glass-armored gopher by the tail. "Not waste food."

Ryan stood with the panga in his fist as Jak made his way out of the glass house. J.B. and Doc exited next, followed by Ryan.

"Think it'll be good eating?" Dean asked, rubbing a hand over his stomach.

"The glass will probably come off with the skin," Krysty commented.

"Not worry," Jak said. He had recovered from his encounter with the vines and was obviously proud that he'd procured dinner for the friends. "When finished, taste like chicken."

Ryan nodded as he wiped his panga clean. It probably would at that.

"TRIPLE STUPE," Grundwold said, hitting the young sec man hard across the face.

A spray of blood and a single tooth flew out of Rory O'Brien's mouth as his head snapped to the left. He spit once before speaking. "I just wanted to get a closer look at them, see what kind of blasters they were carrying. I thought the glass house would be plenty of cover."

Grundwold's hand came back across O'Brien's face, and this time his knuckles struck him full on the cheek. There was more blood this time, but all of the young man's teeth remained, however loose, inside his mouth. "You nearly gave away our position. They've got blasters and long knives and they probably know how to use them. If they hadn't got caught up in those tanglers, they might have seen you and the baron would have had to kiss those two breeders goodbye."

O'Brien's eyes widened in fear at the mention of the baron. "Just trying to do my job, Chief."

"Yeah, well, you've got a new job now, starting as

soon as we get back to the farm. And if I ever find the lavs aren't clean enough to drink out of, your next job will be in some death trap of a mill shoveling black dirt with your bare hands."

There was a look on O'Brien's face that hinted he wasn't too pleased with the demotion.

Grundwold erased the look of displeasure with a hard punch that caught O'Brien flush under the right eye. "Understood?"

O'Brien wiped at the blood that was beginning to pour out of his nose. "Yes, sir."

Grundwold looked at his bloody knuckles and shook his head. "Now get out of my sight."

O'Brien, doing as he was told, was gone in an instant.

Chapter Four

The friends decided to eat the gopher while it was fresh. They set up a spit in the middle of a crossroads so they could see anyone approaching. Doc, Dean and J.B. foraged for firewood, while Jak took a great deal of pleasure in skinning and gutting the animal that almost cost him his life.

When Doc and Dean got back with the wood, Ryan whittled a long stick of green wood with his panga and gave it to Jak, who used it to skewer the gopher lengthwise. Then he placed the stick on the upright branches embedded in holes in the asphalt and checked to make sure it was balanced as it turned.

In minutes the fire was burning hot in the spit and the aroma of cooking meat made the friends' mouths water. Unfortunately the smell would also attract the attention of every mutie for miles around.

"J.B., Krysty, Dean and Doc," Ryan called, "take up a four-point perimeter. Triple red."

While Jak seasoned the meat with a few herbs, Mildred made sure the gopher cooked evenly over the spit, and it wasn't long before the meat was cooked well enough to eat. Jak cut seven portions from the animal, pierced the meat with sharpened branches and handed them out to the group so they could all eat while on lookout against a mutie attack.

When Jak handed Dean his piece, he stood over the boy waiting to hear him offer an opinion. "Taste like chicken?"

Dean took a bite out of the haunch, chewed the meat and grimaced. "Not really."

"Cannie approaching," Doc called.

Ryan turned and saw one of the thin spiderlike muties coming up the road. "Careful, people," he commanded. "If there's one out there, there'll be more."

"Want chilled?" Jak asked, his Colt Python at the ready.

"No," Ryan said. "Not worth the ammo."

"Then what?" Dean asked. "We can't just wait until they surround us."

The boy was right. While Ryan didn't want to waste precious rounds killing muties, they had to do something before there were a hundred muties around them and they'd have to blast their way out. "Everyone finish eating. Take seconds if you want, but leave the rest behind."

The friends quickly ate what Jak had provided for them, even though the meat was a little tough and hard to swallow. Ryan, Jak and Mildred took seconds, leaving more than half of the huge gopher on the spit.

"Let's move," Ryan said.

"Bon appetite," Doc muttered in the direction of the muties.

In a flash the friends were on their feet, continuing the journey south. By the time the group had taken fifty paces the first few muties were crowding around the spit and tearing at the leftovers. After they'd taken sixty paces, the muties numbered in the dozens and the gopher was all but gone.

THE BASEMENT of the main building on Fox Farm was cold, wet and dark, and smelled of a variety of foul bodily fluids. This was where the problem breeders were brought to be made heavy. It was easier for them if they bred willingly, but it wasn't necessary for them to cooperate. Breeders could still get heavy while being chained to the wall, and they birthed children after nine months in the basement just as well as those breeders who worked on the farm during the day and rutted every night. Their offspring weren't as healthy as those of the farmworkers and they sometimes had to be put down, but it was still better to have them breed than send them away on a slave convoy.

Fox paced under the dim light of an electric bulb waiting for his sec men to bring down the latest breeder who'd refused to rut. While he waited, he walked the length of one of the walls the breeders were chained to. The first breeder was a black-haired girl who'd never rutted before she'd come to the farm. She'd refused every one of the men assigned to her, and when it became clear she'd simply been putting off rutting, Fox moved her into the basement and had his four top studs rut her each night for a month until he was sure she'd gotten heavy. When she didn't bleed at the end of the four weeks, he stopped the rutting. A few months later she began showing of signs of heaviness, and now she was more than eight months along and could give birth at any time.

"How do you feel?" Fox asked.

"Good," she answered, pulling the chains away from her naked legs.

"After the birth, will you be ready to rejoin us on the farm?"

"Oh, yes please," she said, her empty, broken expression replaced by a hopeful smile.

"You'll rut every night, then?"

"Yes."

"And you'll like it?"

"Yes...anything. I just want to get out of here."

Fox smiled. Young ones always came around after just a single term in the basement. "You birth me a child and I'll free you from those chains."

"Thank you, Baron."

Fox stepped forward and took his right foot out of his slipper so she could kiss it. When she did, Fox turned to Norman Bauer, his accountant, who stood nearby watching. "Make sure she's comfortable after the birth...and give her three days' free time in the ward before she starts work on the farm."

Bauer opened the ledger and made a notation.

"Thank you, Baron," she said, kissing his foot again with zeal. "Thank you."

She was beginning to slobber over his toes. Fox pushed her away with his foot and slid it back into its slipper.

Next along the wall was an old blond woman who'd lived on the farm for years. She'd been one of his best producers, giving him twins twice and always producing strong, healthy offspring. But after her last—the thirteenth she'd given the farm—she simply stopped producing. Although she kept on rutting, she'd carefully avoided getting heavy. When Fox brought her into his office for an explanation, she'd simply said, "Enough!" Her declaration made Fox laugh. Retirement wasn't an option for a functioning breeder. A woman bred until she couldn't anymore, and when she was done, she was sold into slavery or traded for a blaster.

As Fox approached her, he smiled and said, "And how are we today?"

She looked up at the baron with an expression of contempt, then lowered her head and spit on his slippers.

Fox stood there looking at the stain and shook his head. "As charming as ever, I see."

"Fuck you!"

Fox's fist shot out and caught her in the right eye. Her head snapped back and slammed against the brick wall she was chained to. Fox stood impassively as she swung her arms and legs to strike back at him, knowing the chains were too short to allow her to touch him. He let her continue her futile attempt to hit him and when she was tired out, he struck her again under the left eye. This time, instead of fighting back, she fell unconscious onto the cold concrete floor.

Fox reached over and put a hand on her bloated belly. She was six months along and everything seemed to be progressing normally. Her fighting spirit would probably produce a similarly spirited offspring that would net him a top price at auction—a couple of blasters or a few barrels of diesel at the very least. The thought put a smile on the baron's face.

He started toward the next breeder when a sec man appeared at the door. It was Kingsley, his number-three sec man after Grundwold and Fillinger.

"It's the outlanders, Baron," Kingsley stated. "They're approaching from the north, heading toward the farm."

"Is Grundwold still following them?"

"If he is, our lookouts haven't seen his party."

"Good," Fox said, "then the outlanders probably haven't noticed them, either." Grundwold's men were the best sec men the farm had, and their talent for stealthily following travelers had once again given Fox an advantage over passing travelers. In addition, he had several options as to how to get his hands on the outlander women. "If they approach the front gate looking to trade for food or lodging, let them in and bring them to me. If they pass us by, give them a polite wave and leave them for Grundwold and his men to handle farther down the road."

"Yes, Baron," Kingsley said and was gone.

AFTER AN HOUR'S WALK along the road, the companions came upon a huge steel fence topped with barbed wire. On the other side stood row upon row of neatly trimmed trees, all covered in green leaves and spotted with a magnificent bounty of ripening fruit.

The friends stopped on the roadway, admiring the view.

"Ah." Doc sighed. "Now, that is what a farm should look like. A virtual cornucopia of all good things to eat."

"It looks almost predark," Mildred commented.

The farm was indeed well kept, Ryan thought. And the wire fence was an absolute necessity considering the number of hungry muties lurking in the area. Still, something about the fence didn't feel right to Ryan. He scanned the length that ran parallel to the road and saw something hanging off the fence a few hundred yards south of their position.

"After that gopher meat, one of those apples would sure taste good," Dean said. "You think they'd miss any apples if I climbed over the fence and picked us a few."

"No," Ryan commanded. "Don't go near that fence."

"Why, what's wrong with it?" Krysty asked.

"Not sure." Ryan headed south toward the object hanging from the fence. As the friends neared, it became obvious that it was the remains of a mutie. It was facing the fence as if in the middle of a climb with its hands and feet tangled in the steel weave. There was little flesh left on its bones, and what there was had been burned and charred black.

"An electric fence?" J.B. asked.

Ryan had never actually seen an electric fence, but he knew they'd existed, especially around military installations in predark times. "That'd be my guess," he said.

"If it's electric, why don't I hear any hum?" Mildred asked.

"Maybe it's not on right now," J.B. suggested.

"It would seem to me that such a massive fence would require an equally massive amount of electricity to electrify it," Doc said. "And since electricity is currently harder to come by than gasoline, where would so much electricity come from?"

"You'd like a few of those apples, too, wouldn't you, Doc?" Mildred chided.

"Look there," Krysty said, pointing in the direction they had come.

Ryan turned and saw a couple of muties behind them several hundred yards down the road, as if they'd been following the group. After they'd stopped, the muties moved off the asphalt and were approaching the northern corner of the fence, staring at the fruit on the other side through the heavy steel weave. Then the first mutie suddenly grabbed the fence and started to climb.

"Nothing happen," Jak said, as the companions friends moved toward the muties for a closer look.

The second mutie scrambled up the fence behind the first, but when they were both halfway to the top, Ryan suddenly heard a dull mechanical thrum slowly rising in volume.

The fence was being charged with electricity.

When the current reached them, the mutant's bodies jerked and spasmed wildly, every one of their muscles twitching and writhing uncontrollably. The air was tinged with the sweet and pungent odor of burning flesh and the sound of sizzling meat. Orange-and-blue flames began to shoot out from the hands and feet of the muties, as well as from their other body parts that came in contact with the fence. The muties' hair and eyebrows burned away like flash powder, the ashes falling to the ground like dirty snow.

"Why don't they just let go?" Dean asked.

"Can't," Mildred replied. "Their muscles are in total spasm. They can't control them to release their hold on the fence."

And then the hum suddenly stopped. The muties fell limp against the fence, their burned hands and feet curled around the steel mesh, refusing to let go. Their flesh had developed a hard outer shell and was producing tendrils of acrid gray smoke.

But the muties were still alive. They were gasping for air and groaning in pain, helpless to free themselves from their agonizingly slow death.

"It's a terrible way to be chilled," Mildred commented. "The electricity isn't even the thing that kills you. It paralyzes your heart, shuts off your breathing and boils the fat under your skin so you're cooked to death from the inside out."

It was a horrible way to die.

"Maybe they can turn the power on at will," Mildred suggested. "And at different sections of the fence, wherever it's needed."

"Or it's governed by motion sensors, turning on the fence whenever motion's detected."

"Which may or may not mean that someone knows we're here, people," Ryan said, knowing he'd just put the friends on triple alert. "But let's just continue on as if we've seen nothing new here."

The companions began to move.

The muties continued to smolder on the fence.

FARTHER ALONG, the friends saw their first sec man patrolling the inside of the compound. He was armed with a longblaster, and wore a good pair of boots. Behind the sec man, about thirty people worked a row of trees, pulling weeds, trimming branches and picking fruit. They all looked to be healthy and well fed. A few of the women looked to be pregnant, but they were still able to help with the farm work.

Within a few moments of the friends' appearance, the first sec man was joined by a second, who came riding up in a small white wag that had an engine that ran without making a sound. There was a heavy blaster set up on a swivel mount on the back of the wag that gave the weapon a 360-degree radius of fire.

The first sec man waved to the friends as they walked along the outside of the fence. Ryan returned the wave, and the others followed suit. But while the first sec man remained where he was overseeing the workers, the second sec man in the white miniwag matched their pace, following them all the way to the farm's front gate.

"Fox Farm," Mildred read the sign over the double steel gate that served as the farm's front entrance. There was a kiosk just inside the gate where a sec man was on duty. The mobile sec man pulled up to the gate. He was joined by several others, all carrying blasters of different makes and models, but presumably all in good working order and fully loaded.

"Greetings, outlanders," the sec man said, climbing out of the small white wag. "What brings you to Fox Farm?"

"Just passing through," Ryan said.

"You're welcome to spend the night here if you like. We have some excellent accommodations."

That was out of the question. The electrified fence was probably just as good at keeping people in as it was at keeping things out. If they stepped through the gate, they might never leave.

"How much?" Mildred asked when Ryan said nothing in response to the sec man's offer.

The sec man smiled. "One of your blasters perhaps, or mebbe some ammunition."

"Thanks for the offer," Ryan said. "But we need our blasters and ammo." He turned to leave.

"Fair enough," the sec man said, "but I can't let you go—"

The friends all made subtle moves for their blasters.

"—without making some sort of trade. How about some food? Apples, pears, grapes, beans... I'm sure you have something of value we could exchange."

Dean was first, producing an extra pocketknife. Jak searched his pockets and came up with a few rounds that didn't fit any of the friends' blasters. Krysty offered up one of her two combs, and Mildred decided she could part with a pair of socks.

"We travel light," Ryan said as the others held up the goods for inspection.

"Not to worry," the sec man responded. "These are all things we can make use of." He turned to one of the sec men behind him. "Three bags."

The sec man hopped into the white miniwag and drove up to a large building to the left of the gate. In less than a minute he came back with three bags filled with fresh fruit and vegetables.

"By the horn of the goat Amalthaea," Doc gasped. "I never thought I'd live to see such a cornucopia such as this."

"Fair trade?" the sec man asked.

It was more than fair, Ryan thought, which made him suspicious. In his experience, all traders always wanted to come out on top in a deal. These people either had far more food than they needed, even for trade, or they were after something else. But judging by how prosperous the farm looked, Ryan decided they could probably afford to be generous with their food—as a sign of goodwill, with an eye toward future trades of more valuable commodities. "Fair trade," Ryan answered.

A sec man opened a small door in the gate at chest height, and the goods were passed through the opening.

"It's been a pleasure," the sec man said.

Ryan nodded. J.B., Doc and Krysty each took a bag, but no one grabbed a fruit, knowing they should keep their hands as free as possible in case something went wrong and they had to grab their blasters.

The small door closed and the deal was done.

"How far is the ville from here?" Ryan asked.

"Just down the road," the sec man said, pointing south. "Hardly any people there, but plenty of places to spend the night."

"Thanks," Ryan said.

They were about to leave when J.B. stepped forward. "If you don't mind me asking, where are you getting your electricity?"

"No secret," the sec man said. "Power station at the falls has been making juice for more than two hundred years."

"The falls," Mildred said. "Niagara Falls?"

"That's them."

"Thanks for the trade," Ryan said, "but we best get moving if we want to get to this ville by dark."

"Mebbe we'll see you again sometime," the sec man said.

Ryan nodded. "Mebbe."

The friends headed for the falls, Mildred and Dean covering the rear until they were out of range of the sec men's longblasters.

Chapter Five

When the outlanders were almost out of sight, Baron Fox came down from his office and strolled out to the main gate to meet with Grundwold.

The sec chief had ordered the others in his team to continue trailing the outlanders while he made his report to the baron. He would catch up to them later.

The baron arrived at the gate wearing his familiar silk bathrobe, but now had a heavy pair of black leather boots on his feet. He took a pipe from a pocket in his bathrobe, filled it with some of the tobacco grown on the farm and lit it with a shiny chrome Zippo lighter, which had cost him a breeder. As always, Norman Bauer was several paces behind the baron, his ledger tucked neatly up under his right arm.

"The one-eyed man's their leader," Grundwold stated.

Fox chugged a few times on his pipe. When it was lit, he clenched it between his teeth and said, "Yes, he seemed to do all the talking for the group."

"He's good with a blaster, too," Grundwold said.

"As they all are, no doubt."

"It would make it hard for me to take them without losing a lot of my men."

Fox grew angry with the sec chief. The redheaded

one was exotic, and her hair was the most beautiful he'd ever seen. Even if she never got heavy, he knew a rich baron or two living outside the eastern villes who'd pay big jack to make a wig or weave out of hair like that. And the dark woman had the best set of breeding hips he'd seen in months. "Sec men I can get anywhere," Fox spit. "I need breeders."

"Yes, sir," Grundwold barked. "What do you want me to do, then?"

"I want you to bring them here," Fox said, blowing a plume of gray smoke just under Grundwold's nose. "Bring me the women...whatever it takes."

Grundwold nodded and looked down the road toward the falls. "What did you give them?" he asked.

"Three bags of fruit in exchange for some trinkets."

"Ripe?"

"Most of the fruit is laced with sedatives. We didn't have time to prepare the fruit in all three bags, but there's a good mix. Should be enough to put a few of them off guard," Grundwold stated. "That's all the advantage we'll need."

"I'll send the wag to the tower after dark."

Normally the sec chief would have a wag at his disposal, but a slave had recently stolen one in an escape and they hadn't been able to trade for a replacement yet. That made the second wag even more valuable, and the baron only wanted to let it outside the complex long enough to collect the new breeders and bring them back to the farm.

The sec chief nodded and said, "We'll bring them

back.'' He started down the road at double-time to catch up with the rest of his men.

''Of course you will,'' Baron Fox said. ''Of course you will.''

''IT MAKES SENSE NOW,'' Mildred said as the friends walked along the road toward the ville that was now less than a mile away. ''The region around Niagara Falls was all farmland. Apple orchards, pears, plums, peaches and plenty of grapes for making some really good wine.''

''No more,'' Jak stated.

''Not after the blast. The whole area was wiped out, except for that one farm.''

''In my day,'' Doc offered, ''Niagara Falls was the site of some of the most exciting theoretical discussion about the possibilities of electricity. Not to mention the incredible feat of engineering that would be required to make it possible.''

''Electricity would sure give the baron or whoever owns the farm one hell of an advantage,'' J.B. commented.

''Like fuel,'' Jak said.

''Better than fuel,'' J.B. replied. ''It's harder to steal. No one can blow it up. And it doesn't have to be refined. It could give them lights, even the power to pump fresh water.''

''So why hasn't the rest of the area prospered?'' Ryan asked. ''If there's power here, why is the ville empty?''

''After two hundred years the power station can't

be producing all that much electricity," Krysty reasoned.

"He probably takes everything the station produces," J.B. stated. "Or destroyed all the power lines, except for those running to his farm."

"I must say the people working on the farm looked healthy enough," Doc suggested. "They must all be doing well for themselves."

"And for other traders," Jak said, lifting the bag of fruit.

Ryan had to admit that the farm looked like a well-run operation. But there was still something about it that bothered him. The electrified fence was a logical defense system considering the type of muties that lurked in the area and the amount of electricity that was available. Still, it seemed to be run a little too smoothly for it to be just a farm, and he'd never seen a farm that was so well armed.

"You know," Mildred said, "there's another thing that Niagara Falls was known for in predark times."

"What's that?" J.B. asked.

"It was the honeymoon capital of North America."

"What's that mean?" Dean asked.

"It means that after people got married, they'd come here to, uh, celebrate by spending a lot of time in bed together."

"Oh."

"So that's why the sec man said there were plenty of places to spend the night here," Krysty said.

J.B. smiled. "Good. I could use a good night's rest."

"Not up to a little honeymoon, John?" Mildred chided.

"Oh, I'll be up for it," J.B. responded dryly.

At that moment they crested a rise in the road and suddenly Falls ville and the lake beyond it stretched out before them. There were dozens of buildings around the ville that had been destroyed by the shock waves from the initial nuke blasts, or the aftershocks that followed. But despite the damage, there were still several structures intact, such as the one that looked like a saucer set upon a knife that overlooked the water, and a cluster of buildings huddled together in the center of the ville.

The lake to the south was as big as an ocean, but was spotted by sandbars and dry patches along the shore. Water flowed over a horseshoe-shaped ridge, but it flowed only over two sections in the center of the horseshoe. The rest of the curve was dry and home to several large water birds.

"The falls have almost run dry," Mildred said. "In predark times you'd be able to hear the water roaring from here. Millions of gallons of fresh water every minute, day and night, 365 days a year."

"Now falls like rain," Jak commented.

"Producing enough electricity to operate one farm, but not enough for an entire ville," J.B. said.

"There's something else I just realized," Mildred said.

"What is it?" Ryan asked.

"If that's Niagara Falls," she said, taking a look at the geography around her, "then we're on the Canadian side of what used to be the border."

Chapter Six

"Being located in Canada would explain a lot about the construction of the gateway," Ryan said.

"Anyone using it would be looking to get out of the country in a hurry," J.B. surmised. "So it probably served as an escape hatch, mebbe for military commanders or politicians."

"But there's such a large underground system of redoubts and installations," Krysty said. "Why would a one-way escape gateway be needed?"

"Things go wrong," J.B. suggested. "Even underground fortresses can be infiltrated, especially from the inside. That gateway could get someone out of one hot spot without the risk of them landing in another one."

Krysty considered J.B.'s reasoning. "So the trip through the gateway was meant to be one-way."

"Someone going through that gateway likely wasn't welcome back in the United States, probably wouldn't want to go back to it, either."

"All this talk of travel has made me rather famished," Doc interjected. "Might it be possible to have one of those delectable fruits we are carrying?"

Ryan took a good look around. He hadn't seen a mutie for some time. Although he had noticed a few of the creatures following the friends earlier on, they had dropped away now that the ville was near. They had another half hour before they reached it, and the route looked like fairly easy going. They had time to snack now while they walked, but when they entered the ville, they would need to be on the alert. "I guess it wouldn't hurt to eat something now."

"I'll have a peach, then," Doc said, quickly pulling one of the fuzzy fruit from the bag he was carrying.

"Me, too," Dean said.

Doc tossed Dean the peach he was about to eat, then pulled a second one from the bag for himself.

"I've got apples and pears in this bag," J.B. said.

"Apricots and plums in mine," Krysty added.

"I'll have a few of each," Mildred said. "My father used to make the best plum sauce in three counties. We'd have it on pancakes every Sunday after church."

Krysty handed Mildred a handful of deep purple and golden-yellow fruits.

"I'll have a pear," J.B. said. "How about you, Krysty, Ryan, Jak?"

"Apple," Jak said.

"Pear for me," Ryan said.

Krysty smiled. "Me too."

"These look good," J.B. said, handing a reddish-green pear to Ryan, and then to Krysty. "Mebbe I'll have one, too."

J.B. fished a pear out of the bag for himself.

"These are truly wonderful peaches," Doc said, admiring the fruit in his hand. "Did I ever tell the story about the man I met who rode with Kit Carson when the red-eyed son of a bitch burned out the peach orchard in Canyon de Chelly?''

"Yes," Ryan answered.

"Heard it," Jak said.

"Many times," Mildred chided.

"Well, it is quite the story...." Doc said, his words trailing off until he bit into his peach again.

And for the next five minutes, the companions walked the roadway in relative silence except for the sounds of crunching fruit and the scrape of their boots on the asphalt.

THE SUN WAS JUST beginning to fall behind the western horizon as they entered the outskirts of Falls ville.

Most of the buildings they'd passed until now were in ruins. One of the buildings had been called Ripley's, with the outside covered with pictures of two-headed goats, men joined at the hip and other common Deathlands mutations. The friends were somewhat confused by the renderings, wondering if the structure was predark or skydark.

"Ripley was a man who collected predark oddities and put them in museums for people to gawk at," Mildred explained.

"People pay jack see this?" Jak asked.

Mildred smiled. "As one of Mr. Ripley's colleagues once said, there's a triple-stupe bastard born every minute."

There were other similar establishments, all of them advertising wonders that were all too common in the Deathlands, many of them having to do with wax.

When the road ended at the water's edge, they turned left and followed the weed-infested trail that ran parallel to the river as it flowed toward the falls. As they came to the falls themselves, the air became filled with a moist chill as the water crested over the falls and crashed onto the rocky gorge below. It was an impressive sight, but the amount of water running over the falls was nothing like what Mildred had said flowed there in predark times.

On their left was the strangely shaped tower that stood some two hundred feet above them and likely gave an excellent view of the falls and the surrounding area. Ryan made a note to check out the tower in the morning light. If the sky was clear, he'd be able to do an easy recce of the area for miles around. Directly in front of them were two buildings that looked to be fairly stable. The first was a large structure fronted by a steel framework that had obviously been covered in glass during predark times, but was now nothing more than a white steel skeleton. On one of the metal ribs a faded green sign read Casino Niagara, which was a special kind of place, Mildred explained, where people gambled away all their jack.

"Why would they do that?" Dean asked.

"For fun," Mildred answered.

Next to the bones of the white skeleton was a much older building. It was also white, but only because that was the color of its stonework. Although most of the building's windows had been blasted out, a few panes were still intact. Some of the pale red letters on the roof had toppled over, leaving the rest of the letters to read her ton-Fall View. It was obviously a hotel, and just as the sec men at the farm had said, there looked to be plenty of places to spend the night.

"That one looks like a fine establishment," Doc said. "Why do we not sleep there tonight?"

"I could use some rest," Krysty said, her hair falling straight down from her head and hanging limply over her shoulders. "Those last few miles really tired me out."

"I'm beat, too," J.B. added. "I'd like to sit down for a while, mebbe have some more fruit and call it a night."

Ryan didn't like the idea of sleeping in a strange building without a recce, but the ville seemed deserted enough and it wouldn't be too hard to find a room on the first or second floor that they could make secure for the night. Besides, he was feeling exhausted himself, and a night in a hotel room, even the rad-blasted remnants of one, sounded good.

"All right," he said. "That's where we'll go. Jak and Mildred, scout the grounds around it and meet us in the lobby."

Jak handed his bag of fruit to Dean, and then the albino and the physician quickened their pace with blasters drawn and ready.

"Are you looking forward to a night in bed, lover?" Krysty asked.

"You have to ask?" Ryan answered.

GRUNWOLD CLIMBED the last few steps to the top of the Skylon Tower slowly. The sec chief had double-timed it to the lookout station from Fox Farm, and his lungs were complaining against the strain. He took a few moments to rest at the entrance to the observation deck, not wanting to show his men any weakness, then entered when his breathing and heart rate had come back down to something closer to normal.

"Where are they?" he asked the sec man on watch.

"They're heading toward the Fall view," the sec man answered, not taking his eyes from the binoculars that were trained on the heart of the ville. "My guess is that they're going to stay there tonight."

"Good," Grundwold said. "Where's the team on the ground?"

"They're a few hundred yards behind."

"Have they been spotted?"

"No. I even lost sight of them myself a few times."

"Have the outlanders been eating any fruit?" Grundwold asked.

"Yes," said the sec man. "They were all eating as they entered the ville. Looked pretty hungry, too."

"Excellent!" Grundwold said with a smile. "That should make them ripe for the picking."

Chapter Seven

"Jak's still scouting the inside. The area outside the hotel is clear," Mildred reported. "And there's no sign that anyone's been through the area in a while."

Ryan nodded. He was glad for the news, but wasn't sure how a ville with so many buildings didn't have more people living in it. Where had all the people gone? It was another question whose answer would probably be forthcoming in time. But despite any misgivings Ryan had about staying in the old hotel, it was getting dark out and the friends needed to find a place to bed down for the night. "All right, let's take a look inside and find a place to sleep."

The friends stepped through the broken glass that had once been the hotel's front door and entered the lobby with blasters in hand. While there didn't seem to be anyone living in the ville, a few of the hungry muties could still be crawling around looking for a meal. But even that seemed unlikely, since there was even less food in the ville than there was in all the surrounding rad-chilled farmland.

As they moved through the lobby, Doc walked behind the front desk to have a look around. "Well, I'm honored to be one of the first guests here since 2001," he said, wetting the tip of a pencil on his tongue and signing the guest book on behalf of the friends.

The hotel was laid out in a pair of long corridors that stretched out in opposite directions from the lobby. It wasn't an ideal situation, but they could probably establish a defensible position somewhere in the hotel, allowing them all the good night's sleep they so desperately needed.

Just then a door opened at the end of the ground-floor hallway. The friends immediately had their blasters raised and ready to fire, but it turned out to be Jak returning from his recce of the hotel's upper floors.

"Long halls, many rooms," the albino teenager reported. "Second floor best. One way up, many ways out."

Ryan nodded. Since the elevators wouldn't be working, the only way up would be by the stairs. But a building like this had to have at least two stairways, maybe even more in case of fire. "Only one stairway?" Ryan asked.

"Locked others. Now let out, not in."

"Are the stairs the only way out?"

Jak shook his head. "Windows. Twenty-four each side, not far to ground."

A ten-foot jump out a second-story window wasn't Ryan's favorite way of escaping a firefight, but with forty-eight windows and a few stairways to choose from, not to mention the possibility of going up, the one-eyed man was satisfied they'd be able to escape in the event of a mutie attack, or worse. Besides that, he was too tired to go any farther. If they didn't stop here for the night, Ryan wasn't sure he'd be able to go on. "Second floor it is, then." He looked at the friends to see who was freshest and could take the first watch. "Jak, you take first watch, hour-and-a-half shifts."

The teenager nodded.

The friends went to the end of the hallway and climbed the stairs to the second floor.

RYAN AND KRYSTY TOOK a room on the east side of the building at the far end of the hallway near one of the locked doors that led to the stairs. The windows on that side of the hotel were mostly whole, looking out over a back alley, which was just as deserted as the rest of the ville.

There were two large beds in the room, both covered with dusty sheets. Krysty took them off the bed and shook them out in a room across the hall, then replaced them on the bed. It had been a while since Ryan had slept in a bed with sheets, and he was looking forward to it.

But before he did, there was something else he'd been looking forward to even more. As he lay back on the bed, Ryan set his SIG-Sauer and panga on the nightstand next to him, then hid his Steyr SSG-70 under the bed. Then, in total comfort, he bit into another of the delicious pears they'd traded for, and watched Krysty slowly getting undressed. Seeing her shed her clothing like this always gave him a little thrill that stirred a desire deep within him. The first hint of her beauty was her gorgeous mane of fiery red hair and her strikingly brilliant emerald-green eyes. Even though she looked tired herself and her hair was hanging almost straight down from her head, she was still breathtakingly beautiful. That beauty was further evidenced as she stood at the end of the bed, slipping off her boots and then her jumpsuit and bra and panties, revealing her full breasts, long, muscular legs and firm buttocks.

Ryan took the opportunity to get out of his own clothes, taking off his jacket and shirt in one smooth motion, and then kicking off his boots and sliding out of his pants.

He was ready for her.

Krysty acknowledged that fact with a smile. "If you're done with that pear," she said, "you might want to try some cherry-tipped golden apples."

Ryan stopped himself from taking another bite and put the pear down on the nightstand.

"I thought you might," Krysty said. She crawled onto the bed and toward Ryan on all fours. As she straddled his legs, she bent down and kissed his hardness once, then flicked her head and dragged her long red hair across his body.

Passion flowed through Ryan, and Krysty seemed to have discovered some newfound energy as her hair was now curling slightly around her shoulders. He reached out for her, pulled her forward and, when she was in position, entered her.

They were lost in the throes of passion for a long, long time.

"DID YOU GO on a honeymoon, Doc?" Dean asked as he prepared his bed in the room he was going to share with the old man.

"Oh, I did indeed," Doc answered, smiling.

"What was it like?"

"It was gloriously wonderful," Doc said, looking out the window at the falls. "My dear sweet Emily and I went on a riverboat ride down the mighty Mississippi. While I knew that she was a lovely woman, I had no idea regarding the depths of her charms. She was warm, vibrant and loving, and even though the word hadn't been in common usage, if people knew about my Emily, the word *sexy* might have been in common parlance long before the turn of century."

"You mean 1900?"

"That's the year."

"So men and women spend a lot of time having sex on their honeymoon?"

"Well, now, yes they do." Doc had turned away from the window and was a little unsure if it was his place to talk about such things with Dean.

"Why is that?"

"It is a tradition that goes back hundreds of years." Doc pulled up a chair next to the bed Dean was stretched out on and sat. He stared out the window again and continued talking. "Honeymoon comes from the term 'honey month.' You see, even though people had always gotten married, they weren't always faithful to each other. So, when a man and a woman married, they went off for their honey month, in which they drank an alcoholic beverage called mead, a sort of beerlike drink that was made partly from honey. The alcohol helped them…well, have sex, and it lasted a month because it allowed the woman to complete an entire reproductive cycle. This insured that the woman's first child was undoubtedly the offspring of her husband, since no other man could have had an opportunity to mate with his wife during the honey month.

"Over time the ritual became unnecessary as there was less and less likelihood of a woman's infidelity. However, the honeymoon still served as an opportunity for a newly wed man and woman to become intimate with each other, so it was maintained as a symbolic bonding period between two soul mates."

Doc looked over at Dean and saw that the boy was already sound asleep. He pulled a sheet over him, then went to the other bed to lie down.

"Honey month, honeymoon," he muttered under his breath as he prepared his bed and made himself comfortable on it. "Honey month, honeymoon."

Minutes later Doc was asleep, dreaming of Emily and the Mississippi nights in which he'd thought he'd found a little piece of heaven on earth.

MILDRED WAS in the bathroom of the room she would be sharing with J.B. She'd taken a clean washcloth from the pile of clean towels she'd found in the bathroom and with a few splashes of water from her canteen, she was now giving herself a quick freshening up before bed.

"How long has it been, John?" she asked, looking at herself in the mirror.

"Too long," the Armorer said between bites of a pear. He'd eaten several of them since they'd arrived in the room and was just starting to feel full.

Mildred drew her hands up over her stomach, marveling at how tight and toned the muscles had become since she'd arrived in the Deathlands. Although she was stockily built, her body had become hard and shapely. She cupped her full breasts in her hands, pleased that they had become firmer, and if she said so herself, more attractive, than they'd ever been in predark times.

"Too long is right," she said over her shoulder. "I can't even remember the last time." Mildred waited for an answer, but there was none. "John?"

"Yes."

"I said, it's been so long, I can't remember when we did it last."

"I don't remember, either," J.B. commented, "but I do know that it was great."

Mildred smiled. "Such a romantic."

She finished up in the bathroom and gave herself one last look in the mirror, putting her hands on her hips and twisting her body from side to side. "You're definitely in for a treat, John Barrymore Dix," she whispered.

She left the bathroom and found J.B. stretched out on the bed closest to the window. His eyes were closed and a half-eaten pear was in his right hand, hanging over the edge of the bed and poised to fall to the floor at any moment.

Mildred hurried to J.B.'s side. "Are you asleep, John?" she asked.

No answer.

"John?" She shook his arm, and the pear fell from his fingers. "Are you all right?"

"Huh? What?"

Mildred stood, hands on hips again and doing her best to look indignant. "I can't believe you'd fall asleep when you knew you had this to look forward to."

J.B. smiled and shook his head. "I can't believe it either." He pulled himself into a sitting position and took one of Mildred's chocolate-brown nipples between his lips. At the same time he let his left hand slide down between her legs, gently feeling the invitingly warm and moist folds of flesh that beckoned for more than the touch of his fingers.

"Are you going to get out of your clothes, John?" Mildred asked. "Or am I going to have to strip you down like a blaster?"

"That would be, uh, interesting," J.B. said as Mildred began to work on his belt.

"More than just interesting, Mr. Dix." She leaned in close, whispering in J.B.'s ear. "I'm going to oil your blaster and pull your trigger. Only in this dream, it's going to fire…round after round, until you're all but out of ammo."

J.B. pulled Mildred close to him, loving her long into the night until they were both spent.

JAK GOT THE MOST comfortable chair he could find and brought it out into the hall. After positioning it in front of the only open doorway to the second floor, he sat down and had a peach.

Down the hall he could hear Doc snoring like someone's grandfather and wondered how Dean was able to sleep with so much noise.

He looked at his wrist chron. Just another hour to go before he could wake J.B. and get some rest himself.

The soft noises continued to resound along the hallway.

One hour was going to seem more like two.

SEC CHIEF GRUNWOLD pulled back the frame of the door so the rest of his sec men could enter the hotel without a sound. They tread lightly over the broken glass strewed about the lobby, their boots making slight crunching sounds as they walked.

"Fillinger," he said, his voice barely above a whisper.

"Sir."

"Do a recce of the hotel, find out where they are and report back to me."

Fillinger was gone without a word, treading silently down the first-floor hallway on his way to the stairs.

"I want at least one man on each of the stairwells, and two outside on either side of the hotel. I don't want these outlanders slipping away."

The sec men scattered, each filling one of the posts Grundwold had outlined. The sec chief remained in the lobby by the front desk, using it as a makeshift command center.

Five minutes after he'd been sent away, Fillinger returned, only slightly out of breath. "They're on the second floor. They've got a sentry posted in the hallway in front of the only unlocked door to the floor. The other entrances have all been locked, so my guess is the rest of them are getting some sleep, taking turns on watch through the night."

"Good work."

"Do you have a plan?" Fillinger asked.

"Not yet," Grundwold said. "Give them some time to fall asleep, and for the sedatives to kick in. Meanwhile, I'm sure I'll be able to figure something out."

Chapter Eight

An hour later, Jak Lauren was having trouble keeping his eyes open. During his entire time on watch, he hadn't heard a sound other than Doc's snoring—which had mercifully toned down as the time traveler fell into a deeper sleep—and he'd found it hard to remain awake and alert.

But now that he'd finished his watch, he was eager to be relieved so he could crawl into bed for some much needed sleep. According to the rotation they'd used of late, J.B. followed Jak. J.B. would be followed by Mildred, then came Doc, Dean, Krysty and Ryan. Jak could have waited for J.B. to come and relieve him, but with a mat-trans jump and a long trek on foot there was no reason why anyone would be getting up from a sound sleep on his or her own.

Jak got up from his chair and went into Mildred and J.B.'s room. They were together on the same bed and fully dressed, J.B. on the right side, closer to the door. Jak nudged the Armorer's shoulder in an attempt to wake him.

J.B. didn't stir.

Jak tried again, this time nudging the man a little bit harder.

Still nothing.

Jak took firm hold of J.B.'s shoulder and arm and gave him a firm shake, as well as tapping him on the side of the head with a finger. That seemed to do the trick, because in an instant J.B.'s eyes were open and his hand was under the mattress reaching for his Tekna. In less than a second he had it raised and pointed at Jak. But even though his eyes were open, the sleep wasn't quite gone from his mind. If Jak's white hair and ruby-red eyes hadn't been so distinctive, J.B. just might have run the teenager through with his blade.

"Your turn take watch," Jak said, his right hand on J.B.'s wrist just to make sure he didn't slip with the knife.

J.B. sighed, opened and closed his eyes several times and tried to bring himself to wakefulness. It wasn't easy. He'd been awakened in similar circumstances many times before, but he'd never had so much trouble rousing himself. "I'll be right there," J.B. said.

"Good," Jak replied, leaving the room. "Tired. Need sleep."

J.B. closed his eyes again, but immediately opened them, knowing that if he allowed himself to drift off, he'd never get up. He sat up on the edge of the bed rubbing his hands vigorously over his face.

"Is everything all right, John?" Mildred asked, awakened by J.B.'s movements.

"Tired is all."

"Do you want me to take your turn?"

"No, I'll be fine."

"Call me early for my shift if you need to," Mildred muttered, sliding back into sleep.

"Sure." J.B. laced up his boots, then grabbed his spectacles and fedora off the nightstand and put them on. He decided to take his scattergun with him. It would cover the entire hallway with a single shot, and the noise would surely awaken the rest of the friends from even the deepest sleep.

"See you in an hour and a half," J.B. whispered, giving Mildred a kiss on the cheek.

Mildred smiled as if lost in a dream.

THE OUTLANDERS obviously knew what they were doing, Grundwold thought. While their choice of spending the night on the second floor of the old hotel at first seemed unwise, a closer look revealed that they had taken up a fairly secure defensive position. There was only one way onto the second floor, but many ways off. A new sentry was watching the entrance, and he'd pulled his chair into one of the room doorways so that it was impossible to take him out with the first shot. At best, a sec man would have to open the stairwell door and rush the hallway, giving the sentry at least an even chance at getting off a shot before he was chilled. That would surely awaken the rest of them, and then all hell would break loose.

When that happened, the women could easily get caught in the firestorm. The baron wouldn't like that at all. He wouldn't care if only one of his sec men came back from Falls, as long as he had the two women with him. After all, a single stud could service dozens of women; it was the women who got heavy and delivered the goods.

As an experienced sec chief with plenty of loyal men under his command, Grundwold knew he couldn't commit all his men to a firefight in the hopes of capturing just two women. But in this situation, what else could he do?

He looked through the glass of the doorway at the open end of the hallway. The short wiry man with glasses and a hat looked to be having trouble staying awake. That was likely thanks to the sedatives in the pears. It was just the sort of advantage Grundwold had been hoping for. If nothing else, they could sneak into the hallway, slit the sentry's throat and then take out the rest of the outlanders as they slept, until they had captured the women or chilled all of the men.

"Kauderer," Grundwold whispered.

"Sir!" the sec man responded.

"Go around and join Fillinger at the door at the other end of this hallway."

"Then what?" Kauderer asked.

"We wait for this stupe in the hat to fall fast asleep, and then we start chillin'."

The sec man smiled. "Yes, sir!"

KRYSTY STIRRED beneath the sheets. She could feel something was wrong. She reached over to check on Ryan. Her lover was there, warm and resting comfortably in a deep, peaceful sleep. She wondered if she should wake him and let him know what she was feeling, but decided it wasn't strong enough to sound the alarm just yet. She'd have a look around, and if she noticed anything unusual, she could wake Ryan.

Slipping out of bed, Krysty was struck by the coolness of the night air. She dressed hastily, slipped on her bearskin coat, then picked up her Smith & Wesson and left the room.

The hall was quiet. J.B. was on watch down the hall, which was some twenty-five yards away. He was sitting on a chair in a doorway to one of the rooms and facing the open door to the stairwell. She'd check in with him later, but first she needed to check out the stairs at this end of the hallway. Something told her that whatever was sending her the danger signals was located at this end of the building.

She looked through the glass in the locked door, peering first down the stairs and then up them. No one was there, but still her feeling of unease persisted. She opened the door and took a single step into the stairwell to get a better look.

Suddenly a hand was on her wrist, and another on her mouth. She was yanked into the stairway, her Smith & Wesson torn from her grasp as she was thrown onto the concrete landing.

The door almost closed behind her, but was kept open by a clip from somebody's blaster.

"We weren't expecting you," a sec man whispered. "But we're glad you could make it."

The second sec man plastered a large piece of silver tape over her mouth, and they both worked to tie her hands behind her back with a strong piece of nylon cord.

"And not even a scratch," the first sec man said.

The second one laughed. "The baron will be pleased."

GRUNWOLD COULDN'T believe his luck. As he'd watched through the glass of the door, one of the two outlander women wandered out of her room, opened the door at the far end of the hallway and was caught on the other side by Fillinger and Kauderer.

And best of all, she'd opened the door and now they were free to enter the second floor away from the end of the hallway being watched by the guard.

"Canady and Edson stay here," Grundwold barked hoarsely. "The rest of you come with me."

He headed down the stairs, padding softly on the steps so as to avoid causing any noise that might alert the sleeping outlanders. When he reached the other end of the second-floor hallway, Fillinger and Kauderer were just finishing tying up the redheaded woman. They had replaced the clip in the doorway with a knife that had been wedged into the door frame. It kept the door open and unlocked and was in no danger of being kicked loose.

"Good work!" Grundwold said. "Do you know which room she came out of?"

"Second one on the left," Fillinger answered.

Grundwold turned to face the rest of the sec men who were lined up on the stairs. "Two of you take her to the tower and wait for us there. If I'm not there in one hour, take her back to the farm and make your report to the baron."

Two sec men grabbed Krysty by the arms and led her away.

"And don't mess with her," Grundwold called down the stairwell. "I want her handed over to the baron in good condition."

He turned to the sec men directly behind him. "Follow me," he told Lewis. "The rest of you cover the hallway. If the outlanders discover us, I don't want any of them coming down the hall. All right, let's go."

Grundwold stepped back from the door, and a sec man opened it for him. He and Lewis padded into the hallway, moving quickly toward the second door on the left. They kept a close watch on the man guarding the far door, but he didn't stir.

They stopped just outside the door to the room, and Grundwold peered through the doorway. There was a man on the bed, asleep. They would chill him and move onto the next room in search of the other woman.

Grundwold entered the room, went around to the far side of the bed and leveled his blaster on the back of the man's head. On the other side of the bed, Lewis drew his switchblade, pressed the silver button at the top of the handle and the knife snicked open.

The man on the bed suddenly stirred, and in a single quick and fluid motion, he had a huge knife in his hand and was slashing it across Lewis's belly. The sharp edge of the monster blade cut through the sec man's jacket and abdomen, spilling blood and entrails onto the hotel-room floor.

Lewis stood there with wide eyes as his hands

reached down in an attempt to keep his guts from sliding out of his body.

Grundwold leaped onto the bed, grabbed the prone man's arm with one hand and jammed the barrel of his Persuader up under the man's ear with the other. "I've got sec men all over the hall. If you make another move, or make a sound, I'll chill you and the rest of your friends where they sleep."

The man's body tensed, as if he were going to try something despite the warning. "We've already got the redhead. If you want to see her alive, you'll do what I say."

That seemed to convince the man that putting up a fight wasn't a good idea.

The man slowly got off the bed.

"You can get dressed, but I'll chill you and your friends in a heartbeat if you try anything."

The one-eyed man nodded, seeming to accept his fate, or perhaps realizing that fighting back at the moment would be futile. Whatever the reason, he cooperated with them and began putting on his pants and boots. When Ryan was dressed, Grundwold picked up the man's knife and blaster and led him out of the room, then down to the end of the hallway where a half-dozen sec men were waiting. As soon as they were in the stairwell, the door closed behind them and the sec men who'd been waiting on the stairs began tying the one-eyed man's hands behind his back.

"Tie his legs, too," Grundwold ordered. "Give him enough slack to walk, but not to run."

"Where's Lewis?" one of the sec men asked.

Grundwold shook his head.

The sec man, a friend of Lewis, stepped forward and threw a hard punch into the prisoner's stomach. Ryan doubled over slightly, but recovered quickly. The sec man threw a second punch, fully catching the one-eyed man's jaw. His head snapped left from the force of the blow, but he showed no signs of pain or fear.

Grundwold swung his arm in an arc and caught the sec man with the butt of his blaster before he could throw another punch. "Take it downstairs, before you wake up the rest of them," Grundwold hissed. "We've still got one more breeder to catch."

The sec man unclenched his fist and grabbed Ryan by the arm, pulling him hard down the stairs. The rope between the prisoner's legs caused him to stumble, then fall down a whole flight of stairs.

The sec men picked him up by the arms, then dragged him the rest of the way down the stairs and out of the hotel.

"Fillinger!" Grundwold said. "Come with me."

Grundwold and Fillinger reentered the hallway and began searching rooms for the other outlanders. Grundwold checked the third room on the left and found it empty. He looked back along the hall where Fillinger had just finished searching the second room on the right.

Fillinger shook his head. The room was empty.

Grundwold waited in the doorway of the room he'd just searched, his lovingly maintained Persuader 500 trained at the man guarding the far door, who still hadn't moved.

Fillinger opened the door to the third room on the right, directly across from where Grundwold was providing cover. He had the door halfway open when he stopped in his tracks and looked over at Grundwold and jabbed his thumb in the direction of the room.

Someone was sleeping in there.

Grundwold kept the Persuader trained on the guard as he moved across the hallway to join Fillinger. Then they entered the room together, with Grundwold again moving to the far side of the bed. When they were in place, Fillinger lowered the barrel of his remade longblaster onto the head of the sleeping outlander while Grundwold reached down to pull back the sheet covering the sleeper's head.

It was truly Grundwold's lucky day. Sleeping on the bed was the other breeder.

"Make a sound and you're chilled," Grundwold whispered in her ear.

She opened her mouth to let out a scream, and Fillinger pressed the blue-steel tip of his blaster even harder against the side of her head.

She closed her mouth and held her tongue.

"If you want to try your luck, you should have gone to the casino next door. We don't play games," Grundwold said. "Put on your boots. You're going on a little trip."

Flashing him a murderous look, but without making another sound, Mildred put on her boots.

Although she was fully clothed, Grundwold enjoyed

the view of the breeder's full, voluptuous figure, but didn't allow the sight to make him careless. "We'll take your blaster, thanks," Grundwold said, picking up the target revolver from the table and tucking it into the waistband of his pants.

Grundwold and Fillinger each took hold of one of the woman's arms and led her to the door. There was something about the look on the woman's face that Grundwold didn't like. She seemed to still want to fight back, and there was a good chance she might do something stupe like try to warn the others.

"Hold it!" Grundwold said.

Fillinger paused at the door, and Grundwold took the rag he used to keep his blaster clean out of a jacket pocket. He wrapped the ends of the rag around each of his hands and pulled it taut between them. Then he pressed the rag between her lips until she opened her mouth and he could push it past her teeth. Finally he tied the rag around her neck, preventing her from uttering a sound.

"You say a word or try to make a sound, the head of the guard outside the door will be turned into wallpaper," Grundwold said. "Understand?"

Mildred nodded.

"All right," Grundwold said. "I think now she's ready. Let's get out of here. And keep it quiet."

Together the sec chief and the sec man quickly ushered the prisoner out of the room and down the hallway. The guard was still there on his chair, his eyes never wavering from the door at the other end of the hallway.

As they reached the stairwell, the door was opened by an attentive sec man, and the three of them were able to pass through the doorway without a sound.

"Get her to the tower!" Grundwold ordered.

At once a pair of sec men escorted Mildred down the stairs and out of the hotel.

"Fillinger, go around to the other door and tell the men there to pull back." Grundwold looked at his wrist chron. "I want everyone at the base of the tower in ten minutes."

The sec men scattered without another word.

Grundwold lingered behind, making sure to give Fillinger enough time to go downstairs, through the lobby and back up to the second-floor landing to inform the others their mission had been successfully completed. When he was sure the sec men had pulled back from the door at the other end of the hall, Grundwold reached down and pulled the knife holding the door in front of him open.

The steel fire door swung closed...and locked, the sound of the locking mechanism echoing through a suddenly empty stairwell.

THE HUGE MUTIE CREATURE was on him. It looked very much like a lizard, but was as big as a horse. Its skin was made up of orange-and-green scales, and each of its forward arms ended with a set of three razor-sharp talons.

The Armorer had confronted the beast before and had lost. This time would be different. This time he was going to chill it, blasting it into a hundred different pieces.

The mutie beast neared, its three-inch fangs dripping gore left from its last meal. J.B. took several steps backward, giving him some time to draw his Smith & Wesson M-4000 scattergun. In a few moments there would be a hole in the creature's chest big enough to drive a wag through, and the whole episode would be little more than a bloody memory.

J.B. leveled his blaster at the beast, squeezed the trigger and heard the terrifying sound of a metallic click of the hammer falling on an empty chamber.

The beast lunged—

And J.B. awoke from his dream before it tore his limbs from his body.

He sat on his chair, gasping for breath. His eyelids still seemed heavy, as if he had been awakened from another mat-trans jump, and hadn't simply dozed off for a few minutes.

Had it been a few minutes?

J.B. glanced at his wrist chron. "Dark night!" he exclaimed. According to the chron, he'd been on watch for more than three hours. How could that have been? While there was no excuse for falling asleep while on watch, why hadn't Mildred or one of the others relieved him?

He ran down the hall to his room to check on Mildred.

She was gone.

He went across the hall to check on Ryan and Krysty...and found a dead sec man from the farm in their room, his belly slashed open, most likely by Ryan's panga.

Ryan and Krysty were gone, but Ryan's Steyr SSG-70 longblaster was still tucked safely under the bed.

What in dark night had happened to them? J.B. wondered. What had happened to him that he could sleep through it all?

He ran out into the hallway, shouting. "Doc, Jak, Dean!"

In moments the three friends appeared in the hallway, blasters in hand.

"What is it?" Dean asked.

J.B. stood in the middle of the hallway with Ryan's Steyr in his hand. "Ryan, Krysty and Mildred," he said. "They're gone."

Chapter Nine

"I can see the head!" the healer cried, sweat dripping off his nose. He'd wanted to call in an assistant hours earlier, but Baron Reichel had forbidden it, not wanting any more people than were necessary to see his wife in such a compromised state.

Reichel ville, on the southern shores of Erie Lake, hadn't been blessed with a newborn for many, many months. *Things* had been born, but they bore no resemblance to children. The baron could ill afford to let it be known that such monsters were born into his family. His bloodline was pure, and his heirs needed to be full norms. If his wife bore him a mutie, the fewer who knew about it the better.

Baron Reichel sat on a bench out in the hall just on the other side of the door to the healer's room. He had been in the room for the longest time, but his constant concern over his wife's agonized shrieks had prompted the healer to ask him to leave, allowing the healer to do his work without the interference and misguided concerns of an impassioned observer.

"You must push," the healer said. "Push harder!"

"I can't," the woman gasped, nearing the point of exhaustion.

The healer believed her. In all his years he had

never seen such a lengthy and painful birth. Everything about the delivery of this child was slow and complicated when in truth there were absolutely no signs warranting complications, or even pain for that matter. But here was the baron's wife, in labor half the day and still hours to go before the child was born.

"You must try," the healer urged, his voice showing far more compassion than normal. Usually he was very hard on women during birth, forcing them to work harder in order to end their ordeal more quickly. But Gayle Reichel had already suffered too much, for too long.

She cut short a moan and pushed.

The child's head moved slightly, no more than the width of several hairs. "Yes, that's it! Very good! Again!"

"It moved?" Gayle asked, her breathy voice filled with both surprise and relief.

"Yes, it's coming.... Now, push again."

She grimaced and tightened her body, tensing her stomach muscles and trying to squeeze the child through a birth canal that was far too small.

"I see an ear!" the healer exclaimed. "Keep going!"

Gayle was almost laughing now. She probably felt the child beginning to move a little more each time. After so many hours, she was happy to see it finally coming out of her body. She closed her eyes, pressed her lips together and grabbed at the wooden rails on either side of the roughly made bed.

Then she groaned sharply...and pushed.

Her fingernails cut into the hard, polished wood of the rails. The child's entire head appeared, followed quickly by its shoulders, neck.

And then...

The rest of its body slid out into the world, almost in a gush. The healer moved quickly, managing to catch the child, then inhaled a gasp. With his eyes closed, he held the child in his hands and for the longest time his mouth moved, but he uttered no sound. Finally he said in a whisper, "Father Death, have mercy on this soul."

BARON REICHEL HAD BEEN waiting for what seemed like hours. The screams of his wife had pained him, and now that they had stopped, he feared the worst.

But as he continued to wait in silence, not knowing what had happened to his wife was far worse than hearing her constant cries of pain. At last he stood and bravely opened the door to the healer's chambers.

The room seemed even quieter than the hall had been. His wife, Gayle, was lying on the bed, her chest rising and falling in a deep and regular rhythm. The healer sat at a desk with his head in his hands, no doubt exhausted by the lengthy birthing.

The baron looked around for the child but didn't see it.

When he closed the door behind him, the healer jumped and looked over at him, his face pale and his eyes wide and full of fear. As the baron moved closer, he noticed the healer looking even more aged and haggard than he remembered.

"Is she all right?" the baron asked in a whisper.

The healer nodded. "Your wife is resting. She will recover in a very short time."

"And what of the child?"

"It is resting, as well…in the bassinet over there." He pointed to a small wooden cradle made of tree branches and lined with straw.

The baron looked at the healer for a long time, knowing something wasn't right. If the child was doing well, the healer would be overjoyed, and his wife would be holding the child to her breast, even in her current state of exhaustion. And then there was the word the healer had used. *It* was resting, he'd said. Not *he* or *she,* but *it.* Something was definitely wrong.

"Can I see—" he wondered which word to use "—it?"

"Perhaps it might be best if—"

"I said, can I see it?" the baron said, much more forceful this time.

Gayle stirred at the sound of her husband's voice. "Is that you, love?" she asked.

The healer knew better than to defy the baron's wishes a second time. "Of course." He got up and walked over to the bassinet, reached into the cradle and took out the bundled child, wrapped tightly in a scarlet blanket.

He handed the bundle to the baron.

Baron Reichel found it awkward to hold the bundle properly, but he eventually managed a firm but gentle grasp. He hadn't held all that many babies in his lifetime, but this child *felt* different from the ones he'd held before. Its body seemed hard and bony, wrong somehow.

The healer turned away, taking up a position near the baron's wife.

Baron Reichel pulled aside the blanket and looked upon an abomination.

The child's eyes were open wide, shining black and glassy in the dim light of the room. There were hard nubs of bones along the crown of its head, almost as if it were the offspring of some mutie lizard.

The baron swallowed, his body shuddering in shock. He pulled the blanket farther aside and saw that the child's two arms were on the right side of its body and a leg was where the other arm should be. A second leg was positioned in the center of the lower portion of the trunk, looking much like a tail.

Baron Reichel felt his knees go weak and his heart begin to pound in his throat, choking him.

This was no child of his.

It was a child of the rad-blasted Deathlands.

He took another glance at the creature and grimaced.

It wasn't even a child.

It was a monster.

He wrapped it back in the blanket and held it at arm's length.

"Have you seen him?" Gayle asked, her voice soft yet proud. "Is he beautiful?"

"Yes, very," the baron said, taking the child out of the room.

"Where are you going with him?"

Her words fell on deaf ears, fading into silence.

Once he was out in the hall, the baron closed the door behind him and pulled his knife from its scabbard.

The thing was grunting in his arms, sounding more like a pig than a child. He placed the blade of his knife under the creature's chin, drawing it evenly across its throat.

Blood splattered onto the floor like rain.

Moments later, all was quiet.

AN HOUR LATER the baron, healer and Reichel ville's sec chief met in the ville's main square. The day was warm, but there seemed to be a definite chill in the air. The baron had called the meeting because it was obvious that something had to be done about the rash of recent mutie births in the ville. It was one thing when the residents of the ville were having mutie offspring, but now that it had happened to the baron, the problem had suddenly come to the fore.

Not only was the ville slowly dying off with no young blood to replace the old, but the baron was growing old, as well, and he was still without a son, or even a daughter, to one day take his place. If he didn't have a norm child soon he would grow too old to hold on to the seat of power long enough for one of his offspring to become the new baron. If his wife couldn't deliver him an heir, he'd eventually be killed by an ambitious sec man.

And Reichel ville would be no more.

"Have you seen the...creature?" the baron asked his sec chief.

The sec chief, a man named Ganley, simply nodded.

The baron turned to the healer. "What's causing these mutie births? Is it rad sickness?"

The healer shook his head. "The site of Reichel ville was chosen because it was far enough away from the hot spots around Pittsville and Detroit." He took the rad counter from his collar. "According to this and the others I've given to people in the ville, we're clear."

"What about our water? Food?" sec chief Ganley asked.

"If we were drinking Erie Lake water, we might be getting rad poisoned, but our water well is over a hundred feet deep. I'm almost certain it's still clean."

"Almost certain?" the sec chief commented.

"What about food?" the baron asked, ignoring the sec chief's comment for the time being.

"We keep the best norm fish we catch for ourselves and process the muties we catch for trade. And we grow our own vegetables, so we're not getting rad poisoning that way."

"Then why was my son born a monster?" the baron bellowed, slamming his fist onto his knee.

The healer swallowed. "On our last trade convoy to the eastern villes, I visited one of the great libraries there. In one of the books I read about something called inbreeding."

"What is that?" the baron asked, his anger gone for the moment, replaced by curiosity.

"Inbreeding has to do with the mating of closely related individuals." The healer paused, choosing his words carefully so as to not incur the baron's wrath. "It is considered undesirable because it increases the risk that an offspring will inherit copies of rare recessive genes from both parents and form disabilities because of it."

"So what are you telling me—the Reichel family's blood is tainted and impure?"

"No, not at all, sir. In the book, it said the same thing happened to predark royal families hundreds of years before skydark.

"Lady Gayle is the daughter of your father's sister, isn't she?" the healer asked.

The baron nodded.

"Well, that means that whatever recessive genes you possess, she would likely have them, too."

The baron looked confused.

The healer took a moment to rethink his explanation. If he couldn't convince the baron that the problem was a real threat, there would be nothing done to correct it. "Think of your genes as being a length of steel chain. The chain has several weak links to it. When you have a child with Lady Gayle, her genes, or chain, has exactly the same weak links as yours, so there are parts of the newborn that are defective because her chain couldn't strengthen the weak links of your chain, only weaken it again."

The baron seemed to understand now. Reichel ville had prospered on the shores of Erie Lake for some seventy-five years. It was a small fishing ville, large enough to have a well-armed sec force, but small enough not to be worth the trouble of raiding, since the only real thing of value they possessed was their experience as fishermen. In seventy-five years no one had joined the ville from the outside, and the population had never risen over 150.

"The same weakening occurred before you were born, each generation weakening the chain again and again until…"

The baron placed his left hand over his right, hiding the fingers of his right hand, which were all half as long as the ones on his left. "How can we fix it?" the baron asked.

"Reichel ville needs new blood," the healer explained. "If you don't bring in some new people with new genes into the ville, you won't have the birth of any new norms to celebrate. Not yours, not anyone's."

Sec chief Ganley cleared his throat. "I know a place where we can trade for men and women," he said. "All of them norms. Good breeders."

"Where?"

"A farm to the north. Across the lake."

"But we're just fishermen," the baron stated. "What can we trade for slaves, fish?"

"Our fish would possibly make a decent trade for an old slave, but surely they'd want more for breeders."

"We don't have to trade with them," Ganley suggested.

"What are you saying?"

"We have a well-stocked armory that we've rarely

had to use. We could form a strong raiding party and simply take what we need from this farm.''

''But they would be armed and prepared for such an attack,'' the baron said. ''We'd lose many of the ville's best citizens.''

''The ville is dying as it is,'' the sec chief pointed out. ''At least this way if we die, we do so trying to save the ville.''

The baron considered it, then said, ''Bring as much fish as you can to trade. If they refuse, use all the blasters and grens we have to take what we need.''

''As you wish,'' the sec chief said.

''The survival of Reichel ville depends on it.''

Chapter Ten

"Get in the wag," the sec man grunted, pushing Ryan hard from behind. The one-eyed man's step quickened, but he didn't stumble. He wouldn't give the stupes the satisfaction. They'd butted him with their blasters, kicked them with their boots and punched him countless times, but he hadn't fallen.

It was partly pride on Ryan's part, but also a matter of survival. If he had been unable to carry on, they probably would have chilled him on the spot rather than drag him all the way back to the farm. If he could hold out long enough, he might get the opportunity to repay them for their kindness.

Ryan still didn't understand how they'd managed to capture him so easily. He was usually a light sleeper and should have awakened at the slightest bit of trouble. Instead he was tired and slow-footed and hadn't even noticed Krysty was gone. If he hadn't been so groggy, he might have been able to chill the second sec man as he'd done the first, but his arms and legs seemed so heavy, he was lucky to get just one of them.

And what about J.B.? These sec men had been able to sneak into their rooms and take them away on the Armorer's watch. These sec men were either something special, and Ryan hadn't seen any evidence to prove that, or the same thing that had slowed him had slowed J.B., as well. Judging by the way they handled themselves and the way they'd treated him so far, Ryan was convinced it was the latter.

The wag was an old double-axled transport with a flatbed in back outfitted with wooden benches to sit on. Ryan had trouble climbing onto the back of the wag, but there was no shortage of sec men willing to lend him a hand. They eagerly grabbed him and threw him into the back of the wag, his head slamming into one of the wooden benches.

"Ryan!" a voice called out.

It sounded like Krysty.

Ryan opened his eye, and there was the titian-haired beauty, on her knees and leaning over him with her hands tied behind her back. He checked to see if she'd been hurt in any way, but she looked to be fine. That was good for the sec men, because if there'd been a scratch on her, there would be even more hell to pay.

"Are you all right?" Krysty asked.

Ryan nodded.

"You don't look all right," Mildred said, coming to Ryan's side and leaning awkwardly over him, her hands still bound behind her, as well.

Ryan tried to say something, forgetting his mouth was still covered with tape.

Mildred turned and wriggled her fingers. Ryan moved closer so that the edge of the tape touched Mildred's hand. A few moments later she had a firm grip on the corner of the tape. Ryan rolled away from her and the tape tore away from his face, taking hair and several patches of skin with it. There was some pain, but at least now he could take deeper breaths and talk.

"Are you two hurt?" Ryan asked, getting up from the floor of the wag and taking a seat on a bench.

"Not really," Mildred answered. "They've handled both of us with kid gloves. Real gentle like, which makes me a bit nervous."

"Is there anyone else?"

"No, just the three of us in this wag," Krysty answered.

"Why do they want us three?" Mildred wondered.

"To work the orchards," Ryan stated. "Those workers we saw on the farm must have been slaves."

"I don't know, lover," Krysty mused. "From the way the sec men were looking at us, I don't think they went to the trouble of capturing us just so we could work the fields."

"Mebbe women are different kinds of slaves," Ryan pondered, not liking the thoughts that were crossing his mind.

Just then a sec man appeared at the back of the wag. "Shut your trap, Cyclops," he barked. "And keep it shut till we get to the farm. Next time you talk, it'll be answering questions from Baron Fox."

Ryan just stared at the man, his gaze never wavering.

The wag started to move.

The sec man eventually looked away.

"WHEN I WOKE UP they were gone," J.B. said as he, Doc, Jak and Dean inspected Ryan's room.

"Ah, a puzzle worthy of the sleuth of Baker Street," Doc commented, inspecting the room a bit more closely than the others.

"Who?" Dean asked.

"Holmes, young Master Cawdor. Sherlock Holmes."

Dean just looked at Doc strangely, as did Jak.

"They must have taken Krysty first," Doc concluded. "And outside of this room."

"Why do you say that?" J.B. asked.

"Some of her belongings are on this night table, so this was her side of the bed. There's no sign of a struggle here, unlike on the side Ryan had slept on." They all looked at the dead sec man, lying facedown in a pool of his own blood. "Also, while there are several of Ryan's bloody footprints in the hallway, leading to the far door, there were none made by Krysty's Western boots."

"But how did they manage to get Krysty?"

"I think the nearby door is the key. I think she must have awakened in the middle of the night, perhaps attuned to some disturbance or danger her prescient ability allowed her to sense was very close at hand. She took her blaster and went to investigate, most likely without waking Ryan. She must have opened the door at the end of the hall to have a look up or down the stairs when she was taken by someone on the other side, most likely the very danger she had ventured out of her room to investigate."

The three friends listened closely to Doc's explanation, none of them able to find fault with his reasoning.

Doc continued, obviously intrigued by the peculiar sequence of events and enjoying the process of deduction. "Once the door was open, the sec men were able to come in and out as they pleased, avoiding detection because you were concentrating on the door at the other end of the hall. They searched each room, working their way down the hallway toward you. They found Ryan first. He was able to chill one of the sec men, but not all of them and they managed to subdue him and take him away. Next they found Mildred and were able to steal her away, as well."

"Dark night!" J.B. cursed under his breath.

"And then they stopped their raid," Doc said, striking the end of his swordstick on the floor for emphasis, "and went back to the farm."

"Why?" Dean asked.

"I think it has to do with the women. I believe that is all they were interested in from the beginning. Ryan just happened to be in the way, and quite frankly I am surprised they did not just kill him where he lay."

"Wake up rest," Jak offered.

"Yes, in all likelihood," Doc said.

"But why would they want just the women?" Dean asked.

Doc didn't answer.

Even so, Dean slowly realized it for himself. "Oh," he said.

"It's my fault," J.B. said. "I let everyone down, just like in my dream."

Doc put a hand on the Armorer's shoulder. "No, it is not your fault, John Barrymore. There's another element to this scenario that I have yet to mention."

"What is it?"

"Well, under normal circumstances, a bunch of local sec men would never have accomplished this feat without one or all of us waking up and killing a fair number of them, if not all. So, the question is, what was different this time?"

"Food," Jak said.

"Exactly, my dear Jak. The fruit we traded for had to have been contaminated in some way, either naturally by radiation poisoning, or on purpose by sec men with a plan."

"Sec men with plan," Jak decided.

"I think you're right," Dean said. "I've never been so tired in my life."

"Nor have any of us," Doc commented. "So don't blame yourself, John Barrymore. You couldn't have helped it."

"Rad-blasted sec men and their baron are gonna have hell to pay," J.B. said through gritted teeth.

"That's the spirit," Doc cheered.

"Let's move," J.B. said, leading the way.

Chapter Eleven

Sec chief Ganley supervised the raiding party that was assembling on the shores of Erie Lake. He had spread word about the raid through Reichel ville, being careful to explain why it was necessary and the dangers the raiders would encounter.

They would be taking two of their sleekest fishing vessels. Each one measured roughly eighteen feet long and was powered by paddlers, four to a side. That meant the ideal number of raiders would be eighteen, giving each boat eight paddlers and a navigator. But while eighteen raiders would move fastest across the lake, they would need more than that when they reached their destination. Ganley decided on twenty-four, which gave each boat ten paddlers, a navigator and a lookout, which was something important to have considering there were plenty of mutie creatures out in the deeper waters in the middle of the lake.

Yet despite deciding on twenty-four raiders, Ganley had no trouble filling out the ranks. He'd selected twenty-three so far and now had to decide on the final spot with five volunteers to choose from.

The first was a boy who was obviously too young. "Sorry," the sec chief said, "but I need some to stay here in Reichel ville to protect it while I'm gone."

The boy was disappointed but not surprised.

Next was an old man whose prime years had come and gone long ago. He walked with a cane, but carried a mint-condition blaster. The blaster would be handy to have with them on the raid, but not if he could only use one hand to fire it.

Ganley shook his head.

The old-timer seemed relieved, as if he'd volunteered simply to save face.

The final three were all women, which mattered not to the sec chief. His only concern was that they be able to fight, and he'd seen women who were every bit as capable as men and often were even more cunning.

The first carried a remade blaster that looked as if it were held together with glue, baling wire and string. She seemed to be uncomfortable holding the weapon in her hand, as if she were afraid it might go off while she held it.

"Let me see you change clips," the sec chief said, pointing to the blaster.

"That's the thing that holds the bullets, right?"

Ganley nodded.

She fumbled with it, then said, "I'm sorry, it was my man's blaster. He never showed me how to use it because it was always by his side."

"Mebbe you can stay here in the ville and learn."

The woman nodded and walked away.

The next woman was young and lithe, and was dressed in little more than rags. Her only weapon was a sharpened stick, but there looked to be bloodstains on the end of it.

"Is that the only weapon you have?" the sec chief asked, getting up from his seat.

The woman nodded.

"The place we're headed will have plenty of well-armed sec men. I need blasters." He reached for the stick with his right hand.

In a blur of motion, the woman swung the stick away from his grasp around the back of her neck and ended up with the pointed end directly under the sec chief's chin. She pressed the tip firmly against his flesh, until a single drop of blood ran down the shaft.

"But there'll be plenty of close-in fighting, too," Ganley said, "and sharp sticks can kill just as easily as a round from a blaster."

She pulled the point from his chin.

"You're in."

Ganley looked for the last volunteer, but she had already turned and was well on her way back home.

"We leave in an hour."

THE WAG WAS in good condition and carried them comfortably over the weed-covered roads toward Fox Farm. Judging by the smell of lubricating oil coming from the wag's underside, this baron had plenty of jack to spend on the things that were vital to his operation. Ryan had made a mental note of the sec men's blasters and aside from a few well-put-together remades, they all had quality weapons. Sure, the baron had an advantage with an unlimited supply of electricity, but he was obviously trading more than just fruit.

"What do you think they did with J.B., Doc and Dean?" Mildred asked, her voice masked by the throaty rumble of the wag's diesel engine.

"I think they're fine," Ryan answered. "The sec men left the building after they got Mildred, so they all probably got a good night's sleep."

"How long do you think it'll be until they come after us, lover?" Krysty asked.

"Couple days, mebbe," Ryan said. "They'll need to come up with a plan."

"So we should just relax and make the best of things for the next little while."

"Yes." Ryan nodded. "And try to figure a way—"

Ryan's words were cut off by the butt of a long-blaster that caught him square in the jaw.

"No talking until you see the baron, Cyclops!" said the sec man riding in the back of the wag. He raised his blaster again and moved to strike a second blow, but Ryan—with his hands still bound behind him—managed to get out of the way in time, and then put a boot into the man's midsection. He pushed as hard as he could, sending the man back into his seat, where he hit the wooden bench with a thud.

He got up again, intending to strike Ryan, when the wag began to slow, then came to a full stop.

"Get them ready," someone called from the cab of the wag. "Baron Fox is waiting."

At the mention of the baron's name, the sec man relaxed his stance. Ryan was curious about what the baron might be like considering that the mere mention of his name could put fear into one of his sec men's eyes.

The wag jerked forward again, and when they were past a heavy steel fence, the gate closed behind the wag, securing them inside the compound.

Ryan figured he wouldn't have long to wait before he and the baron met face-to-face.

After a short drive the wag pulled into a barn that was full of barrels, bushel baskets and jars. There were remnants of a couple of wags, but they looked as if they'd been stripped for parts. Off to one corner stood an electrical transformer and rows and rows of what looked like batteries. Other items crowded the end of the barn closer to them, everything from farm tools to barrels of diesel and oil, garden tools and power generators, everything a farming operation might need to produce food and keep it guarded until it could be traded for other useful items.

At the other end of the barn was a collection of seven miniwags. These were small, two-man vehicles that ran on electricity. Each of the seven was currently attached to a wall-mounted box that was more than likely the source of electricity that kept the miniwags' batteries charged.

"I wish J.B. could see all this," Ryan muttered under his breath as he eased himself off the end of the wag's flatbed onto the dirty, straw-covered floor of the barn.

A half-dozen sec men ringed the three friends. The rest made their way out of the barn, their mission having been completed. That surprised Ryan since most of the sec men he'd known would have hung around to hear some words of compliment from the baron, but these men obviously weren't interested in that.

Just then, a small door opened up at the far end of the barn and a man—most likely the baron—entered the building. He was followed by a second man, unarmed, who remained several steps behind and carried a large black book under his arm.

The baron was dressed in a shiny, multicolored bathrobe and wore an equally shiny pair of black boots. He was also smoking a pipe. The man looked pleasant enough, Ryan thought, but if he'd learned anything over the years, it was that looks could be very deceiving, especially where barons were concerned.

"How many men did you lose?" the baron asked, looking over the three friends as if he were inspecting cattle at auction.

One of the sec men stepped forward. Ryan figured him to be the sec chief. "Just the one. This one chilled him," he said, pointing his blaster at Ryan.

"That why you brought him here?"

"No, sir. If we chilled him, he might have awakened the rest. He—"

The baron nodded as if he weren't interested in what else the sec chief had to say about Ryan. His attention was suddenly drawn to Mildred. He walked over to her and examined her more closely. After being pushed around and getting on and off the wag with her hands tied behind her back, her clothes had become disheveled and her shirt had opened halfway down her chest. The baron put a hand on her cheek, gauging the texture of her skin and pulling her lips back to examine her teeth.

"Nice," he said. "Very nice."

Mildred jerked her head away from the baron's touch, and the man laughed.

"Spirited, too, I see. I like that. I like that a lot." He lingered in front of Mildred for a few moments, putting a hand on her neck and letting his fingers roam down her chest, under her blouse and over one of her breasts.

Mildred didn't move. Instead she stood by impassively, letting the baron squeeze her breast and tweak the nipple. But when he finally looked her in the eye, she said, "You better be enjoying that, mister, because you're going to be paying the price for doing it."

The baron withdrew his hand from her breast, seemingly unsure what to make of the dark-skinned woman. And then he laughed. "Oh, that's good. I like that," he said. But then just as quickly, the humor was gone from his voice. His eyes narrowed and he moved in closer to Mildred's face. "I wonder if you'd be just as courageous with a red-hot angle iron shoved up your ass."

Mildred said nothing, wisely deciding not to press her luck with so many armed sec men around.

The baron moved down the line to Ryan, standing in front of him for long time while his eyes moved up and down his frame. "So, you chilled one of my sec men."

Ryan said nothing.

The baron turned his head slightly to the side. "What'd he do it with?" he asked the sec chief.

"Bastard big knife," the sec chief said. "Cut his belly wide open the second we woke him up."

The baron nodded, obviously impressed. He reached over and flipped up Ryan's eye patch. Instead of being disgusted by the empty socket, the man seemed intrigued by it.

The baron replaced the eye patch and puffed on his pipe. Then he reached between Ryan's legs to fondle his genitals.

Ryan wanted nothing more than to put his knee into the man's groin and then stomp on his neck as he flopped around on the ground, but he knew it would be the last move he ever made. So instead of fighting back, Ryan followed Mildred's lead and did nothing.

"Hmm," the baron said. "You just might prove to be a useful addition to my operation." He took his hand away and ran his fingers through Ryan's hair. "Ruggedly handsome. You wouldn't have any problems finding a breeder to rut with, would you?"

The baron moved on to Krysty.

"Ah, saved the best for last, I see."

He stepped in front of her, then did a slow walk around her so that he could appreciate her from all angles. There was a wide smile on his face.

"I knew she was attractive from afar," the baron said, "but I had no idea..."

Krysty's sentient hair was curled tightly around her head and shoulders, and the rest of her body looked just as uncomfortable with the baron's attention.

"The possibilities…" the man muttered. There was a fire alight in his eyes.

He stood there in front of Krysty for the longest time, simply looking at her body.

The sec men seemed to be getting tired of just standing around. Finally the sec chief asked a question. "What do you want us to do with them?"

The baron turned to Ryan and Mildred and said, "Put these two in gen pop, working the orchards."

"And the redhead?"

"Take her to my quarters and make her comfortable," the baron said. "I've got something special in mind for her."

Chapter Twelve

Two boats full of raiders, blasters and fish shoved off from the southern shore of Erie Lake before the sun was at its highest point in the sky. Sec chief Ganley took the navigator's position of the first boat, since he was the one in charge of the mission and it was only right that he take the lead. Later, when they were out of view of the people of Reichel ville who'd gathered to send them off, he would take his turn paddling, just like everyone else.

The plan was to travel along the southern shore of Erie Lake until dark, then make camp for the night and set out the next day on the second leg of their water journey. Then, sometime on the second day, they would land at the old garrison that guarded the mouth of the river there.

Another night's rest and they'd make the final part of their journey overland, heading straight north until they hit upon their destination. Ganley wasn't happy about having to travel so far overland, but it was easier and safer than risking the river and the treacherous falls at its end.

"Stroke...stroke...stroke..." the sec chief called out, keeping a steady pace.

Despite the extra passengers and the load of dried

fish, the boats were making good progress. Perhaps they wouldn't be spending as much time on the water as he'd thought.

J.B., JAK, DEAN and Doc left the hotel, slightly burdened by Ryan's, Krysty's and Mildred's belongings. J.B. had wanted to leave the bags of fruit behind, but Doc insisted that they take the food with them. Even though the fruit had been tainted by some sort of drug, Doc thought that he'd be able to make use of at least one bag during their trip.

J.B. didn't press the matter. If the old man wanted to take the fruit, then he was free to carry it himself.

The four friends moved slowly through the ville's blasted core. While they were always on the lookout for anything of value that they could use, especially now that they had to rescue the others, it was clear the ville had already been picked clean by local barons, travelers and muties. Plenty of useful items were likely still hidden away inside the ville, but they didn't have time to search blindly through dozens of homes and buildings looking for needles in haystacks.

As they walked past the large high tower that overlooked the falls, J.B. stopped to look up at the great concrete needle.

"What are you thinking?" Dean asked.

"That there was someone up there yesterday watching us enter the ville."

"Think someone there now?" Jak asked.

"Don't know."

"Want find out?"

J.B. thought about it, then said, "Yeah."

They headed toward the tower and entered through the smashed entryway. The little shops inside had been cleaned out of the most useful items, and only little trinkets bearing pictures of the falls remained. Dean picked up a few and stuffed them in his pockets.

Jak checked out the routes to the top. The elevators weren't working, but the stairs were clear. There were no signs of any sec men guarding the base of the tower, which meant that the top would likely be clear, as well. "Take stairs," Jak said when he'd finished his recce.

J.B., Dean and Doc followed the teenager into the stairwell. They had gone up three flights when Jak suddenly stopped and turned.

"Muties," he said to the friends behind him.

J.B. looked up the twisting staircase and could see three of the thin, spiderlike creatures standing on the stairs above them, unmoving and seemingly wary of the friends.

"Let's blast them," Dean suggested, always eager for a fight.

"No," J.B. commanded. "We can't shoot around corners, and there's no telling what kind of ricochets we'll get off this concrete."

"Want go back down?" Jak asked.

"Mebbe," J.B. said.

"But you would very much appreciate getting a good lay of the land from the vantage point offered by this magnificent tower, correct?" Doc asked.

"Yeah, a good recce of the area would be real helpful."

"Then might I try something I have in mind that I think will rid us of these muties and get us to the top of the tower without firing a shot."

"I'm open to suggestions, Doc," J.B. said.

Without another word, the old man took several steps toward the top of the tower. The muties backed away from him, matching his movements step for step and keeping the distance between them constant. When he reached the next landing, Doc stopped and put about a dozen pieces of fruit on the floor, then rejoined J.B., Jak and Dean.

"What now?" Jak asked.

"Patience," Doc said. "Give them a minute."

But seconds later the muties were coming down the stairs and tearing savagely into the fruit.

"Let us go," Doc said, leading the way.

The friends had their blasters at the ready as they passed the feeding muties, who were so ravenous they didn't stop eating to even look up as they passed.

In seconds the four companions were again hurrying toward the top of the tower, the sounds of hungry muties fading slowly behind them.

"What about on the way down?" J.B. asked.

"I think we shall find them rather cooperative at that point," Doc answered.

"They're just going to let us pass?" Dean questioned.

"No, I suspect they will all be quite fast asleep by then."

MILDRED AND RYAN WERE led out of the barn by three sec men. Two of the white electrically powered mini-wags were waiting for them.

"Get on the back of the wag," a sec man ordered.

The two friends climbed up onto the wag with their backs to the driver. The other two sec men got into the second wag and when the driver pulled away, they followed.

"Where do you think they're taking us?" Mildred asked Ryan.

"Probably to work the fields with the rest of the slaves," Ryan answered.

"What do you think they'll do with Krysty?"

Ryan shook his head slightly. "Don't know."

"She'll be all right. She can take care of herself."

"It's not Krysty that I'm worried about."

"Who then?" Mildred asked.

"The baron. I'm worried Krysty will chill him before I get the chance to do it."

They continued to roll past the trees. Ryan tried to gauge how fast they were traveling so he could get an idea how big the farm was, but he stopped trying after a while. There was no point to it. Fox Farm was a huge operation, probably growing enough fruit and vegetables to supply several eastern villes.

The wags began to slow, and Ryan craned his neck to have a look around. People were working in the trees, picking fruit under the watchful eyes of even more sec men. Others crawled over the ground on all fours pulling weeds from the earth between the trees. These people were also watched closely by sec men, and every once in a while one would get a blaster butt slammed into his back or thigh.

"Get out!" the sec men in the second wag ordered when the miniwags came to a stop.

Ryan and Mildred got off the wag and stood with their hands still bound behind them. A sec man overseeing the workers approached, pulled a knife from a scabbard on his belt and cut them both free.

"Start picking!" the sec man in charge of the work detail shouted.

Ryan and Mildred headed toward the trees that were being picked by the rest of the crew and started working themselves, trying to keep busy while they attempted to figure out how things worked out in the fields.

At the edge of the stand of trees a sec man and a woman were having what looked like a rather heated discussion. Suddenly she dropped down on her knees in front of him and for a moment it looked as if he were going to chill her with his blaster. But instead of shooting her, he shouldered his weapon and began unbuttoning his pants.

The workers had stopped picking fruit and were now watching the woman provide the man with a sexual favor.

"Keep working!" another sec man shouted.

Slowly the pickers went back to doing their job. Ryan and Mildred began picking fruit like the others, but Ryan was still able to watch the couple out of the corner of his eye.

The sec man had pulled out his cock and the woman had taken it in her mouth. He was thrusting against her, holding her head roughly in place. The rest of the workers had gotten back to work as if nothing out of the ordinary was happening.

When the man was done, he pushed the woman away and did up his pants. She walked back toward the others, a resigned expression on her face.

"What kind of place is this?" Mildred asked.

"Don't know," Ryan answered. "But before we know for sure, let's just get busy picking fruit."

WHEN THEY REACHED the top of the tower, J.B., Jak, Doc and Dean spent a few minutes admiring the view. Even though Mildred had said only a small amount of water was flowing over the falls, they were still an impressive sight.

But more important than the view of the falls was that they were better able to see Fox Farm from the top of the tower, and could get an idea of its layout. It was located on the northwest corner of an intersection between two roads that had long ago been overgrown with weeds. The farm had to stretch a mile or more in each direction because the far northern corners of the fence were just visible from their vantage point.

Two large buildings stood near the front gate of the complex where the friends had traded for fruit. Set back from the gate was a large rectangular two-story building, which seemed to be the focal point. A tower rose from its center, allowing the sec force to oversee a large portion of the farm. If they were going to rescue Ryan and the others, they would definitely have to take the main building. If nothing else, the tower would have to be knocked over because one or more sec men positioned inside would be able to cover the entire farmyard with a carpet of blasterfire, taking down everything in its path.

Behind the main building were rows and rows of trees that stretched to the north. The shapes and sizes varied, and in between a few of the rows were patches of brown soil that were probably used for growing vegetables.

To the left of the orchards were two rows of tiny cabins where either the sec men or farmworkers lived.

"A lot of places to hide once we're inside," J.B. said.

Jak nodded in agreement. "Have to fight house to house. Tree to tree. Many sec men get chilled."

"It occurs to me that things might go better for us once we're inside if we know where Ryan, Krysty and Mildred are being held," Doc commented. "Otherwise, we could be looking for them for a long, long time."

J.B. nodded. "We're too far away for that now. We'll still have to do another recce when we get in closer, mebbe even one inside the fence."

"But what about the electricity?" Dean asked.

Yes, J.B. thought, what about that?

Off to the left stood a big wooden barn that was probably used for storage of either food or equipment, or both. Smaller sheds stood to the north side of the barn, and it was possible that the farm's arms and munitions were kept there. But connected to the shed were several thick cables that were strung over the fence and continued toward the west, before turning south toward the falls.

"Electricity might not be as big a problem as we thought," J.B. stated.

"MAKE YOURSELF comfortable," Baron Fox said, a bit of a feral smile on his face. He had changed out of his boots and into his slippers, but as always he was still wearing his brightly colored silk bathrobe.

Krysty was glad to sit down on the couch in the baron's office, having gotten little rest before being taken from the hotel in the middle of the night.

"Can I get you something to eat or drink?"

Krysty thought of the fruits that had made them all sleepy and careless. She could only imagine what might happen to her if she got drowsy now. "No, thank you," she said.

In addition to the baron, several men were inside the room. Most noticeable was a man standing just inside the door like a piece of furniture. He said nothing, hadn't even moved, and Krysty thought there was something dangerous about how quiet he was. He looked to be thinking all the time, and what was going on in the room at that moment didn't require all that much thought. There were several sec men, too, but they all seemed giddy as prepubescent teens. They were dangerous, too, but in a way that was different from the man with the book under his arm. The sec men would chill you at any moment; the other would chill only when the time was right.

"You're rather beautiful," the baron said. "Did you know that?"

"I've been told once or twice."

"Unzip your jumpsuit."

Krysty shook her head. "No."

The baron smiled. "All the breeders who come to Fox Farm are like you at first. They resist, or they have crazy notions about love, but I assure you I can be very persuasive."

"I'm sure you can be."

"You see, your options right now are very limited. You can make it easy on yourself and rut with me willingly, or I'll have you chained to a wall and force you to breed."

Krysty said nothing.

The baron walked over to the door and knocked on it three times. A moment later the door opened and the man with the ledger under his arm reappeared, followed this time by three sec men. The sec men surrounded her and leveled their blasters at her head.

"Now," the baron said and smiled. "Unzip your jumpsuit to your waist."

Krysty slowly complied, taking her time to give herself the chance to think.

Mildred had once told her about a predark defense tactic for women in this situation suggesting a woman should cooperate with the man until she found a safe way out of her predicament. And if she never found a way out, then she should keep cooperating because that way at least the man might not chill her, which was something he was sure to do if you resisted. It seemed like triple-stupe advice, but Krysty wasn't sure what else she could do at the moment.

Of course, she could always call on the power of Gaia, the Earth Mother, if she needed to. Although it would leave her weak and vulnerable afterward, it wouldn't be so bad if she was able to chill the baron and a few of his sec men along the way. She decided she'd keep Gaia as a last resort, calling upon her if and when Mildred's predark strategy didn't work out.

"Excellent," the baron said as she finished. "Now, take it off."

Krysty hesitated for a second, but then did as she was told, slipping her arms out of the jumpsuit so that the top part of it fell around her waist and left her upper body exposed. It was possible that the man didn't want to do anything other than look.

"All of it!" he said. "And the undergarments."

When she finally stripped, she could hear a few approving words being muttered by the sec men in the room. At another time she might be flattered, but right now she was feeling sick to her stomach.

"A natural redhead, I see," the baron observed. "You are now my prize breeder. Your offspring will bring top jack for years to come. Congratulations."

Krysty was about to tell the baron to go fuck himself, but decided it might be wiser to hold her tongue for just a little while longer.

"Sit down," he instructed.

Krysty sat again, crossing her legs and folding her arms across her chest.

The baron opened his bathrobe to expose himself as

if he were drawing back curtains. He was hard, but his cock was small for a man of his height.

"Spread your legs!"

She uncrossed her legs and slowly spread them apart, wondering if the predark instructions Mildred had told her about had been made up by men like this baron. She didn't seem to be any closer to finding a way out of this situation.

She readied herself to call upon the power of Gaia.

The baron was now standing directly in front of her, his small erection just a few inches from her face.

"Take it!" he said.

The sec men in the room chuckled at that.

"I said take it," the baron repeated.

This was where it ended, Krysty thought. She reached out with her right hand and gently caressed the baron's scrotum, feeling his testicles sliding around inside his sack. With her left hand she took hold of his cock, her fingers able to reach all the way around the thin shaft, and then some.

"Ahh," the baron sighed. "That's good."

Krysty, ready to invoke the name of Gaia, prepared to squeeze as hard as she could with her right hand. She also tensed her left hand, ready to give his scrotum a hard twist.

"Enough!" the baron said, pushing Krysty back in her chair.

She released her hold on the baron's genitals.

"I don't want to scar you, my pretty one," the baron said, doing up his bathrobe. "I know an East

Coast breeder who is partial to redheads, and I doubt he'd pay much jack for, uh, damaged goods.''

Krysty began getting dressed.

"But first you have to give me an offspring.''

"Who do you wish her to rut with?'' the man with the book asked.

"I imagine there will be many who'll want her,'' the baron said. "But only the strongest man on the farm would be worthy of her, so we'll have a gladitorial-type contest for her. Men, battling each other to the death for the privilege of rutting with this vision of beauty.'' The baron looked out the window at his orchards. "Yes, men brutally chilling each other, spilling blood, guts and gore, all for the right to mate and make new life with this woman.''

Krysty wanted no part of the baron's mad plan, but as long as she played along with it, she'd be safe and able to try to get in touch with Ryan and Mildred so they could begin to figure out an escape plan.

The baron turned to two of the sec men in the room. "Take her to one of the private lounges and make sure she's comfortable. I want her to look good for the combatants.''

The sec men nodded and led Krysty to the door.

The baron turned to the man with the book, and took his riding crop from the pocket of his bathrobe. "Send me a breeder,'' he said, whipping the crop against his hand. "And make her red-haired if we have one.''

"Yes, baron,'' Norman Bauer replied. "Right away.''

Chapter Thirteen

Doc had been right about the muties.

When the four friends were done making their recce of the area from the observation level of the tower, they found the fruit gone from the stairs, and the three muties fast asleep on one of the landings.

"So you see, John Barrymore," Doc said, as they carefully stepped over the sleeping muties. "It wasn't your fault that you fell asleep on watch. The fruit had a similar effect on all of us."

J.B. nodded, feeling a little better, but only a little. So there was a reason why he'd fallen asleep on his watch. It still wasn't anything but an excuse.

They made it down from the tower without further incident and began the journey northwest toward the farm. When they reached the outer edges of the ville, where the ruins of the old city ended and the ruins of the old farms began, they decided to take a short break to eat what little supplies they had with them. Doc was still carrying the bag of fruit, but none in the group was hungry enough to eat any. Instead, they made do with a few pieces of jerked beef J.B. had with him, and a bag of nuts Jak had squirreled away in one of the pockets of his jacket.

"Any more peanuts in the bag?" Dean asked Jak.

"Ate them."

A sound erupted behind them just then, like the snap of a twig or the fall of a rock. All four of the friends had their blasters drawn a second later and were searching the nearby tangles of weeds for a sign of what was there.

They could see nothing unusual.

"By the three Kennedys!" Doc exclaimed, rubbing a knot that was rising up from his head.

"What was it?" J.B. asked.

"If I'm not mistaken, it was a stone." Doc searched the ground around him and found a small round rock by his feet. "As I suspected," he said, holding up the offending rock.

Other rocks hit the ground around them, then stopped.

J.B. looked in the direction the rocks had come from. There was no movement in the weeds now, and whoever had thrown the rock had likely moved on.

"Jak, Dean," J.B. whispered. "Find out what's out there."

Jak nodded and hurried off toward the weeds while Dean made a wide circle to the right.

"Are you hurt?" J.B. asked Doc.

Doc rubbed his head. There was probably a sizeable lump there, but the skin wasn't broken. "Only my pride."

J.B. smiled.

"I would like to know why it is that I am the one

who was first to come across such misfortunes on this trip?''

"Lucky, I guess," J.B. said.

JAK MOVED THROUGH the weeds as quietly as a cat and as quick as a snake. His lean, muscular build and acrobatic athleticism were well-suited for this sort of hunt. If there was anything out there, he would either catch it or chill it long before it ever saw him.

He pushed aside the tangle of weeds in front of him with the six-inch barrel of his .357 Magnum Colt Python and peered into the undergrowth. He couldn't see anything, but that didn't mean much. After all, whoever was out here couldn't see him, either.

Jak crouched and moved deftly to his left, careful not to disturb any weeds or otherwise alert his prey to his presence. With his acute sense of hearing, Jak detected Dean making his way toward him from about twenty-five paces away. With one of his friends so close, Jak holstered the Colt Python and fished inside his jacket for a pair of leaf-bladed throwing knives. Even if he could positively identify an enemy through the weedy underbrush, the man-stopping power of the Colt could easily punch through a body and still chill Dean, even if he was standing dozens of yards away.

And then he saw it—the flick of a weed and the flash of color distinct from the pale green and sickly yellow of the weeds.

Jak moved in for the kill. If he was lucky, it would be a coon or squirrel and they'd soon be eating something better than jerky and nuts for breakfast.

Jak positioned a knife in his right hand for throwing and parted the weeds in front of him for a better view.

He reared back with his right arm...and saw Dean looking back at him, the boy's Browning Hi-Power leveled at Jak's head.

The albino teen relaxed his arm; Dean lowered his blaster.

Jak jerked his head to the left.

Dean nodded, moving away from Jak so he could circle whatever it was his friend was hunting in the brush.

Jak moved left and saw that the growth of weeds ended a little farther on. That meant that whoever or whatever was moving in that direction would either have to double back soon or make a run for it over open ground.

Either way, Jak would have them.

As the two youths neared the edge of the tangle of weeds, Jak caught sight of some color low to the ground. The color was pale, like the white of his own skin, which meant there was a good chance it was one of the spiderlike muties.

Jak readied the throwing knife again and prepared to move aside the final few weeds separating himself and the unsuspecting mutie. When he had a clear view of the creature, he'd throw the knife at its neck. The blade would penetrate a few inches, chilling it in a matter of seconds—quick, precise and almost painless.

Jak prepared to pounce.

He moved his left hand across his body, ready to push the weeds aside, almost as if he were about to open a sliding door.

One...two...three...

The weeds were suddenly gone, and he had a clear view of his prey. He reached back to throw the knife and realized it wasn't a mutie at all, but a young woman.

And a pretty young woman at that.

"Hi there," she said with a smile and a wave.

Jak slowly lowered his throwing arm. "Hi."

Chapter Fourteen

"Who are you planning on rutting with tonight?" a hard-muscled, blond-haired man asked Mildred.

"Excuse me?" she replied.

"Tonight," he said. "Who are you rutting with?"

"I don't *rut*," Mildred said, doing her best to ignore the man.

"But everyone ruts at night. It's our reward."

"Well," Mildred said, continuing to pick peaches and place them in the basket slung around her hips. "I'm not everyone, and I don't rut. Understand?"

Another young man, this one tow-headed, came up to the base of the tree Mildred was working at and said, "Is she rutting with you tonight, or is she free?"

"I saw her first," the blonde said.

"But mebbe she wants me instead."

Mildred stopped what she was doing and watched the two men fight over her. The scene seemed quite unreal, but although she thought it a pathetic display of machismo, she still found the attention quite flattering.

"I saw her first. So if she's going to rut with anyone tonight, it'll be me," the blonde stated, jabbing himself in the chest with an outstretched thumb. "Unless you want to do something about it."

"Maybe I will."

The blonde stepped away from the tree. He was naked from the waist up, all of his muscles well-defined from days working in the orchards. He had on a pair of short pants that were ragged and torn, revealing equally sculpted thighs and calves.

The dark-haired one was no slouch, either. What he didn't have in muscle tone, he made up for in mass, outweighing the other by thirty pounds, at least. As a result, they were a good match for each other, and Mildred was curious to see who might walk away the victor.

Everyone else seemed curious, as well, as most of the slaves had stopped picking by now and had become interested in the men's squabble. It even sounded as if there were bets being placed, with the blonde being the early favorite.

The dark-haired man didn't make a move for several seconds and, thinking there would be no fight, the blonde waved him off and turned back toward Mildred. That's when the other took the chance to throw a punch that struck the blonde square on the back of the head at the base of the skull. The fair-haired one's head snapped forward, and he fell to the ground.

As the dark-haired one carefully stepped over the other to catch Mildred's attention, the blonde on the ground kicked the other's feet out from under him and in seconds the two men were rolling around on the ground, punching wildly.

The sec men seemed to be enjoying the contest.

Their weapons were lowered and they were cheering on their favorite.

After several minutes the combatants seemed to tire. They were roughed up, with a few scrapes and bruises, but neither of the men was bloody. Finally the dark-haired one slapped his right arm onto the ground three times and the blonde released him. The two men got onto their feet and the dark-haired one walked away to resume his work.

The workers got back to work.

The sec men began exchanging jack.

The blonde walked over toward Mildred, a bit of a proud grin on his face. "So," he said, "you'll be rutting with me tonight, then?" It was as much a statement as a question.

Mildred had no intention of having sex with this man, even though it seemed to be the natural way of things on this farm. Still, she had the feeling that simply saying no to the man would probably cause problems. She had to think of something else to tell him, and fast.

"Well, then?"

"I'd like to, honey, but it's, uh, my time of the month."

"I don't mind."

"But I do," she said.

There was no anger or disappointment on the man's face. He simply nodded in acceptance of this fact of life. "Tomorrow, then. Or when you're first able."

He was persistent, Mildred thought. "It might take a while," she said.

"I'll rut with others in the meantime," the blonde said. "But when you're ready, I'll have you first."

Mildred couldn't imagine she'd still be here picking fruit in a few days' time, but if she promised this man, maybe the word would get around and the others might not be inclined to proposition her. "Sure," she said. "When I'm ready, I'll let you know."

The blonde smiled. "My name's Eric. I'm one of the best rutters on the farm."

"I'm Mildred," she said, admiring his physique. "And I bet you are at that."

Eric left her then, returning to work.

The women working the nearby trees eyed her warily. "Maybe the men won't be the only ones I'll have to worry about here," she muttered under her breath.

"THIS WAY!" The sec man pointed down a long, wide hallway that had several doors and ended at another corridor. When Krysty hesitated, he gave her a hard push from behind that nearly sent her sprawling.

She regained her balance and continued slowly, familiarizing herself with her surroundings so she wouldn't lose her bearings in what seemed like a maze of doors and hallways. The rough treatment aside, the sec men seemed a little too casual about guarding her, slinging their longblasters over their shoulders instead of keeping them trained on her. Krysty considered spinning, slamming the heel of her hand into the nose of the one behind her and taking his blaster, but she doubted she'd be able to do much after that. Even if she could chill the sec man in front of her before he chilled her, she had no idea where she was in the building, and she'd need an escape route.

"Second door on the left is your room," the sec man behind her said.

The first sec man opened the door for her, then stepped back to let her enter the room.

There was a bed at the far end, and a large window covered by steel bars overlooked the common area in front of the main building. Closer to the door were two large, comfortable-looking chairs and several pieces of furniture with doors and shelves that could be used for storage.

The sec man who'd been behind her followed her into the room and switched on the lights. Krysty was startled for a moment by the light from the electric bulb, but retained her composure.

"There's running water, too," the sec man said.

Running water and a hot bath would be nice, Krysty thought. She was on her way to the bathroom to try the faucets there when she heard the door close behind her.

And the lock snicked into place.

She spun on her heel to find the sec man standing in front of the door, a grin on his face.

"What do you want?" Krysty asked.

"There's two kinds of breeders on Fox Farm," he began. "Smarts and stupes."

"Is that right?"

The sec man nodded. "The stupes put up a fight and wind up in the basement for nine months chained to the wall."

"And the smart ones?"

"They rut with anyone who wants to, sec men especially." He unslung his longblaster and pointed it at Krysty.

"Sec men like you?" Krysty asked.

"I knew you were a smart one," the sec man said, replacing the longblaster on his shoulder.

"What do you want me to do?"

"You can suck my cock for a start," he said. "My friend's, too."

"Sure." Krysty better understood the predark theory now. If she cooperated with the sec man, he'd put himself in a vulnerable position. Already the man had his blaster over his shoulder instead of in his hands and pointed at her head.

"Well, all right."

She walked to the bed, sat on the edge and beckoned him with a curl of her right index finger. The sec man joined her, undoing his belt, which held a hunting knife and several boxes of ammo, and unbuttoning his pants.

"Let me see it," Krysty ordered, feigning breathlessness.

Without hesitation the man let his pants fall, allowing his erection to bob and waver in front of her like a flagpole in the wind.

"Do you like it, bitch?"

"Uh-huh," Krysty answered.

She reached out with her hands, taking hold of his cock with her left hand and hefting his scrotum in her right. "What's my reward for doing this?" she asked.

"For starters, you won't get beat as bad as others do."

"Oh, that sounds fair."

"You bet."

And that's when Krysty simultaneously squeezed and twisted her hands as if she were wringing water from a damp towel.

The sec man let out a yelp, his body snapping straight and unable to move.

Krysty gave him another hard twist, the force of it lifting him onto his toes. Sweat began to bead on his forehead, and tears leaked from his eyes. She let go of his scrotum and reached down with her right hand to pull his knife from its sheath. It was a four-inch hunting knife with a serrated edge on one side and a straight-edge on the other. She came up with the knife quickly, slashing it from right to left, slicing off the tip of the sec man's cock.

He screamed.

She let go, pushed him away with a hard shove and slid the knife under the bed.

He stumbled backward, then reached down between his legs to grab hold of his severed member. He tried to staunch the flow of blood with his hands, but it still flowed freely through his fingers and down the insides of his legs.

"Rad-blasted slut!" the sec man screamed, holding himself with one hand and trying to pull up his pants with the other. He finally let go of his pants and brought around his longblaster.

The door burst open and a second sec man entered the room. "Put it down!" he said.

"But she cut me."

A third sec man entered the room. Krysty recognized him as the sec chief named Grundwold. "Did she reach into your pants and pull it out for you, too?" the sec chief demanded.

"He was going to hurt me," Krysty said. "Mebbe even chill me. I was only defending myself."

The sec chief looked at his two sec men with contempt. "Get out of here, before the baron hears about this." He pushed the bleeding man in the direction of the door.

"But—"

"Never mind," Grundwold said. "Or mebbe you want to explain to the baron what just happened here."

The two sec men left without another word. Once outside the room, the injured one grunted and groaned his way down the hall.

Grundwold stopped in the doorway before he left the room. "You try and relax, mebbe get some sleep. The baron wants you looking your best."

"That's kind of him."

The sec chief nodded and left the room, closing the door behind him.

Krysty fished under the bed for the knife. She wiped off the blood and slipped it into her boot.

Who knew? Mebbe it would come in handy.

RYAN WAS HAVING troubles of his own.

Although he was doing his best to do the job that

was required of him and be as inconspicuous as possible while doing it, the addition of a new slave was bound to attract attention.

"Are you spoken for?" asked an older woman with scraggly brown hair. She was obviously several months' pregnant and wasn't too concerned about concealing the fact, or she would have felt the need to cover her bloated breasts, which rested on her distended belly like eggs in a frying pan.

"Yes, I am," Ryan said, taking a bite out of a fresh peach.

"Who?" the woman wanted to know. "You just arrived. How could you—?"

"You can't rut with him," a second woman said. She was younger by about ten years, rake thin and without child. "That's not your choice to make. You're already heavy."

"But I want him," the pregnant one said. "He's strong and handsome. Maybe even a little mysterious."

"But if the baron catches you rutting without permission while you're already heavy, he'll chain you up until you birth."

"Who's going to know? Who'll tell the baron? You?"

The younger woman just smiled.

"Why, you bitch," said the older one. She threw her fist forward and caught the other woman flush in the nose. Blood began to drain from one of the younger woman's nostrils, but that wasn't stopping the older woman from trying to hit her again.

The young woman dropped to the ground and took the older one's legs out from under her with a spinning leg trip. The older woman fell on her rear, and her enlarged breasts seemed to bounce and jiggle for the longest time. The younger woman was about to give her a hard kick in the abdomen when another slave came by to break up the fight.

"That's enough, both of you!" he shouted, giving the smaller woman a stiff kick in the legs.

"Hey," Ryan called out, jumping down from the tree.

"You stay out of this, One-eye."

He gave each of the women another kick in the legs, and they finally stopped clawing at each other.

Ryan wasn't impressed.

He was a big man, well muscled with a body covered with scars, including several around his neck. There were leathery stripes of healed-over flesh down and across his back, likely the result of dozens, maybe even hundreds of lashes inflicted by sec men over the years. He had short-cropped hair and a full beard, and in many ways he reminded Ryan a bit of Major Gregori Zimyanin, which gave Ryan all the more reason to stop the man from beating the two women.

"Your next kick will be your last," Ryan said calmly, his fists clenched by his side.

The big man ignored Ryan's comment and pulled the two women apart.

The women were done fighting, but still eyed each other warily.

"Beth," he said to the older woman, "you know

you can't rut until you've birthed the child. If you need to rut, it can be arranged. I could even see to it personally.'' He helped her off the ground and sent her on her way.

Then he turned to the other woman. "And I swear, if you had hurt Beth's offspring in any way, you wouldn't have been rutting with anybody, not the one-eye, and not anybody for a long, long time."

"But I wanted him tonight, Andy," she said, looking up at Ryan with something like fire in her eyes.

"There'll be plenty of time to rut with the one-eyed dog later," Andy said. "He's not going anywhere."

The young woman still didn't seem satisfied, but she stomped off without further protest.

When she was gone, Andy turned to face Ryan. "This is my work detail, One-eye. I keep the peace here any way I see fit, including giving breeders a kick when they got it coming."

"What are the sec men for?"

"To make sure no one tries to escape. As long as our group makes our quotas, they don't give a shit what goes on between us."

Ryan stepped forward, halving the distance between them. "Including when one of you gets chilled?"

Without warning, Andy threw a punch at Ryan's head. He dodged the blow and struck Andy's head with his left elbow. There was a definite crack of bone on impact, and Andy fell to the ground, dazed and unable to get up.

Ryan broke a branch off a nearby tree and was about to run the jagged edge of it through Andy's ribs, when a sec man fired a round at Ryan. The bullet zinged past the one-eyed man's head and slammed into the peach tree behind him, sending splinters in every direction.

"Leave him alone!" a sec man shouted as he walked over to where Ryan stood over the prone Andy. "Get back to work!"

Ryan tossed aside the branch and stepped away from the still groaning Andy.

The sec man helped Andy to his feet, and although the big man didn't say anything, the look in his eyes told Ryan that it wasn't over between them.

Only beginning.

Chapter Fifteen

"What's your name?" J.B. asked the young woman Jak had brought out of the weeds.

"Clarissa," she answered.

She was probably in her early twenties and had dirty blond hair that was all in a tangle. Her clothes were pretty worn-out, with large tears in both her T-shirt and pants. And although dirty, her skin was clean of any signs of rad sickness. She looked pretty much like a norm, but one could never tell in the Deathlands.

"Why were you throwing rocks at us?"

"It wasn't just me throwing rocks," she stated. "There were muties out there, too, you know."

"All right, then, why were you and the muties throwing rocks?"

"To get your food."

"But we don't have any food," Dean said.

"You've got more than we have, and that's enough. We watched you eat and wanted some of your food."

"And you were going to get it by throwing rocks?"

"I thought we could scare you off. You know, force you to leave a few crumbs behind."

"With rocks?"

Clarissa shrugged. "We're hungry. We'll try anything to get some food."

"We?" J.B. asked.

"Me and the muties."

"You're with the muties."

"Always."

J.B. just looked at her, trying to figure out the woman. She didn't seem afraid or even worried about what the friends might do to her. And she was definitely a norm, but instead of living with other norms she seemed to be living with, maybe even leading the muties.

Very strange.

"I wonder if you and your mutie friends might still be hungry?" Doc asked.

"We're always hungry."

"Well, perhaps we can make a trade."

J.B. wasn't sure what Doc had in mind, but he seemed to have a plan.

"Trade for what?" She eyed him suspiciously.

"For some information."

"About?"

"The area around here. And about Fox Farm."

"Sure," she said. "What have you got to trade?"

Doc smiled. "This bag of fruit."

Without a word, Clarissa took the bag from Doc and began pitching peaches, pears and apples into the nearby weeds. The muties there began to feed. She took a few of the fruits for herself, turned back to face Doc and J.B. and said, "Ask away."

J.B. moved in closer. "Three of our friends went missing last night, and we found a sec man from Fox

Farm dead in one of the rooms of the hotel we were staying in.''

''Are your missing friends women?''

''Two of them are.''

Clarissa nodded. ''They took the women for breeding. Not sure why they'd take a man, though. They've got more of them than they need on the farm.''

''For breeding? I don't understand.''

''Fox Farm grows food. Best around for miles— hell, it's the *only* food around for miles. See, Baron Fox knows all about electricity, so he came out here a few years ago with the idea of using the power from the falls to start his own little barony. With the electricity he was able to rework the soil and bring in freshwater from the bottom of the lake. But the more he grows on the farm, the less there seems to be for anyone on the outside. The land here's good for growing, but any time we've tried to plant something the weeds grow so fast everything gets choked off. That's why the baron has so many slaves working for him. They spend most of their time pulling weeds.''

''Slaves?'' Dean repeated.

''Sure, that's why there's an electric fence all the way around the farm. It keeps animals and muties out of the orchards, but it doesn't let anyone out, either.''

''We thought as much about the fence,'' J.B. said, nodding.

''Uh, excuse me, dear lady,'' Doc interjected. ''But you mentioned something about breeding.''

She took another bite of an apple, eating slowly now that she'd eaten a few fruits and had sated some of her hunger. "One of the reasons they grow a lot of fruit is for trade. They supply a few big eastern villes with fresh produce, so the farm is well stocked with everything like linen and soap, sugar and clothes."

"Blasters?" J.B. asked.

Clarissa laughed. "All kinds. Maybe a few grens— I can't be sure since I don't know a lot about weapons. There's a lot of them, though, I know that."

"What about the breeding?" Doc repeated, looking a little frustrated.

"Well, the other reason they grow so much food is to feed the slaves. See, they all work hard pulling weeds and picking fruit, and at night they rut. All night, every night."

"What does she mean by rut?" Dean asked.

"Rut," Doc answered, "is a vulgar term meaning to have sexual relations, especially intercourse."

"That's right, rut," Clarissa said. "Baron Fox trades in fruit and vegetables, but he also trades in slaves and babies."

"Babies?" Dean seemed confused.

"Since everyone is rutting every night, the women are getting heavy all the time. And since most of the offspring are norms, they are worth a lot to couples in the eastern villes who can't have kids of their own because of rad sickness or whatever."

"So that's how he's been able to become so rich," J.B. concluded.

"An offspring a few months old can net him a new blaster. Ten or twelve of them is good enough for a wag in perfect running order. He's got convoys heading east every month or so. Last few months he's been shipping every other week. There's even couples that have heard about the operation and make the trip to the falls just to see him. He usually gets their wag, so the smart ones bring two.''

J.B. thought about Mildred. "What happens to women on the farm who don't want to rut?"

"They all do eventually. The baron doesn't care if you want to or not, and I think he even likes it when the women put up a fight. The ones who resist usually get beaten for starters. Then the baron will deny them food and water for days, and contact with all other people for months...just about anything a person needs to survive. Most of the women succumb, some don't, but even the holdouts get heavy in the end. They wind up chained to a wall in the baron's dungeon where they are force-bred until they're made heavy.

"But even when you get heavy, the punishment isn't over. Willing breeders don't rut when they're heavy if they don't want to, but the ones who resist can be rutted by anyone—sec men usually—right up until they birth. It's no wonder that after they've delivered an offspring, the women are only too happy and willing to rut like the rest of them.''

Everyone was silent for several moments.

"It would seem to me that we must try to rescue Ryan, Krysty and Mildred as soon as possible," Doc pondered, "or our friends won't be the same when they come out."

"My thoughts exactly," J.B. said.

"I have question," Jak stated.

"What is it?" Clarissa asked.

"If baron takes women, why you here?"

It was a good question. All four of the friends looked to Clarissa for an answer.

"I was inside," she stated.

J.B. looked at her skeptically.

"About a year ago my family was part of a wag convoy heading east to a new ville my uncle was starting up in Roads Island. But when we came through here, Baron Fox's men captured my family and brought us all to the farm. My mom didn't last long. She put up a bit of a fight, but since she was old and couldn't get heavy anymore, she was sent to the sec men's lounge for the stupe bastard's entertainment. She didn't last long there, and died just a few weeks after we were captured."

Clarissa paused to let out a sigh and take another bite of her apple.

"My dad was an older man and found the orchards hard work. When he learned about what had happened to my mother, he went mad and attacked a group of sec men with a stick. They chilled him before he could strike a single blow. After that, I knew I couldn't stay on the farm, so I tried to escape. It took me three tries, but I finally did it by dressing up in a sec man's uniform, stealing a wag and driving it through the front gate. I've been living on the outside for about eight months now."

"Why stay here?" Jak asked. "Not go away?"

Clarissa looked sad. "My sister's still inside. She resisted the baron a lot more than I did, and she ended up in the dungeon. She was heavy when I got out, and she might be ready to birth in a few weeks. After I escaped, I wanted to leave, to get as far away as I could, but I just couldn't bring myself to do it. Knowing I'm on the outside waiting for her is probably the only thing that's keeping her alive in there.''

''Try save her?''

Clarissa shook her head. ''No, what could I do by myself?''

''What about the muties?'' Doc asked.

''They wouldn't be much help in an attack. Throwing rocks and tearing things apart with their teeth is about all they're good for. If I could get them inside the complex, they might do some damage, but I can't get them past the fence.''

''That's not what I meant,'' J.B. said. ''They let you live with them without them hurting you?''

''Yes.''

''And even now, they aren't attacking us.''

''That's because I don't want them to. You see, I feed them whatever I can spare.'' She threw the cores of her apples and pears off into the bushes. ''They consider me a sort of savior.'' She threw back her head and ran her fingers through her dirty blond hair. ''There isn't anything they wouldn't do for me.''

''Do you think if you told them to attack the farm, they'd do it for you?'' J.B. asked.

''Attack the farm?''

''We're not leaving our friends inside,'' J.B. stated.

''But that would be crazy. There's only four of you, and that place is like a fortress.''

"That, my dear girl," Doc piped up, "is why we can use all the help we can get. Mutie or otherwise."

"You could help us, too." J.B. leaned in closer to her. "You know your way around the farm and could lead us to where we want to go."

Clarissa said nothing but looked to each of the friends in turn.

"We could get your sister out along with our friends," J.B. suggested.

"You four are serious, aren't you?"

"I have been a part of this group a long time, young lady," Doc announced, "and I can assure you beyond a shadow of a doubt that we take such matters very seriously."

"Okay, but even if I help you and convince the muties to come along for the ride, you're still going to need more weapons to break in to the place, and to break out."

"Some heavier blasters would be nice," J.B. said.

"A few grens would be useful in causing diversions too," Doc mused.

"More ammo," Jak said.

"And a wag," Dean added.

"Yes, and a wag," J.B. echoed.

"If you had some of those things, you really think you could free my sister and your friends."

"Other slaves, too," Jak muttered.

"Okay." She nodded, as if she'd just taken a step from which there was no turning back. "I know a place where we can find some of the things you need."

Chapter Sixteen

The crew broke for lunch, which was served in the orchard off the back of a rebuilt electric wag that had burners and coolers and all sorts of things to help prepare food and keep it hot or cold as required. Ryan was given the choice of vegetable soup or some sort of meat stew. He decided on the soup, since he knew that the vegetables were grown on the farm but he couldn't be sure where the meat for the stew had come from.

The man in the greasy clothes behind the food counter spooned out the soup into Ryan's oversize mug, then put a large bread roll on the tray beside it. Farther along, an overripe tomato was put on his tray and finally an empty glass, which could be filled up with water from one of the spouts that extended off the end of the wag.

Ryan filled the glass, drank and then filled it a second time. He turned to find Mildred. She was sitting in the shade under one of the peach trees, eating the stew. Ryan joined her.

"How's the food?" he asked.

"Had better. Had worse," she answered.

"How's your back?" Ryan leaned backward to ease the pain in his lower back. He was in terrific physical shape, and his muscles were as taut as iron bands, but nothing could have prepared him for hours of being hunched over and looking for weeds. He'd get used to the work eventually, but he wasn't planning on being there long enough for that.

"It's been better."

Ryan sat beside Mildred and began to eat. The soup was as good as any he'd tasted. When he was done eating it, he broke his roll into chunks and used it to soak up the broth. When he was about to bite into his tomato, a middle-aged dark-haired woman, heavy with child, sat in front of Mildred and Ryan.

"I don't think Purvis likes you much," she said.

"Is that his name, Purvis?" Ryan asked.

"Yes, Andy Purvis. He's the leader of our crew."

"Not much of a leader if you ask me," Mildred said, chewing on a piece of meat from her stew.

"I don't think he's going to forget what happened today. Be careful tonight. He'll be looking for you."

"Why? What will happen tonight?"

"We'll work the fields until a few hours before sundown when the white wags will come out to bring us back to the main house. In back of the main building we'll be able to wash ourselves and freshen up. Then we all go to the dining hall for dinner, which will probably be soup and stew again."

Ryan nodded, wondering if he might try the stew tonight.

"After dinner there'll be some sort of entertainment on the dining-hall stage."

"Entertainment?" Mildred's eyes widened. "What kind of entertainment?"

"You know, like in a gaudy house. Someone might do a strip dance. Sometimes the baron comes out and tells a few funnies, and one time he showed us a pre-dark sex vid. That was interesting."

"And you have these sorts of shows every night?" Mildred asked.

"Yes," she answered, as if Mildred had just asked a silly question.

"Why?"

"It's supposed to put everyone in the mood to rut."

"Is that what happens after?" Ryan asked.

"Yes, after the shows everyone who wants to rut pairs up, or you can go to the big room where a lot of people get together at one time."

"What if you don't want to rut?" Mildred wondered.

"If it's your time, like you said, no one will bother you. Or if you're not feeling well, you can take a room by yourself. Some people prefer that."

"So," Ryan said. "Sounds like we have an interesting night in front of us."

Mildred nodded. "*Interesting* is a good word for it."

"Anyway, if Purvis is going to try anything, it will probably be in the showers or during the entertainment."

"Thanks for the warning," Ryan said. "But why are you telling me this?"

Her eyes darted left and right, and she moved her

head ever so slightly to see if anyone was near. "I don't like him. I don't like him at all."

"What's not to like?" Mildred quipped. "A man who beats women the way he does can't be all bad."

"No, he's dangerous. If he thinks you're a threat to his position as alpha male on the crew, he'll try and chill you any way he can."

"What about the sec men?" Ryan turned his head in the direction of the guards, who were all sitting on folding chairs that had come off the wag. They seemed unconcerned about the crew under their charge.

"They don't care about the men. It's the women who are valuable to the baron. Anyone hurts a woman, especially a breeder, they're chilled on the spot. Purvis is hard on the women in his crew, but none of us has ever stopped breeding because of it."

"What a prince," Mildred said.

"There's some worse overseeing other crews, but not many," she stated.

Just then the a sec man blew a whistle to let them know it was time to get back to picking fruit and pulling weeds.

"Just be careful, mister," she said. "He'll chill you if he has a chance."

Ryan got to his feet. "Not if I chill him first."

That put a smile on the woman's face. "I was sort of hoping that might be the case. You look like you've chilled people before. I bet you have, haven't you?"

"A few," Ryan said.

"All right," a sec man bellowed. "Stop yapping and get back to work."

Chapter Seventeen

"Stroke! Stroke! Stroke!" Sec chief Ganley cried as he kept the two boats on pace to reach their destination by dark.

While they had often spent entire days out on the water, they had never ventured so far out into the lake before. Neither had they ever paddled so hard for so long. When they reached the southern shores of the lake, they would be exhausted and would be hard-pressed to set up camp for the night. There was also a question of food. They had brought some with them, and there was plenty more they'd brought to trade, but after such a hard day, dried fish would hardly be a fitting meal. They could do with something fresh.

"Rhonda," he called, breaking the rhythm for just a moment.

A woman in his boat turned. "What?"

"Take the bow. If you spot anything in the water, spear it. We could use a decent, fresh meal tonight."

"Yes, sir!" she said with a smile.

The woman climbed up through the center of the boat and replaced the man who'd been stationed there with a blaster for most of the day.

Ganley watched her get settled, then tie one end of a rope to a ring on the blunt tip of her spear and the other end to the bow of the boat. Then she got into position, spear raised and ready to be thrown at anything that might swim by.

"Stroke! Stroke! Stroke!"

Ganley had called over four hundred strokes, and Rhonda's throwing arm hadn't wavered. Ganley had been impressed with her moves when he'd screened the volunteers, and he'd later found that there was no one better in the ville with a spear. And now he could see why. She was like a cat who would wait hours for a mouse to peek its nose out of a hole. The second it did, the cat would pounce and the mouse would never know what hit it.

"Stroke! C'mon, just a few more hours. Stroke! Rhonda will have us a supper like never before. Stroke!"

And then, as if the fish had been waiting for the proper introduction, Rhonda thrust her spear into the water.

The paddles stopped moving, and necks craned for a glimpse of the water in front of the boat.

"What is it?" Ganley asked.

"Sturgeon," Rhonda answered, pulling on the rope.

"Excellent!" Sturgeon was a large bony fish with five rows of bony plates down its back. They'd said that in predark times the fish's sucking mouth had been used to feed off the bottom, but now its wide mouth had adapted to the times and was used for scooping up dead fish floating on the top of the water.

"How big?"

"Couldn't tell. Only saw one of its plates."

This far out there was no telling how big the sturgeon could get. The lake was big enough, and the supply of dead fish almost unlimited because of rad poisoning.

The crew on the boat waited as Rhonda continued to pull in the line. But before she got the fish to the boat, there were shouts and a commotion coming from the crew of the second boat.

How big was it? Ganley wondered.

And at that moment, the sturgeon's enormous tail flipped up out of the water, rocking the second boat and throwing several of its crew into the water.

Seeing that, Rhonda began stabbing the enormous fish in the back, again and again. Blood began to spurt up from the back of the giant fish and into the boat.

Several of the other crew drew their blasters.

"No!" Ganley ordered.

Rhonda was leaning over the bow of the boat, moving her spear up the fish's body, and was now poised to strike its head. She reared back and plunged the spear deep into the sturgeon's brain.

The fish convulsed several times, throwing up a red froth under the other boat and hampering their efforts to pull it out of the water. Finally the giant fish was still and floating on the surface of the water. It was twenty-five-feet long, its bony ridges breaking the water like armor plates on a war wag.

"Tie off the tail!" Rhonda called to the other boat.

"We can't take it with us," Ganley said.

"I know that, but we have to eat." Rhonda tied off

the snout and the giant fish was suspended between the two boats.

Rhonda secured her spear to the boat, tied a mesh bag to her waistband, then unsheathed her knife and dived in the water.

Ganley watched her expertly cut more than a dozen steaks from the fish's tender underbelly and toss them into the boat. And then, she disappeared under the water for several minutes only to reappear with a smile on her face and a bag full of caviar.

Ganley couldn't believe he almost hadn't allowed the woman to come along on the trip.

"WHERE?" the Armorer asked.

"Across the bridge, on what used to be the American side," Clarissa said. "There's an old museum, the Niagara Aerospace Museum. It's in a shopping mall."

"An aerospace museum?" J.B. wasn't impressed.

"Yeah, it's got a lot of great stuff in it, like—"

"Like airplanes and helicopters."

"That's right."

"Even if those things could still get off the ground," J.B. argued, "none of us know how to fly an airplane."

"There's mostly that sort of stuff, and other things like training simulators and testing equipment, even some airplane and rocket engines."

"You mean to tell me, young lady," Doc interjected, "that in all this time no one, especially the local baron, has visited this museum and stripped away everything that might be of some value to someone trying to survive in the Deathlands?''

"The museum in the mall's been stripped clean, sure, but I know how to get to the museum's underground storage facility. That's where they kept all the spares, even moved a few of the museum's best pieces when the nukes started to fall. It's also where I stashed the wag I stole.''

"What's there?'' J.B. asked, suddenly more interested.

"There's an airplane that's got some pretty big blasters on it for one thing.''

Jak eyed the young woman skeptically. "How you know, and not others?''

"Some of my mutie friends live under the mall, and they've made their home pretty secure.''

"And why,'' J.B. asked, "will the muties just let us come in and take the stuff away?''

"Because I'm going to tell them what you're going to use it for, and…you're going to give them food.''

"We don't have any food,'' Dean offered.

"No,'' J.B. said, "but mebbe we can get some on the way.''

No one said a word for several long moments.

Finally, Jak rose to his feet. "Let's go.''

"I'm afraid we're going to have to put off our trip to the museum for a few hours yet,'' Doc pointed out. "Or at least until our guide, Sleeping Beauty, awakens to show us the way.''

J.B. looked over at where Clarissa had been sitting. The young woman was now on her side, sleeping soundly after eating so much of the sedative-laden fruit.

"Mebbe it's for the best," J.B. said. "Give us a chance to recce the farm."

The Armorer got to his feet and stretched his legs. "Doc and Dean, stay here. Jak and I are going to see exactly what we're up against."

The old man nodded. Dean looked disappointed about being left behind, but nodded just the same.

"How much time before she wakes up, Doc?"

"Two hours would be my guess."

"Okay, then," J.B. said, glancing at his wrist chron. "See you in two hours."

THE WHISTLE BLEW about an hour before sunset and a series of white miniwags pulled up to where the crew was working in order to take them back to the main building for cleanup, a hot meal and the rest of the evening's activities.

Ryan joined Mildred so they could watch each other's back on the way in. He kept his eye on Purvis, too, making sure to always keep the man in front of him so there would be no surprises.

As they neared the wag, the woman who had be-friended Ryan earlier in the day came up alongside Mildred. "Don't worry. He won't try anything until we get to the main building. There'll be sec men on other wags keeping an eye on everything. They like a peaceful ride in at the end of the day like the rest of us...." Her voice trailed off and she seemed to gasp for breath.

"Are you all right?" Mildred asked, putting out an arm to steady the woman.

"Tired is all," she responded with a strained smile. "I could use a warm meal and a good night's rest." Her smile turned into a grimace and she clutched her belly.

"You don't sound all right to me," Mildred stated.

"Oh!" she gasped, louder this time.

Mildred grabbed her with two hands. "What is it?" But she didn't need to hear an answer to know what was going on. There was a dark wet spot on the ground between the woman's legs, and greenish-brown water was running down the inside of her thighs.

A sec man came running. "What's wrong with her?"

Mildred eased the woman over to a tree and sat her in a squatting position to allow for the free flow of the fluid. "Her water's broke. She'll be having the baby in the next few hours."

"Why is she so dirty?"

"It's muconium staining," Mildred stated. "Her amniotic fluid is stained with a substance that's coming from the baby's digestive tract. It could be a sign that the baby is in some kind of distress."

"How do you know that?" the sec man asked, looking at Mildred strangely.

Mildred hesitated. She tried never to reveal to anyone that she was a medical doctor, since such people were worth more than blasters to barons and villes. If the baron here found out, she'd never be allowed to leave, or even be given the chance to escape. But if she denied her medical knowledge right now, this woman and her baby might both die a slow and painful death. "I know a little bit about healing," she admitted.

The sec man turned to the others. "This one's birthing. Bring another wag."

A couple of sec men took off in one of the white electric miniwags.

"They'll be back in a few minutes, to take you to the nursery." He turned to Mildred. "You're going with her."

Mildred nodded.

The woman let out another cry of pain.

Mildred placed a comforting hand on her shoulder. "Don't worry," she said, wondering what the woman's name was. "What's your name, sugar?"

"Jasmine."

"Don't worry, Jasmine," Mildred said. "It'll be all right."

J.B. AND JAK ARRIVED at the farm just before sundown. No crews were working the orchards at that time of day.

"Quiet," Jak said.

J.B. nodded.

The courtyard between the main building and the front gate was illuminated by several lights, turning the area from night into day. A couple of sec men on foot out by the gate and another few up in the lookout towers, which provided them with a view of the entire farm. Intermittently, lights would come on inside the orchards.

"Looking someone?" Jak asked.

"I think it's just a test," J.B. answered. "Make sure the lights work if they need them, but they probably don't need them all that much because of the fence."

The two friends moved in closer, and after just a few paces they could hear the faint hum of electricity. "Like I thought," J.B. said, nodding. "They keep the electricity on through the night to keep out the animals and muties. A couple of squirrelies inside the fence could ruin a whole crop."

"Worse for us?"

"No. The electricity shouldn't be a problem." J.B. said nothing more, but moved quickly and silently around the perimeter of the farm to the west side where he'd seen the power lines.

As he suspected, the high-tension wires that brought electricity to the farm were strung up at the top of several forty-foot poles. The wires were almost impossible to get at and would be difficult to cut. Regardless, the wires were a definite weak point in the farm's defenses and something they could take advantage of somehow.

"Problem?"

"Mebbe, mebbe not. At least now we know what we're up against."

"Have plan?"

J.B. shook his head. "Not yet, but I'll think of something once we know what kind of weapons we'll be using."

Jak nodded. "Think she tells true about weapons?"

"I sure hope so, because if she isn't, Ryan, Mildred and Krysty are going to be in there for a long time."

Chapter Eighteen

Ryan watched Mildred tend to the woman named Jasmine and knew he'd be on his own the rest of the night. He climbed onto the wag and took a seat near the back where he could keep Purvis and everyone else in front of him.

A full-figured blond woman with ample hips and even more ample breasts took the seat across the aisle from Ryan. "You rutting with anyone tonight, honey?" she asked.

"Yes, I am. Sorry."

"Aw, we could have a lot of fun together, honey." As she spoke she pressed her breasts together with her arms to create a long line of cleavage between them.

"Oh, I'm sure we could have."

"Mebbe another time, then?"

"Mebbe."

"I'll keep my motor runnin' for you."

Ryan didn't answer, but instead focused his attention on Purvis, who had just climbed onto the wag. He stared at Ryan a moment, then took a seat at the front among the sec men.

Outside, a smaller wag pulled up and Mildred and the woman got in. After a few moments they drove off, heading back to the main building at a good clip.

"Does your friend know what she's doing?" a voice asked.

Ryan turned and saw a man on the seat in front of him. "You say something?"

The man nodded. "I said, does your friend know what she's doing?"

"Who are you?"

The man looked around suspiciously. "I'm her mate. She's carrying my child."

Ryan looked closely at the man. He seemed genuinely worried about the woman bearing his child, which was probably a dangerous thing to be doing on this farm. "She's in good hands," he said. "So is the child."

"Appreciate it." A smile eased the tension in the man's face. "My name's Brody, by the way."

"Ryan." They shook hands then, Ryan's gaze locked once again on Purvis.

"He doesn't like you much."

"And I don't like him."

"You could use someone to watch your back."

"You're probably right."

"Consider it watched."

The wag started moving.

"Thanks," Ryan said.

IT WAS DARK by the time J.B. and Jak returned from their recce of the farm.

"Just in time," Doc greeted them. "Our sleeper has just recently awakened."

Clarissa stretched her arms and legs. A few yards

away, the muties were also rising from their fruit-induced sleep. "What happened? One minute I was talking to you, and then the next I was fast asleep."

"The fruit," Doc explained, "which came courtesy of Fox Farm, seems to have been laced with some sort of sedative."

"And you gave it to me to eat, knowing that?"

"You were hungry," J.B. stated. "It wasn't lethal, and we didn't have anything else to give you...or your friends, to eat. Besides, it was either that or chill you."

She looked at the Armorer for a long time, probably wondering if he was kidding or serious. "I believe you would have, too," she said at last.

J.B. remained silent.

"This museum you spoke of," Doc said. "Is it close enough to travel to in the dark, or should we find some other accommodation for the night?"

"Not a good idea to be out at night."

"Know safe place?" Jak asked.

"Sure."

"Okay, we'll rest up tonight, and tomorrow we'll hit the museum."

J.B. turned to Clarissa. "Lead the way."

MILDRED WAS LED into a well-lit and very clean room in the basement of the main building. A row of beds stood against each wall, ten to a row, twenty beds in all. All but four of the beds were empty.

Sitting at one end of the room at a desk was an old woman who had to be in her sixties. She was gray haired, hunched over and the knuckles of her hands were gnarled with arthritis.

"Two at once," the old woman said when Mildred brought Jasmine into the nursery.

"No," Mildred said. "I'm just here to help her."

"You a midwife?"

"No, not exactly."

"Healer?"

"Sort of."

"Oh well, welcome, then. I could use the help. What's her story?"

"Her water's broke and she's had some muconium staining."

"Is that like dark water?"

"Yes."

"She may be overdue, then."

"That's right." Mildred had wondered if the old woman would be in the way, but it was obvious that she'd delivered plenty of babies in her time and knew what she was doing.

"Here, honey," the old woman said, taking Jasmine's hands and placing them on her nipples. "Touch them, twist them and pull on them for the next little while."

"What will that do?" Jasmine asked.

Mildred wondered about that, too, but then remembered that nipple stimulation released the hormone oxytocin, which caused the uterus to contract. But how did you go about explaining that to a woman born and raised in the Deathlands?

"It will help make the baby come out," Mildred said, deciding the simplest explanation was best.

The old woman nodded her approval, then turned to Mildred. "Now, help me get ready."

Mildred smiled. There'd been so much chilling in her life recently, it would be wonderful to help bring some new life into the Deathlands.

"My pleasure," Mildred said, rolling up her sleeves.

"DINNER'S SERVED in twenty," the sec man shouted as the crew exited the wag. "Show starts in an hour."

"The showers are this way," Brody stated.

"What if I don't want a shower?" Ryan asked.

Brody shook his head. "Everyone's got to go through. The baron likes his people to be clean when they rut. Protection against disease, healthy offspring and all that. Besides, the water's hot, and it'll make you feel good after a day working in the orchard."

Ryan entered the large room where both men and women were getting undressed. About half of the women were noticeably heavy, and all the men looked fit and healthy.

Brody gave Ryan a plastic crate with the name of a predark dairy imprinted on the side. "Put your clothes in the crate. You can get them washed if you want, or you can put them on again after your shower. Up to you."

Although his clothes could probably do with a wash, he decided he'd put them on again. If they went into the wash, there was no telling when or if he'd get back the same clothes.

Ryan stepped into the shower. Brody stood off to the side, keeping an eye out for Purvis while Ryan washed up. The one-eyed man was grateful for the chance to wash the blood, dust and grime from his body. He put his head under the water, which was both fresh and warm thanks to the farm's unlimited supply of water and electricity, and let it flow over him like a river.

As he soaped up and rinsed for the last time, Ryan caught sight of Purvis at the exit to the showers. He decided to ignore him for the time being, knowing that the man wouldn't do anything while so many slaves were still in the showers with them.

But with Purvis standing there and looking for a fight, the others rinsed off quickly and left, leaving Ryan and Brody alone with him.

Purvis was as tall and as muscular as one might expect from the dominant male of a work crew. He also looked as if he'd been in a few fights during his time on the farm. Several of his teeth were missing, his nose was caved in and there was a bite-sized chunk of flesh missing from the outside of his right thigh.

"Your time has come, One-eye," Purvis said, taking a couple of steps into the shower.

"He doesn't want any trouble, Purvis," Brody argued. "He doesn't know how things work on the farm, that's all."

Ryan decided to say nothing for the moment, giving

Purvis the chance to back out of this without getting hurt.

"You got that right, Brody. He don't know shit about what he's got himself into."

"He made a mistake is all," Brody reasoned. "He was thinking like an outlander, not like a slave. Forget it this time, and it won't happen again."

There was a slight grin on Purvis's face. He was obviously enjoying hearing Brody talk.

But Ryan didn't like it at all.

"No, it will happen again," Ryan said. "It will happen every time you beat on a woman, Purvis, or anybody else who's done you no wrong."

"You're all talk." Purvis took a few steps closer.

"I've been called a lot of things," Ryan said, "but never that."

The big man hesitated. He gestured to Brody. "I don't like the odds."

Ryan nodded. "Get out of here, Brody!"

"But—"

"Get out!"

Brody left without another word.

"Pack your bags, One-eye," Purvis said. "You're about to board the last train west."

Ryan said nothing, too busy assessing the situation to waste time on more talk. The water was still running in the showers. It helped drown out their voices so the sec men couldn't hear them, but it also made the floor of the shower very slippery. Purvis was a head taller than Ryan and probably outweighed him by fifty pounds. So if Ryan was to have any chance against the bigger man, he'd have to move fast, strike first and strike hard.

"C'mon, One-eye, I'm waiting."

Ryan crouched, pushed off from the wall and slid across the smooth tiles of the shower floor. He struck Purvis's legs while still moving at a good clip, and the big man toppled, landing hard on his shoulder.

Before the man had time to recover, Ryan was on his feet again. He kicked out with his right foot, catching the side of Purvis's head with his heel. The blow seemed to have little effect on the downed man because he managed to get to his feet as if he'd received little more than a tap on the shoulder.

"You're fast," he said. "I'll give you that."

Ryan decided if it worked once, it might be worth trying again. He knelt, got onto his hands and swung his feet out in a wide arc, taking Purvis's feet out from under him again. This time the big man fell backward, landing hard on his back and striking his head on the hard, wet floor.

Purvis seemed to be in pain so Ryan moved in to take advantage. But when he got close, Purvis reached out and grabbed the one-eyed man's feet, pulling him off the floor. Ryan managed to break his fall with his hands, but still landed heavily on the tiles, smacking the right side of his face hard enough to see bright sparks of pain flashing behind his eye.

After his heavy falls, the big man was slowly getting stronger, and Ryan knew that if he managed to get close, it was possible that he would be smothered in his grip.

A crowd of slaves had gathered at the entrance to the shower, but there were still no sec men in sight, which meant that only one of them would be walking out of the showers alive.

Ryan backed away from Purvis until his back touched one of the shower room's tiled walls.

"You can't run from me, One-eye." Purvis grinned, taking the move as a sign of weakness.

But in truth, Ryan was merely putting as much space between himself and the big man as he could. A second later he was off running, leaping through the air and throwing his shoulder and all of his body weight into Purvis's chest.

There was a large whoosh as Ryan knocked the air out of the man's lungs, and then a hard smack as Purvis fell backward with Ryan on top of him.

Purvis gulped for air.

Ryan took hold of the man's head and kept slamming it onto the hard tile floor until the back of his skull was crushed. Blood leaked onto the shower floor.

He let go of the big man's ruined head and looked over to the shower entrance. The slaves were gone and in their place were two sec men. They didn't look all that surprised to see a dead man lying on the shower floor. If Purvis was anything special, you sure couldn't tell from the sec men's expressions.

"What happened to him?" one of the sec men asked.

"Slipped on some soap," Ryan answered.

"Second one this month," the other sec man commented.

Chapter Nineteen

"Are we there yet?" Dean asked. The sun had set, and the boy was feeling tired.

"Almost," Clarissa answered as she led them up-river to some unknown destination.

"Patience, my dear boy," Doc said. "If the woman leads us to a safe place in which to spend the night, the peaceful rest we will receive will be more than worth the walk."

"There it is," she said, pointing off into the distance. "Just behind that rise."

The companions continued on, followed tirelessly by a group of muties, like seagulls trailing behind a ship hoping to catch something churned up by the ship's wake.

When they reached the rise, J.B. stopped abruptly and grabbed Clarissa by the arm. "There's nothing here," he said, taking another look around. "If you double-cross us, it'll be the last thing you ever do."

"No double cross. You wanted someplace safe, so I'm bringing you to my home, or at least the place I've been living these past few months."

"But there's nothing here."

"Nothing on the surface, but there's plenty underground. Follow me."

Again the friends placed their trust in their female guide. When they reached the bottom of the rise, they came upon a concrete kiosk in the middle of the field.

"This looks like the place where we arrived," Dean whispered to Jak.

"Same, but different."

There was a door on one side of the kiosk. Clarissa opened it and gestured to the four friends. "After you, boys."

"What's this?" J.B. asked.

"An entrance to a water tunnel."

"That leads where?"

"To one of the power plants downriver," Clarissa answered. "I can't be sure which one, since most of them aren't operating anymore and to find out I'd have to walk some five miles in the dark. I figured it's not that important."

J.B. followed the other three friends inside. "What about the muties?"

"They're content to wait for me outside at the entrance until I reappear in the morning."

"I must say that is an excellent security measure," Doc said.

"For some reason, they don't like going underground, or the dark," she said, closing the door and making sure it was locked.

The tunnel was indeed dark. With the door closed, J.B. couldn't see his hands, even when he held them directly in front of his face. "Anyone have a gas lighter?" J.B. asked.

In answer, a small point of light came on to J.B.'s left, illuminating Jak's pale figure.

But a moment later another, much brighter light came on in the tunnel. "There's a few live wires around the falls," Clarissa said, twisting a plastic connector knob onto the ends of two wires. "You just have to know where to look, and not use so much that Baron Fox would notice someone is stealing juice from him."

"Wow!" Dean gasped, his neck craning to take in the enormous size of the tunnel.

"Wow indeed," Doc echoed.

"Big," Jak said.

They were standing at the bottom of a huge concrete tunnel that was roughly fifty or sixty feet across and stretched out in both directions for what seemed like forever. It was like a redoubt, J.B. thought but the tunnel was completely cylindrical—like a blaster barrel—and there seemed to be no end to it.

"And this carried water to the power stations downriver?" J.B. asked.

"When there was water to be carried there," she answered.

But despite it being dry, there was still a soft wash of sound echoing through the tunnel, as if the river's ghost still haunted the caverns beneath the city.

"Now it's just a safe place to sleep."

"An excellent idea, my dear," Doc said.

"What is?"

"Sleep."

"Be my guest."

She had transformed a section of the tunnel into a living space, with several sleeping places made of grasses and twigs.

The companions settled in.

THE FOOD in the farm's cafeteria was as good as one would expect from a farm. The soup and stew had both been made fresh, and Ryan was amazed to find real bits of meat floating around in both.

He took a seat on a bench at one of the tables near the exit, and Brody sat with him. When they'd left the showers, there had been plenty of activity among the sec men as they got rid of Purvis's body and cleaned the showers for the next crew coming in. Ryan wondered why they didn't get the slaves to do the job for them, but figured it was easy to keep the man's death secret from the baron if they handled the problem themselves.

"Nobody will miss Purvis," Brody explained. "But if the baron catches wind of what happened, he might want an explanation. They'll tell him the man slipped on some soap and that will be the end of it."

"But that was what happened," Ryan said with a wink of his eye.

"You'll do all right here, Ryan."

Halfway through the meal, Mildred came and joined Ryan, sitting across the table from him. "Aren't you eating anything?" Ryan asked when he noticed Mildred had no tray in front of her.

"Nursery workers get fed first, and best," she said,

running a hand over her stomach. "I didn't think I'd ever eat steak again."

"How is...?" Brody began, then hesitated, looking around to see if any sec men were listening. "How is Jasmine?"

Mildred looked surprised.

"Mildred," Ryan said, "allow me to introduce Brody. He's the mate of the woman you took to the nursery."

"Pleased to meet you," Mildred said, shaking the man's hand.

"Jasmine?" Brody said.

"She's fine," Mildred answered. "It was tough going for a while, but she's doing real well now."

"And the baby?"

"A boy."

Brody smiled.

"Correct me if I'm wrong," Ryan said, "but you're not supposed to have attachments to the children born here."

"I have a son," Brody said.

Mildred looked over at Ryan. "That's right. The baby was taken from the mother and is now being taken care of by someone else in the nursery. I found out when the baby's six months old he'll be shipped off to a family down south."

"No," Brody said, obviously heartbroken.

"But you knew that would happen?" Ryan said.

"It doesn't matter if I knew," Brody answered. "That's my boy, my flesh and blood. I told myself a thousand times that this would happen, that we'd lose him, and I tried to prepare for it, but nothing can prepare you for losing your child like that.''

Mildred reached over and held Brody's hand.

Ryan looked at the man, understanding a little of what he was going through. Ryan himself had gone through life in the Deathlands never knowing of the son he had. But then, just days after meeting the ten-year-old child for the first time, there had been a bond between them that grew stronger every day. Brody's bond with his newborn was being broken against his will and it hurt the man deeply.

''You may be reunited with your woman and your son yet,'' Ryan said. ''In a couple of days this whole place is going to be turned upside down.''

Brody shook his head in despair and gestured toward Ryan and Mildred. ''Who's going to do it? You two?''

''Mebbe us, mebbe help from outside, mebbe both.''

''You mean there were more out there with you?''

''Four more.''

Brody's smile was wide and bright. ''I'll help you, then. Whatever you need, I'll see that you get it.''

''I need you to stay strong,'' Ryan said. ''For your son.''

Mildred nodded in agreement.

''You got it.''

THERE WAS a knock at Krysty's door.

''Yes?''

The door opened and a short, heavy bull of a sec

man entered the room. "The baron wants you to join him in the cafeteria in twenty minutes."

"All right."

"And he wants you to wear this." The sec man's lips pulled back to reveal a smile full of black holes and broken teeth. In his grimy hand was what looked like a few slips of black fabric.

"What's that?" Krysty asked.

"It's what the baron wants you to wear."

"But what is it?"

"Clothes for a gaudy slut."

"And he wants me to wear them?"

"That's right. He's gonna parade you around to the slaves as his new prize."

"And if I don't put on the clothes?"

"He said I could have you myself," the sec man said, his big beefy tongue slobbering over his bruised and swollen bottom lip. "So if you don't want to put it on, I think mebbe we should stop wasting time and get right down to business."

Krysty considered her options. There was no way she'd let this foul creature lay a finger on her, but even if she resisted all his advances there'd be three more sec men outside the door, all too eager to help him.

"Give them to me!" she snapped.

The sec man looked disappointed but handed over the clothes.

"Wait outside!" she said, pointing to the door.

Reluctantly, the sec man left the room.

THEY CLEARED their food trays and sat back down in their seats in anticipation for the entertainment portion of the evening. The lights in the cafeteria were turned down low, while the lights on the stage at one end of the room were turned up bright.

A middle-aged woman dressed in a black shift walked onstage, and the room slowly grew quiet. "We're in for a special treat tonight. Instead of our usual show, Baron Fox himself has a special surprise for us."

Everyone stopped what they were doing and directed their focus onto the stage.

"And now, here he is, the giver of all good things, Baron Fox."

A round of applause.

The baron walked out onstage with Krysty in tow.

"Krysty!" Ryan exclaimed.

"You know her?" Brody asked.

"That's his mate," Mildred answered. "She was captured with us, but the baron seemed to take a shine to her."

Ryan turned to Mildred. "What is she wearing?"

"I believe that's lingerie, and she makes it look good."

Krysty was wearing a lacy black chemise and panties, and a pair of black mules with three-inch heels.

"Greetings," the baron said. "Today we were very fortunate to come upon new breeding stock."

A smattering of applause.

"As you can see, this one is absolutely exquisite. I believe she is the finest female we've had on the farm for some time." He walked around Krysty admiring her form. ''But rather than have her placed in gen pop and rutted by any who chose to or for me to choose an exclusive stud, I believe she deserves only the best. For that reason, I've decided to hold a little contest, a gladiatorial contest in which the victor will be the only one allowed to rut with the red until she is heavy and an offspring is birthed.''

A wave of excitement seemed to course through the assembled slaves, and the cafeteria was filled with the drone of voices.

''The contest will take place tomorrow afternoon in the courtyard between the main building and the front gate,'' the baron proclaimed. ''Work will end early so that all may watch.''

That brought a cheer.

When the room quieted, the baron continued. ''Fighters will be able to leave the arena by one of two ways. Chilled, or by their own will. The last one left will claim the prize.'' He paused to admire Krysty one last time. ''Those interested can give their name to Norman Bauer.''

Norman Bauer was standing off to the side of the stage. There was a rush of men heading toward him.

''Survival of the fittest,'' Mildred said. ''Evolution in action.''

''What do you mean?'' Ryan asked.

''Charles Darwin was a scientist during Doc's time who proposed the modern theory of evolution,'' Mildred explained. ''His principle of natural selection basically said that the strongest survive, and that a species continues to evolve through natural and sexual selection.''

''Meaning what?'' Ryan asked.

''Meaning this contest will determine who among the men here is the strongest and it's only natural that the strongest male mates with the strongest female so that the species produces the best possible offspring.''

Ryan nodded, then got up from the table.

Brody stood, as well.

''Where are you going?'' Ryan asked.

Brody put a hand on Ryan's shoulder. ''There'll be at least a dozen men in that ring and every one of them is going to want to chill you. If you're going to break out of here in the next couple of days, you'll need to be alive to do it. And to stay alive in the arena, you're going to need someone watching your back, and that's me.''

''Thanks, Brody,'' Ryan said, grateful to have the help. ''You're a good man.''

''You're a good man, too, Ryan,'' Brody responded. ''Let's just hope that for the sake of your woman, you're also the best.''

Chapter Twenty

Sec chief Ganley was first off the boat as they came aground on the south shore of Erie Lake. The beach stretched some twenty feet back from the water, and beyond that was a tangle of deadwood and choked forest.

The sun was just beginning to set, and they would have to hurry to set up camp. Ganley posted a pair of guards at opposite ends of the campsite where the beach met the forest, and then led the expedition to find firewood for the night.

Deadwood proved easy to find, and thirty minutes later they had a roaring fire burning on the sand and a rack of sturgeon steaks cooking on a spit.

"What are you hoping to find when we get there?" Ganley asked as the group huddled around the fire waiting for the fish to cook. "What kind of mates do you all want?"

"My woman's got to have all her teeth!" one of the group called out.

"Mine should have breeding hips," another said.

"My man's gotta be strong," Rhonda said. "Stronger than me."

"Not many of those around," someone quipped.

Ganley agreed. "Seeing you in action, Rhonda,

makes me think that there is no such man on the planet.''

''No, he's out there somewhere,'' she said, turning to look over the surface of the water. ''And I'm going to find him.''

After a moment's silence, punctuated by the crackling of the fire, Rhonda looked at Ganley and said, ''What about you, Chief? What are you looking for on this trip?''

The sec chief smiled. His only intention was to lead the mission and return as many people safely to the village as he could. The thought that he might take a mate back with him had never even occurred to him. ''I'm just looking to get you all back to Reichel ville alive.''

''Come on, Chief, you must have a preference.''

''Well, she would have to be healthy, but that's obvious.'' He paused a moment further to consider the question. ''I've always liked red hair....''

''See, I told you. Everyone has things they like.''

''And dark skin. One or the other.''

''Well,'' Rhonda said, getting up to check on the fish. ''We'll see if we can find one or the other for you. Or maybe even both.''

The travelers smiled and laughed.

''Fish is ready,'' Rhonda said.

''Eat up, everyone, then get some rest. We've got a long day tomorrow, and it starts with the sun.''

Chapter Twenty-One

Ryan spent the night in a cabin with Mildred. After he'd signed up for the contest, several women not yet matched up for the night came around asking Ryan if he'd been spoken for.

"He's with me," Mildred said, changing her story from earlier in the day.

"Besides," Ryan said, "I need my strength for tomorrow and you look like you'd tire me out."

That sent the women away with smiles on their faces.

Both Mildred and Ryan enjoyed a good night's sleep, but when the sun came up they were roused out of bed by sec men banging on the side of the cabin.

"We're burning daylight, people," the sec man shouted. "If you want to watch the contest today, you've got to start work that much earlier."

The two friends went to the cafeteria for breakfast, and afterward Mildred was led to the nursery and Ryan joined Brody and the rest of his crew out in the orchards.

"Have you ever seen one of these contests before?" Ryan asked Brody as they began pulling weeds.

"A couple times."

"What are they like?"

"The first one I saw had only two men in it. This couple had been kidnapped on their way south and the woman was put up for battle. Her man signed up, but so did Purvis. This guy put up a good fight, but wouldn't give up and in the end Purvis had to chill him to make him stop fighting. Thing of it was, I don't even think Purvis wanted the woman, since she was already a little on the old side."

"And the other time?"

"This young girl, beautiful in just about every way. More than a dozen signed up for it, but most backed out early when they saw that Mog had entered."

"Who's Mog?"

"Big man," Brody answered. "Stands six-five, six-six, weighs near three hundred pounds. He's the farm's alpha male and pretty mean, too, meaner even than Purvis."

"He's signed up for this contest?"

"Oh, yeah," Brody nodded. "He has to if he wants to maintain his position."

"And how many others?"

"I checked this morning before getting on the wag. Eighteen so far. Might be more, might be less by the end of the day."

Ryan nodded. "What about weapons?"

"No blasters, of course. But when the contest begins, an assortment of hand weapons will be thrown into the arena, everything from sharp sticks and clubs to chains and maces."

"So why haven't the others joined together to get rid of this Mog?"

"There are those loyal to him. They watch his back, and he rewards them with breeders they might not have otherwise."

"How many loyals does he have?"

"Many, but only three are signed up so far."

"So that makes four altogether, Mog and his loyals."

"Yes," Brody said.

Ryan nodded. "Then our chances are good."

GANLEY GOT THE BOATS back on the water shortly after the sun came up on Erie Lake.

"With any luck," he said, "tonight will be the first of many we spend with our new mates."

A cheer erupted from the two boats, but then quickly died down as the sec chief settled into the regular rhythm of, "Stroke! Stroke! Stroke!" that would have them on the north shore by midafternoon and then on to their destination by nightfall.

THEY USED the Rainbow Bridge to cross the river below the falls, but if they had a wag with them on the way back they would have to try a different route. The Rainbow had been twisted and broken by movement caused by the skydark nukes on either side of the river. The bridge could handle people on foot, but anything heavier, especially a wag, and the whole bridge could collapse into the gorge below.

The Whirlpool Rapids Bridge farther downstream was a possibility, but J.B. didn't like the creaking sound the steel girders made whenever the wind blew with any strength.

"So even if we find a wag, we might not be able to get back with it," J.B. stated.

"No, there's another bridge farther south," Clarissa reported. "It's stable and strong. It's the one Baron Fox takes on his way to the eastern villes all the time."

J.B. was satisfied.

After crossing over onto the American side, they found the ruins of Niagara Falls Boulevard and took the road east, followed by an ever present gang of muties.

The ville on the American side had sustained more damage than its Canadian counterpart. The houses, all made of wood, had burned to the ground in a firestorm, and the few remaining buildings were scorched black. A fine dust covered the ground and anything that had remained on the street.

They crossed a highway and saw on their left the remains of an airport. They were mostly small planes with single engines, none of them with any weapons. J.B. had often wondered if he could get such a vehicle running, and perhaps even take it into the skies one day, but he knew that such thoughts were best suited for another time, perhaps when the companions were done roaming the Deathlands and he had the time and the patience for such tinkering.

"The museum's just on the right," Clarissa said.

J.B. adjusted his spectacles on the bridge of his nose. "Looks like a big gaudy house."

"It might have been at one time," Clarissa agreed. "If 'mall' is another word for 'gaudy house.'"

Doc cleared his throat. "In my day a mall was a large area, usually lined with shade trees and shrubbery and used as a public walk or promenade. But I believe in later years it was used to describe a large retail facility containing a variety of stores, restaurants and business establishments, often housed under a single roof."

"They had stores for wags and blasters in predark times?" Dean asked.

"No," Clarissa answered, "but they had lots of space inside for a museum."

"Why no one else find?" Jak asked.

"The museum is cleaned out, but not by people looking for wags. It's all in storage belowground."

J.B. nodded. "If the people who ran the museum knew skydark was coming, they might have moved the museum pieces to protect them from damage."

Clarissa picked up her pace. "This way."

They started down a ramp that led to a large roll-up door. A sign on the right read Deliveries Only.

J.B. pointed to the sign. "I guess we're just going to have to break the rules."

Doc shook his head. "On the contrary, John Barrymore. Whatever we find down there will help us deliver Ryan, Krysty and Mildred from a life of slavery."

J.B. gave Doc a thin smile.

Clarissa lifted the large roll-up door until there was a foot-and-a-half gap between the bottom of the door and the pavement. "That's all I can open from the outside."

"More than enough," Jak said, rolling into the garage.

Dean crawled through on all fours.

J.B. slid under the door on his back, not wanting to roll over his blasters.

Doc got to the ground more slowly than the others, the joints of his knees crackling and popping in protest the closer he got to the ground. "I do hope that you intend to provide us with a more dignified way of getting out of this place."

Clarissa said nothing, following Doc inside and rolling down the door behind her.

There was a long line of loading docks where goods would have been loaded and unloaded from transport wags almost every day of the year. But now it was vacant for the most part, except for the far corner of the garage.

"That's the stuff down there," Clarissa said.

"Dark night!"

"What?" Jak asked.

But the Armorer didn't answer. He was already running toward the small cache of ancient items stored in the far corner of what was basically a concrete bunker.

The others followed.

There wasn't a LAV among the collection, but there was a decent-sized wag—the one Clarissa had stolen from Baron Fox—that would suit their needs with a little bit of work.

"That's a P-39," J.B. said, standing in front of the green World War II fighter airplane.

Dean came up behind J.B. "What's a P-39?"

J.B. pointed to the winged relic. "That is a Bell P-39 Airacobra. It was made in this part of the country and used by the air force for ground attack in World War II."

Doc tapped the aircraft's wings with his swordstick. "Don't tell me it's almost as old as I am."

"Not quite, Doc," J.B. answered. "Just about 150 years old."

Jak looked at the old machine skeptically. "Not know how to fly."

J.B. shook his head. "Not interested in flying. If I was, I'd use that helicopter over there to land right inside the compound. No, the P-39 just happens to be armed with four .50-caliber machine blasters and a 37 mm cannon."

"Hot pipe!" Dean exclaimed.

"Hot pipe, indeed," Doc echoed.

"If we can find some ammunition for those blasters in these stores and secure the blasters onto the transport wag Clarissa stole—" he pointed to the wag "—we'll be able to rescue Ryan, Krysty and Mildred in style."

"Easy say," Jak said with a bit of a smile. "Harder do."

Clarissa piped up then, agreeing with Jak. "That's right. You're talking about all of this as if it's as easy as changing a round in a blaster."

J.B. was about to say something to the woman, but was cut off by a wave of Doc's hand.

"My dear lady, I believe our albino friend is merely teasing his friend. The fact that what John is proposing is extremely difficult is only more of a reason why he will succeed. I have seen this man do some astounding things with blasters and wags, and I have learned never to doubt his word. I've also seen that look in his eye. This metal bird's big blaster will not only provide the means for him to rescue his friends, but it will also provide him with no small amount of pleasure. There is a light in his eyes, and he is eager to find out what a round from a 37 mm cannon can do. And, quite frankly, I am rather curious about that myself. So you see, our weapons expert will not fail. He will succeed and he will do so gloriously. There is simply no other way."

J.B. had stood back while Doc spoke, and now that he was done, J.B. nodded. "Yeah, that sounds about right."

"So, instead of telling the weapons master why something will not work, I suggest you begin opening crates over there and help out in the search for tools and ammunition."

"All right, I believe," she said. "Where should I begin?"

"Open all the crates. Any tools you find, bring them to me."

"All right, let's do it," she said.

They began opening the crates and lockers piled on the loading docks, first with their bare hands, and then with hammers and crowbars after Dean found a few of the tools stored in a locker.

"This looks like it might be something," Dean later called out from a corner of the underground garage.

J.B. stopped his work on freeing the P-39's cannon and walked over to where the boy was hunched over a wooden crate marked with a symbol that looked like an exploding rock. He looked down into the crate over Dean's shoulder, and even though he could only see the base of the shells, he knew exactly what he was looking at.

"Those are the 37 mm cannon shells," J.B. stated. "Take them out and line them up on the concrete."

Dean began to lift the heavy munitions out of the crate and set them down on the loading dock. Each shell weighed more than a pound, was an inch and a half in diameter and over four inches long. When Dean was done, there were sixteen shells lined up in a row and with the shells gone, the belt that fed them into the cannon was discovered in the bottom of the crate.

The Armorer picked up a few of the shells, examining their seals and general condition. "They're in good shape. If half of them fire, it'll be more than enough."

"John Barrymore, come here," Doc shouted.

J.B. hurried to Doc's side. He was sitting on a pile of smaller crates that had the same stencil mark on them as Dean's crate. "What is it?"

"A gift."

J.B. reached into the crate and pulled out a belt of .50-caliber rounds for the P-39's machine blasters. The belt and shells still had an oily sheen on them. He pulled the belt from the crate and began walking the length of the loading dock until the end of the belt appeared and he could see both ends clearly. Then he placed the belt on the floor and began pacing out its length. It took him nine steps to get from one end to the other. "The whole nine yards," he said with a gleeful smile.

Doc gave him a confused look. "I am afraid I do not understand."

"The belt is twenty-seven feet long and full of ammunition. It's as much as you can load into one of these machine blasters. In the Pacific Arena in World War II, pilots would use the expression 'I gave him the whole nine yards' to say that they used up all their ammunition against the enemy."

"How do you know that?" Clarissa asked. She'd come over to join J.B. and Doc, along with Dean.

Doc turned to the woman and said, "There isn't anything having to do with blasters and bullets that J.B. does not know about. Even the most insignificant and trivial bits of information are stored within his brain, sometimes to the exclusion of other, more valuable bits...as we have just been witness to."

"It also means," J.B. said, realizing Doc was just having some fun, "that we'll be able to use two of the machine blasters rescuing Ryan, Krysty and Mildred."

"And my sister," Clarissa added quickly.

"Yes." J.B. nodded. "And your sister."

That seemed to please her to no end.

"Now that we've got the ammunition," J.B. said, "let's see if we can get the old bird to give up the blasters."

KRYSTY ATE her breakfast in her room under the watchful eye of a young sec man who looked harmless enough. His gaze never wavered from her body the whole time she was eating, and Krysty couldn't be sure if he was doing his job or simply getting an eyeful.

She decided that if he was enamored with her, then maybe she could use that to her advantage.

"That's a nice blaster you've got there," she lied. It looked like a Smith & Wesson Model 18, but the different metal shadings betrayed its status as a remade. It was a .22 rimfire that wasn't good for much more than plinking cans off fence posts, but the young sec man seemed proud of it.

"Thanks," he answered. "It's been a friend to me."

"I had a Smith & Wesson myself," she said, unzipping the front of her jumpsuit, as if she were warm.

"Really?"

"Yes, a .38-caliber Model 640."

"Wow, that's a big gun for a..."

"For a what?" she asked. "For a woman?"

"For such a pretty one, at least."

"A woman's got to protect herself. There are a lot of bad people out in the Deathlands."

"I've seen a few of them."

"But when they brought me here, they took my blaster from me." Krysty drew the zipper a little lower, exposing her full breasts enclosed in a lacy bra. "I know I can't ever have it back, but I've been wondering what they might have done with it."

"Oh, it's likely in the armory with the others," the sec man said, licking his lips like a dog. "They brought all the outlanders' blasters down there. I've seen some of them. Quality stuff."

"The other sec men haven't taken them for themselves yet?" Krysty said breathlessly.

"No." He shook his head. "Everything that comes into the farm like that belongs to the baron. He'll probably have a shooting contest in a few days to see who deserves to have the best blasters. Then the rest of us will upgrade with blasters being used by more senior sec men." He looked at his remade .22. "Maybe I'll have to give up my crippler for a man-stopper."

"Where is the armory?"

"Down in the basement of this building. It's right next door to the nursery."

"And who has keys to it?"

"Baron Fox, of course."

"Of course."

"Sec chief Grundwold does, too. And the armory's quartermaster, of course."

"No one else has a key?"

"There might be a few others." He shrugged. "The lock's mostly to keep people from wandering into the room by mistake. The door's not all that strong, so if someone really wanted to get in, all they'd have to do is break down the door."

Krysty nodded, sat up straight in her chair and began zipping up her top. "That was a great breakfast," she said, smiling. "But the company was best of all. Will you be bringing my lunch?"

"I could try and get the duty if you like."

"Oh, yes, I'd like that very much."

"Consider it done."

"See you then."

The young sec man smiled as he lingered in the room, finally bumping into the door frame on his way out.

REMOVING THE 37 mm cannon from the nose of the P-39 was proving more difficult than J.B. had thought it would be. The engine was behind the pilot's seat and drove the propeller by way of a long extension shaft. That allowed the nose of the aircraft to house the cannon, firing directly through the propeller hub, along with a pair of .50-caliber machine blasters sitting in the top part of the nose. The blasters had been easy to take out, but the gearing and shaft driving the engine proved to be an obstacle to the removal of the cannon.

"How's it coming, J.B.?" Doc asked.

"I don't think we're going to be raiding the farm tonight, Doc."

"Stubborn," Jak observed, coming up alongside Doc.

"That's a good word for it."

Doc rested an arm on the plane's wing. "Is there anything we can do to help?"

"Something to eat would be nice. And a warm cup of coffee sub."

Doc, Jak and Dean all turned to look at Clarissa.

"Are you boys good with those blasters?"

Doc sighed. "Must you ask?"

"Okay, then, do you like fish?"

"Haven't had any for a while," J.B. said.

"Well, there's a spot below the falls where you might be able to shoot some for dinner."

"Shooting fish in a barrel?" Doc asked.

"Something like that."

"Doc stays with me," J.B. commanded. "You two go with her. We'll need enough to get us through today and tomorrow."

Jak and Dean followed Clarissa out of the underground garage.

"And Jak..." J.B. called out.

The albino turned.

"I don't want to hear anything about the ones that got away."

Jak unholstered his .357 Magnum Colt Python. "No worry. Fish not escape."

WITHOUT PURVIS LOOKING over the crew, work in the orchards was almost pleasant for Ryan and Brody. They were pulling weeds again, but no one was pushing them hard, since most everyone's thoughts were on the afternoon's contest.

At morning break, an older man approached Ryan, standing over him and Brody as they drank some much needed water.

"I know what you did to Purvis," the old man said.

Ryan was cautious. "He a friend of yours?"

"No, sir! He was no friend of anyone on this crew, especially the women."

"So I gathered."

Brody was growing suspicious of the old man. "You got something to say, old-timer?"

"Only this." He paused and licked his lips with his tongue. "The women, them over there—"

Ryan looked to where the old man was pointing and saw six women huddled together in a circle. Two of the women waved at him. Ryan waved back.

"They're grateful for what you done, and they want you to know they'll be cheering for you today."

"Thank you," Ryan said.

"And they wanted me to give you this." He held out his fist, turned his fingers over to catch the sun, then opened his hand. In his palm, a shiny bit of metal glinted in the morning sunlight.

"Brass knuckles," Brody said.

"I've been keeping them in case Purvis ever wanted to roll me. I wouldn't have stopped him, but I might have at least broken his nose." The old man laughed then, a dry, wheezing sort of laugh.

"Weapons like this are allowed?" Ryan asked, taking the brass knuckles from the old man and slipping them over the fingers of his right hand.

Brody nodded. "The others will be trying to bring everything they can in with them, too, from spikes to knife blades."

"What about the sec men?"

"They'll be looking the other way."

Ryan nodded, pressing his brass-ringed fist into the palm of his left hand. It would certainly do some damage, and it was comfortable enough that he could still hold a sword or club in his right hand while the knuckles were on his fingers. "Thank you, to you and the ladies."

"No, thank *you*," the old man said. "Today's been almost like a holiday without that bastard Purvis around. So even if you get chilled in the arena, you've already done us a good deed."

"You're welcome," Ryan said. "I guess."

CLARISSA BROUGHT Jak and Doc down to the river where the water ran fast in a swirling froth of water and foam.

"There are fish here?" Jak asked.

"Not here." Clarissa gestured across the river. "There's a whirlpool on the other side. With the lower water level, the fish get trapped inside it, swirling around and around. We've tried to catch them all sorts of ways, with our bare hands and with sharpened sticks, but the fish are too fast."

They began walking across the river, the water being just low enough for them to be able to make it on foot—if they were careful.

"And we're supposed to shoot them?" Dean asked.

"Do you see any other food around?" Clarissa responded with her own question.

"No, but I—"

Suddenly Dean's voice was gone as he slipped on the rocks and fell under the water.

"Dean!" Clarissa shouted.

He was hanging on to a jutting rock with both hands, the flow of water trying to push him downstream. "I can't pull myself up," he said, swallowing a mouthful of water in the process.

Jak took off his coat and extended his left hand to Clarissa. "Grab hand!"

She took it.

He then extended his arms and took one sleeve of his jacket in his right hand. He swung the jacket toward Dean so the other sleeve fell near the rock he was clutching.

Dean reached for the jacket, which was fluttering in the flow of water, but when he let go of the rock with one hand, he was nearly swept away by the river. He was forced to grab hold again with two hands.

"Jak, look!" Clarissa screamed.

Jak glanced downstream and saw what looked like rocks moving against the flow. "What is it?"

"A mutie fish," she shouted. "A big one, muskie or salmon, maybe even a mutie sturgeon."

The fish was getting closer, its huge mouth open wide to catch everything the river sent its way. It scooped up dead fish and other refuse without ever having to move more than a few dozen feet left or right. If Dean let go, he'd be swept away by the water into the fish's belly in seconds.

"Hang on, Dean!" Clarissa shouted.

Jak kept trying to work his jacket into position, but he was short by a couple of feet.

"Give me pants," he said.

Without hesitation, Clarissa slid off her pants, stepped out of them and tied one of the legs to Jak's jacket sleeve. Then she held Jak's arm while he tried reaching Dean.

This time the pant leg landed over Dean's hands. With a quick movement of his right hand, the boy grabbed the pant leg. Then, with it securely wrapped around his wrist, he let go of the rock.

"Pull!" Jak said, straining against the current.

"Jak, the fish!"

The albino teen looked past Dean. The fish was swimming against the current toward their fallen friend, as if Dean were bait at the end of a line. They continued to reel him in, but they couldn't pull fast enough. With a mighty flip of its tail the fish lunged forward, its upper lip brushing up against Dean's boots.

"Hurry up!" Dean yelled.

The fish kept coming, and Jak realized that even after they pulled Dean in, the mutie fish would still be able to move upstream against the current with its belly against the bottom and water flowing through its gills to breathe.

The shallow rapids weren't any protection against this fish. They were all in danger.

"Take jacket," Jak said, handing the sleeve to Clarissa so she could hold on to it with him while he pulled his .357 Colt Python from its holster.

Dean, seeing the big six-inch barrel of Jak's blaster pointed in his direction, ducked his head, plunging it under the water to get it out of the way.

Jak fired off two rounds that smashed into the fish's great head. The powerful rounds punched holes in its skull and tore big bloody swaths through its soft body. Chunks of blood, brain and meaty flesh exploded out the sides of its body. But it was still moving for Dean. Jak squeezed off another two rounds, catching the fish in one of its eyes with the first shot and blowing away the entire left side of its mouth with the other.

Blood began to turn the river around the fish a pinkish red, and it began to lose the battle with the current and slowly started to float away.

With the danger of the fish now gone, Clarissa and Jak were able to quickly pull Dean to safety.

"I've done a lot of things in the time I've been with Dad," Dean commented, when he was back on his feet and squeezing water out of his clothes. "But I never thought I'd be used as fish bait."

Jak stood in silence, watching the big fish float downriver, toward the lake. "Fish getting away. Not tell J.B."

Clarissa began putting on her sodden pants. "Well, we can always try the whirlpool. That was the plan in the beginning anyway."

But then the fish was caught by an eddy in the river, and it turned sideways against the current. As if by design, it washed up on the north shore, across the river from Whirlpool Point. They'd be able to cut as many steaks as they wanted out of the fish, and the carcass would feed Clarissa's mutie clan for days to come.

"Hot pipe!" Dean exclaimed. "We'll tell J.B. all about it. He won't believe a word of it, but we can tell him."

They hurried across the river.

"WHERE'S THE FISH?" J.B. asked when the door to the underground garage rolled up and Jak, Clarissa and Dean slid under the bottom gap.

"Floating in the river," Dean answered.

Doc rubbed his empty stomach. "Are you saying that you did not chill a single fish?"

"Chilled one fish," Jak said, a burlap sack slung over his shoulder.

"Just one," J.B. said, working to loosen something in the cockpit of the P-39. "Don't tell me. All the rest got away, right?"

"Nope." Dean smiled. "After Jak chilled that one fish, it floated downriver and we didn't need to chill any more."

"Washed up on shore," Jak said, dropping the sack at Doc's feet.

"But a half-ton fish was too big to bring back here," Clarissa said, "so we decided to bring back fifty pounds of fish steaks instead. Hope that's enough."

Doc was speechless for a moment, then asked, "What sort of fish?"

Clarissa held up one of the neatly cut slabs. "Sturgeon."

"Is that good eating?"

"No worry," Jak said. "When finished, taste like chicken."

BRODY REJOINED the crew later in the afternoon. "I bet all the jack I had on you at ten to one," he told Ryan. "You're sitting at eight to one now."

"What about you?" Ryan asked.

"Me," Brody shrugged. "Something like twenty-five to one, but that's just being kind. No one's put any jack on me, not even me. Come to think of it, nobody's put any jack on you except for the people in this crew. They've all bet on you."

A sec man approached them from behind. Ryan's muscles tensed, ready to strike the man or his blaster if the situation required it.

"All right, you two, your work is over for today," the sec man said. "Catch a ride on the wag back to your quarters. The baron wants you rested up for tonight's entertainment."

The two men stopped pulling weeds and headed for the wag.

Ryan didn't like to chill anything for sport, but it appeared he wouldn't be having any choice in the matter this time around.

Chapter Twenty-Two

Baron Fox sat back in his chair behind his desk, looking through the pages of another one of his tattered predark skin mags.

"Nineteen have signed up for the contest, Baron," Norman Bauer said after waiting several minutes for Baron Fox to finish with his mag.

The baron didn't lift his eyes from the page. "Who is favored?"

"Mog. One to four."

The baron nodded. "Who's got the best odds next after Mog?"

"The one-eyed outlander," Bauer reported. "Eight to one."

That seemed to catch the baron's interest. "The outlander has signed up to save his woman, has he? Oh, that's precious."

"From what the sec men tell me, this one-eye is a very dangerous man."

"Really?"

"We can't prove it, since none of the slaves will come forward, but the talk is that the one-eye must have chilled Purvis in the shower his first day in the orchards."

Baron Fox put aside his mag. "In the shower?"

"Everyone says Purvis slipped on some soap, but he and the one-eye were the last ones in the showers."

"He chilled Purvis in the shower, with his bare hands?"

"Smashed his head on the tiles, it would seem."

The baron was excited by the thought of it.

"Tell Mog's crew," he said at last. "A week free of work for the man who chills the one-eye."

THERE WAS A KNOCK on the door to the nursery.

"Come," Mildred said. She was watching over Jasmine, making sure the woman was comfortable. She was still experiencing afterpains in the abdomen and was showing a bloody vaginal discharge. The latter was beginning to clear up, but the pains were still as sharp as ever. And then there was the depression that followed delivery, made worse by the absence of the newborn child.

A sec man entered the nursery first, followed by Krysty Wroth.

"Krysty!" Mildred said warmly. "What brings you here?"

"The baron," she answered. "He wants me to get checked out to make sure I'm healthy for the winner."

"Girl, you're one of the healthiest females I've ever known. But if the baron wants you checked out, then we should do that in the examination room." Mildred smiled and led Krysty away from the sec man and into a small room at the back of the nursery.

When the door was closed behind them, Mildred

turned to Krysty. "Looks like they've been treating you well."

Krysty nodded. "The best of everything."

"Ryan's signed up for the contest," Mildred said. "And you saw that woman out in the nursery. Her man will be fighting alongside Ryan."

"It's good to know he's not alone."

"His work crew's behind him, as well."

Krysty lowered her voice some. "I found out that our blasters are being stored in the armory near here. They'll be having another contest, a shooting contest between sec men to see who gets them."

"Hopefully we won't be here that long."

Krysty nodded. "The door's locked, but I've been told it can be easily broken into."

"Maybe I'll do that when the time comes."

"My guess is tomorrow."

"Mine, too."

Just then the door to the examination room opened, revealing a sec man standing in the doorway.

"Can I help you?" Mildred asked, her hands on her hips.

"Keep the door open," he said. "So I can hear what you're saying."

"I was just telling her that her female parts are in fine working order and that's she's going to make the champion one happy man."

The sec man smiled and turned away from the open door.

JAK AND CLARISSA COOKED the fish steaks over an open fire near the entrance to the underground garage.

As usual, there were muties hanging around on the other side of the garage door, but they'd all gorged themselves on the sturgeon carcass in the river and were now just waiting for instruction from their goddess, Clarissa.

J.B. had managed to free the 37 mm cannon from the P-39 and was now in the process of stripping it to check for dampness and rust.

"Will it fire?" Doc asked, peering over J.B.'s shoulder.

"I think so."

"Any thoughts on how you might mount such an infernal weapon?"

"Thinking about bolting it onto the side of the wag, but there's not much solid steel to mount it on," he explained. "If we had any more than sixteen shells to fire, the cannon's recoil would eventually tear the whole side off the wag. Should hold together till we're done with it, though."

"What about aiming it?"

"I'll have to point the wag where I want the round to go. Probably have to use a round or two to calibrate the cannon, mebbe put an X onto the windshield marking the target at a hundred yards or so."

"Ah, a precision weapon, I see," Doc teased the Armorer.

J.B. smiled. "In some ways it's like your LeMat, Doc. With this thing, all I have to be is close. The half pound of hot lead will do the rest."

Doc smiled, knowing J.B. was in his element. "When do you think it will be ready?"

"Not tonight," the Armorer said with a disappointed sigh. "I still have to mount the .50 calibers and then test the guns, and that should be done during the day. So I'm afraid Ryan will have to wait one more night."

"I could do with another night's sleep myself," Doc said. "That and a bite to eat." He turned in the direction of Jak and Clarissa, who had now been joined by Dean. "I say, Master Jak, is dinner close to being served?"

"Not yet," the albino said. "Take time if want taste like chicken."

Doc was forced to go hungry another fifteen minutes, but forgot all about the wait when he discovered that sturgeon steaks did indeed taste like chicken.

And very tasty chicken at that.

Chapter Twenty-Three

There was a carnival atmosphere in the air.

The slaves had gotten off work early and many of them had broken out their private stocks of booze, most of which the baron had given them as reward for good breeding.

An eight-point ring had been mapped out in the courtyard about fifty feet across, with tall wooden stakes being pounded into the ground and connected to each other by a length of medium-gauge chain. Each stake was topped with a red flag, and the chain was painted bright red to clearly denote the perimeter of the circle.

Slaves and sec men gathered around the outside of the circle. Those eager to be spattered with sweat and blood sat on the dry, hard ground just a few paces back from the chain, while less bloodthirsty spectators kept farther back of the makeshift arena, sitting on an assortment of crates, boxes and chairs.

Baron Fox appeared on the wooden stage that had been constructed years earlier for such outdoor spectacles and addressed the crowd.

"This is a happy time at Fox Farm," he began. "We have birthed more offspring in the past month than in the previous three months combined, and it's all because of you!

"So, as a small token of my appreciation for so many jobs well done, I have arranged a special entertainment for this evening. Like gladiators from a long ago time, these men will be testing their strength, courage, desire and spirit in a fight to the finish. Ten men will enter the circle...."

Over in the main building, Ryan stood behind the closed doors, waiting for his time to enter the circle. "Only ten?"

"A few must have dropped out," Brody explained, "signing up just for show and an early quitting time. Or the sec chief might have tossed out a few men he thought would only get in the way."

"...and in the end, only one will remain. The victor!"

"To the victor go the spoils!" the crowd shouted in unison. "To the victor go the spoils!"

The baron looked pleased. He nodded and Krysty was led out onto the stage by a pair of sec men. She had changed yet again, this time into a short skirt and skintight tank top that highlighted all of her curves. She was still wearing her cowboy boots, but a studded collar had been added to her neck.

The baron put out his hand to calm the crowd. "The spoils, yes! Here she is, a shining example of feminine perfection, hot, fiery and a worthy prize for the strongest, most virile male on the farm. Their union will produce a beautiful offspring."

The baron placed his hand on Krysty's breast. She

tried to move away, but the sec men behind her held her in place.

The sight caused Ryan's blood to boil with anger.

"Easy, my friend," Brody said. "You've got to chill a few other men before you can get close to him."

The baron continued. "But before any of that can happen, we must first decide which of these brave males will be allowed to be drowned in this woman's ample feminine charms. And so, I give you sec chief Grundwold, who will remind you all of the rules."

The crowd let out a long, loud cheer.

The baron, waving to the crowd, sat on the purple throne set atop the stage. Krysty was brought by his side and was made to sit on pillow at his feet. A chain was attached to her dog collar, with the other end locked to one of the throne's purple legs.

Grundwold stepped forward. "The last man left standing in the circle is the victor. Rest periods will be called for the removal of bodies from the circle. Wounded combatants can leave the ring of their own free will, or they can be forced out at any time by another combatant, or they can be chilled!

"And so, let the game begin. And as always, to the victor go the spoils!"

The doors to the main building were opened by a sec man standing in the courtyard. "Get out there, you two!"

Ryan and Brody stepped out into the hot afternoon sun and walked along a path kept clear by sec men that led into the circle. There were a few cheers for the two men coming from their own crew, but everyone else kept quiet, saving their loudest cheers for the others.

When Ryan and Brody reached the far end of the circle, they turned to see a white miniwag pull up and two sec men step off the back, heading for the circle. The noise level among the slaves remained constant, but the sec men who were scattered around the courtyard and up in the towers all whistled their approval.

"Richmond and Salazar," Brody said. "They're the two meanest sec men on the farm. I doubt they'll go up against Mog and his animals, but if they've entered the game it means they're looking to chill someone."

Ryan understood, and he hated the two men instantly. He'd seen plenty of sec men go mad from the power they had over people. These men enjoyed beating slaves and had probably chilled dozens over the years. Their first few had been a mistake, the result of a combination of overeagerness and not knowing when to quit. After the first few, however, chilling got easier, until they needed to chill someone like an addict needed jolt. They were here for some fun, to chill and inflict pain and then back out of the fight like cowards. Ryan would see to it that they didn't leave the circle in the same shape they entered it.

The doors to the big barn opened next, and two pale creatures scrambled across the courtyard and into the circle. Their skin was white, covered by a layer of grime. The rest of their bodies were covered in tattered clothing, and their exposed arms were as thin as blaster barrels. Tufts of black hair stood up on their heads, patches of it coming low on the forehead and shading eyes that were sunk back deep in their sockets. Tongues lolled uselessly out the sides of their mouths as both of them sniffed at the air.

"That's Laslo and Hambly."

"Muties?"

"Mostly," Brody answered. "They're more norm than mutie, but they aren't allowed to rut with the rest of us. The baron keeps them in the barn to shovel shit and clean toilets. Every once in a while he gives them a nonbreeder he's all done with since once they go into the barn, they don't usually come back out alive. They've probably got their sights set on your woman."

"That's all they'll get of her, too."

The crowd began chanting as one. "Mog! Mog! Mog!"

"Here he comes," Brody said.

Ryan turned toward the orchard closest to the courtyard. Walking between two rows of plum trees, almost as tall as a tree himself, was what had to be the man called Mog.

He stood over six and a half feet tall, and his naked upper body bulged with well-defined muscles and flesh that was covered with a road map of scars. His head was shaved above the ears, and his remaining hair was cut short, bristling straight up from his head in a sort of cocomb that split the sides of his skull in two, like a wedge. Half of his left ear was missing, and his nose looked as if it had been broken several times.

"Mog! Mog! Mog!"

Mog was obviously the crowd favorite, getting slapped on the back by men and women alike all the way into the circle.

"And he's as mean as he is big," Brody said. "The sec men wanted to recruit him into the ranks, but he refused. Said he'd rather be a slave than a rad-blasted sec man."

Ryan appreciated the sentiment. "Looks dangerous enough."

"When he first arrived, the sec men had trouble keeping him in line. He broke the necks of two men the first week."

"Why didn't they chill him?"

"Baron wouldn't let them. Mog's offspring bring in top jack for the farm. Baron even gave him his own personal group of breeders."

"Sounds like he's got a good deal going. What's he doing here?"

"I think he wants Krysty for himself."

Ryan remembered something the Trader used to say and muttered it now under his breath. "A chilled man has no desires, no wants."

"What was that?"

"Nothing," Ryan answered, craning his neck to see the three men walking in Mog's shadow. "Who are they?"

"Dorfman, Billingsley and Foghat. They're Mog's cronies and will be watching his back, like I'll be doing for you. Stab you in the back if they can. Makes no difference to them."

''Thanks for the warning.''

''Well, all of them will stab you in the back if they get the chance.''

Ryan nodded. ''That's what I figured.''

''Chill or be chilled.''

Grundwold entered the circle carrying a canvas duffel bag filled with weapons. When he reached the center, he upended the bag and let the contents fall to the ground. Piled in a heap were several lengths of heavy chain, an assortment of knives, a few long wooden pikes and a few rusty swords. However, included in the jumble were several newer pieces, including Ryan's own panga.

Seeing the knife's eighteen-inch blade, Ryan moved closer to the center of the circle.

''Back off, One-eye!'' Grundwold bellowed. ''You start anything while I'm in the circle, and my snipers will blow a hole through your skull big enough to drive a wag through.''

Ryan looked at the armed men in the towers and took a cautious step backward.

Mog moved closer to the circle's center, as well, but instead of calling the man on it, Grundwold simply hurried out of the circle.

''Makes no difference to me, outlander,'' Mog said, gesturing to the weapons. ''I'll chill you with whatever you leave behind.''

Ryan watched the giant man stop a few paces from the pile of weapons and wondered if he meant what he'd said, or was merely trying to put Ryan off.

''Take what you want,'' Brody said. ''Hurry!''

Ryan reached for his panga, slid his fingers around the handle and pulled it roughly out of the bottom of the pile.

Brody grabbed a six-foot-long pike, selecting the best weapon to keep the others at bay.

The sec men and muties also reached for the weapons, the sec men picking out knives and the muties selecting the aged swords. True to his word, Mog and his men took what was left behind. The giant took a length of chain for himself, while Dorfman, Billingsley and Foghat ended up with a knife, pike and sword respectively.

"I can chill you with a chain as easily as a blaster, One-eye," Mog said, his voice a low, deep rumble that boomed out of his cavernous chest like a cannon shot.

Outside the circle, Grundwold raised his hands. "Ready?"

The question was answered by a rumble of shouts and whistles from the crowd. They were more than ready, for blood and chilling.

"Fight!"

The circle came alive with movement.

Ryan stepped back from the center, expecting Mog to swing the chain in his direction, but instead he quickly turned to the left, whipping his arm out and catching the mutie named Laslo in the neck. The chain tore into the mutie's neck, embedding itself three inches into the flesh, causing a gout of blood to spurt up from the open wound.

Hambly looked at his partner with stunned fascination as Laslo desperately tried to pull the chain from his neck. Blood was pouring over the dying mutie's shoulder as he fell to his knees, still vainly trying to work the chain free.

Mog took a step toward Laslo, wrapped the remaining length of chain around the part of the neck that remained, and then pulled with both hands. The blunt chain ripped through the mutie's flesh like a dull blade, tearing his head from his shoulders and sending it spinning into the air.

The flying severed head, blood still draining from inside, caught the attention of the crowd and most of the combatants.

But not Ryan.

He used the opportunity to move right and slash at the leg of one of the sec men. He caught Salazar on the right leg just below the knee. The man let out a yelp of pain as his pant leg was slashed open and blood began to pool around his right foot.

"You should have chilled me with that blow, One-eye," Salazar said, clutching at his bleeding leg. "'Cause I'm gonna make you pay for it."

The sec man lunged forward, but stopped himself in midstride when he found the sharpened tip of Brody's pike between himself and Ryan.

"Let him come," Ryan said, moving the pike aside with his left hand. "You just watch that the other poor excuse for a sec man doesn't interfere."

Richmond heard the comment and sneered at Ryan. "Don't chill him, Sally," he told Salazar. "Leave a bit of his worthless life for me."

"You got it." Salazar grimaced, still bleeding.

Ryan stepped back to keep his distance from the approaching sec man. On Ryan's right, the second mutie, Hambly, had his hands full trying to stay away from Mog. The giant appeared to be toying with the man, putting on a show with his chain that the crowd seemed to be enjoying since they were still shouting, "Mog! Mog! Mog!" louder than ever.

Salazar's knife was about the same length as Ryan's panga, but that's where the similarities ended. Ryan's blade was sharp, and the balance of the weapon was excellent. Salazar, on the other hand, seemed to be fighting his knife, not sure whether to lunge or slash with it.

And there was another advantage Ryan held over the sec man. Salazar's wounded leg continued to spill blood. If the cut hadn't slowed him, the loss of blood was sure to. All Ryan had to do was wait, but in this arena, waiting was a luxury he might not have time for.

"What's the matter, One-eye, don't want to stand and fight?"

Ryan thought of the Trader's saying about those who run away being able to run away another day, but that didn't apply here. If he ran, his fight was over and one of these creatures would end up with Krysty.

His best friend.

His lover.

The thought of her made Ryan stand his ground.

He planted his boots on the dry, dusty ground and threw the panga back and forth from his left hand to his right. The move had been intended to confuse Salazar and let him know that Ryan was equally good with the knife with either hand, but it had also captured the attention of the crowd, who appreciated a fighter with some showmanship and flare.

Even Mog and the others were watching Ryan now.

But he refused to put on a show for their entertainment. Chilling was a matter of survival, not people's amusement. He stopped tossing the panga back and forth and held it before himself to guard against an attack.

Salazar had no problems about putting on a show, however. He tried to emulate Ryan's prowess with his knife, but was handling the weapon awkwardly. Ryan followed the flight of the knife from one hand to the other, waiting for his chance.

It came on the third time the knife was in Salazar's left hand. He fumbled with it, having to adjust his hand slightly to firm up his grip on the knife.

Ryan wasted no time.

In a flash, his right boot shot up from the ground, kicking Salazar's hand, breaking several finger bones and sending the knife spinning through the air.

Salazar looked stupidly at his empty right hand, as if the knife had suddenly betrayed him.

Ryan followed the kick with a hard left cross to the side of the sec man's face. Teeth and blood flew out of a corner of his mouth, much of it landing outside the ring, and his eyes rolled up in their sockets. He fell to the ground in a heap, his head slamming hard into the ground.

Richmond stepped forward to help his fellow sec man, but Brody kept him back.

Even one of Mog's men, Foghat, moved in to keep Richmond away.

Ryan stepped forward and looked over the fallen guard. ''If you agree to leave at the break, I won't chill you, sec man.''

''Fuck you, outlander!'' Salazar spit on Ryan's boot and pounded a fist weakly against Ryan's thigh.

Ryan flipped the panga so that it was pointing down and plunged the tip of it into Salazar's chest. The knife stopped when it was through his body and had come up against the hard-packed ground beneath it.

A faint pulse of blood bubbled up around the panga's blade, and a crimson line leaked out of the corner of the man's mouth.

The crowd grew silent.

A bell rang to signify the first break.

Ryan and Brody were still alive, and there were two fewer opponents to worry about.

Chapter Twenty-Four

Sec chief Ganley helped pull the second boat onto dry land and began overseeing preparations for another night on the shore. The volunteers were near exhaustion after fighting the wind and current on Erie Lake throughout the long afternoon. Some had gone off into the nearby forests in search of firewood and anything else that might be useful to them.

There was plenty of fresh fish to eat, but Ganley would allow them to break into some of the dried stores they'd brought to trade if anyone wanted. The following day would be a long one, and they'd need all the rest and strength they could manage.

A sudden scream came from somewhere inland.

Ganley ran toward the sound, followed closely by several of the others.

When he reached a small stand of trees, Ganley stopped in his tracks. He frantically searched the deadwood and pale leaves of the trees, but could see nothing in the afternoon shadows.

"Help me!" The scream was fainter this time, but clearly a man's scream.

The scream had come from somewhere up ahead and to the right. Ganley headed toward it, signaling to the others to fan out to the left and farther right.

With each step the sounds of the man's scream grew

fainter, replaced by another noise more sinister in nature. It was wet and sloppy and mixed in with the unmistakable sound of bones snapping and muscle and sinew being torn apart.

And then he saw it.

Russell Duncan, a young fisherman in his early twenties on the mission to bring home a wife, was lying in a small clearing while his body was being torn apart by several pale white, sickly-looking mutants. They were tearing Duncan's flesh open with their bare hands and taking bites from his open wounds with their teeth, shredding the skin and muscle with vicious jerking motions of their heads.

There were four of them feeding on the body.

"No!" Ganley cried out, but none of the muties seemed to notice. Others began trying to scare the muties away, but they all remained where they were, feeding.

Ganley raised his blaster and fired nearly a dozen shots. He was careful with the first shot, making sure he placed the round in Russell Duncan's skull. When the body went limp and he knew the young fisherman was dead, he opened fire on the creatures in earnest, peppering the muties with a hail of blasterfire, throwing them back and away from the corpse and ripping holes in every part of their bodies.

He walked over to the remains of Duncan's body and grabbed the man's jacket collar. He began to drag the corpse toward the beach where they could bury it properly and with an appropriate ceremony.

J.B. HAD THE FOUR .50-caliber machine blasters out of the P-39. All of the parts had been fairly well-preserved, and a few of them still had a light sheen of oil.

"I thought we would only be using two of these blasters?" Doc asked.

"We are," J.B. answered. "I'm going to use the best parts out of the four to make two."

Doc sat and watched the Armorer work. There was pleasure to be had watching someone who thoroughly enjoyed his work, and that was J.B. He had quality blasters to fiddle with, and he looked just like a boy in a toy store. There was a strange look of pleasure on his face, as if he couldn't wait to fire the .50 caliber, or to see the 37 mm cannon blow apart the side of a building.

Doc envied the man's simple pleasures and wished he could become so lost in something. Instead, he spent his time thinking of his dear Emily and the two children they'd had together, Rachel and Jolyon.

With all the talk of breeding going on the past couple of days, Doc took solace in the fact that he had sired two of the most beautiful and vibrant children in all of the eastern states. They would have lived their lives out long ago, and while he was sure that Emily had raised them right, he often wondered about what they made of their lives, and if his family name or bloodline had lived on into skydark.

J.B. tried the gun he'd been assembling, pulling the trigger and gauging the action by the sound the mechanism made. He looked pleased.

"Impressive!" Doc commented.

"Rate of fire of five hundred rounds per minute, a

muzzle velocity of 895 mps, and a range of 10,000 feet,'' J.B. said with a look of pride on his face. ''This blaster can destroy any soft target it can reach, and that includes buildings.''

Doc nodded, silently wondering if it might have been better if none of his descendants had survived the nukecaust.

Chapter Twenty-Five

"How are you?" Mildred asked. She had been assigned to the circle to help with the wounded combatants. She hadn't had much to do so far except pronounce two of them dead.

Ryan looked over his arms and shoulders. "Not a scratch on me yet."

"Try and keep it that way," Brody said. He had suffered a cut on his right arm.

"Intend to," Ryan said.

"I don't think Richmond and Hambly are likely to team up this next round. Something about sec men and muties that just don't mix. If anything, Richmond will be after you, wanting to give you payback for chilling Salazar. Hambly will either be taken out by Mog and his men, or he'll be hugging the edge of the circle hoping a wound will take him out at the next break."

"Can't he just quit?"

Brody shook his head. "He could, but that would make him a laughingstock."

"On your feet!" called Grundwold.

Ryan and Brody stood along with the others.

"In this round, all combatants will remove their shirts," the sec chief ordered.

Ryan took off his shirt. The crowd seemed to enjoy the sight of bare, bloody and sweaty flesh.

"Ready?" the sec chief bellowed.

The crowd screamed its approval.

"Fight!"

As Brody had suggested, Mog and his men went after Hambly, allowing Richmond the chance to go after Ryan.

Brody made sure Dorfman, Billingsley and Foghat remained with Mog and didn't try to take out Ryan amid the confusion.

"You're good with the knife, Cyclops," Richmond said, calling Ryan by the name the sec men on the farm seemed to favor.

"Better to be quick with a knife than quick with my mouth."

Richmond was a tall, lanky man. Ryan estimated they weighed about the same, but Richmond stood about three inches taller. Unlike the knife scars he'd seen on other sec men and slaves here, Richmond had a big round blaster scar on his right shoulder that was about three inches across. The wound was set back in the flesh about an inch, as if someone had scooped out a patch of flesh with a knife. "You want me to put down the knife, Cyclops?"

Ryan shrugged.

"No problem." Richmond dropped his knife onto the ground and kicked it to the edge of the circle.

Meanwhile, Mog and his three men had Hambly, the mutie, surrounded. Billingsley was poking him with his pike while Foghat was slashing at his back with his sword. There was pale red blood flowing over the mutant's equally pale flesh, making him look like a predark barber's pole. Every once in a while, Hambly would make a break for the circle's edge, but Mog would always catch him and pull him back for still more torture.

As Ryan was dealing with Richmond, he noticed what was going on out of the corner of his eye and knew he'd have no trouble chilling Mog when the time came. He was too careless and casual in his way, and Ryan would take full advantage of it when the time came. He looked back at Richmond and threw his panga to the ground where the tip dug into the hard, dry earth and stuck, leaving the handle to quiver slightly in the sun.

"I'll get more pleasure chilling you with my bare hands anyway," Richmond said, moving closer. "That way it will happen slowly and with plenty of pain."

Ryan said nothing, concentrating solely on Richmond's hands and feet.

Dorfman, one of Mog's cronies, wandered over toward Richmond and Ryan, looking for a chance to chill one of them while they fought. But Brody stepped forward, waving the sharp end of his pike in Dorfman's face, and the man backed off.

Richmond lunged at Ryan, but the one-eyed man was able to move left, out of the way. Richmond turned, a slight smile on his face, then lunged again, this time feigning left, then moving right. Ryan again stepped to the side, but this time as Richmond passed him, he put out a knee, catching the sec man in the thigh and sending him spinning to the ground.

Richmond spit dust and dirt from his mouth and rolled onto his back, expecting Ryan to be right there towering over him.

But Ryan was standing well back, waiting for the sec man to regain his feet.

"You'll be sorry you didn't try to finish me off, Cyclops!"

"I'll make you the same offer I made your friend," Ryan said. "If you leave at the next break, I won't chill you."

Richmond said nothing for several seconds, then began to laugh. "You're gonna spare my life, slave!"

"I'm no slave," Ryan said.

Richmond grabbed a handful of dirt and dust and threw it in Ryan's face. The one-eyed man had been expecting as much from the sec man and turned his head to the right, causing the grit to sting his face and fall harmlessly against the patch over his left eye.

Ryan moved in, not giving the downed sec man any more time to get back to his feet. But before he could get his hands on Richmond, the man had a knife in his right fist. He gave it a flick and a four-inch blade appeared, as if out of the air.

The crowd had noticed Richmond's weapon and realized he had brought it into the ring with him. They began to boo and throw rotten fruit and vegetables into the circle. Ryan was hit in the back by an overripe tomato.

Grundwold got up from his chair, looking as if he

might stop the fighting or force Richmond to drop his weapon, but the baron motioned for Grundwold to sit down, then waved his hands, signaling that the combatants continue their fight.

Ryan ducked low and kicked at Richmond's feet, sending the sec man spinning onto his back. Without hesitation, he kicked him again, this time hard in the stomach.

Richmond sputtered and coughed up a mouthful of bile, but still managed to slash at Ryan's leg, splitting the fabric of his pant leg open at the knee.

Brody moved in with his pike to pin the sec man down, but Ryan waved him off. "I don't need your help!"

The crowd roared its approval and turned its attention away from Mog's battle with Hambly. The mutie had been cut and slashed so many times that he would probably bleed to death before the next break. But that hadn't stopped Mog from continuing the torture, cutting off pieces of the mutant's body just to see how long he could remain standing. The sadistic punishment had held the crowd's interest for a while, but paled in comparison to the drama of the close contest being waged between Richmond and Ryan.

Richmond slashed at Ryan with his knife, forcing the one-eyed man to back away. When a few yards separated them, the sec man reached behind his back and produced a second knife. For a moment it seemed he might toss it to Ryan to make it a fair fight, but it soon became apparent he had no intention of doing anything of the sort. He came at Ryan with both knives leading the way.

Ryan backpedaled from the slashing steel, then tripped on something on the ground and fell onto his back.

A groan of disappointment washed over the crowd as it looked as if Ryan would be chilled, but the one-eyed man grabbed a handful of dirt and flung it at the face of the approaching sec man, just as the sec man had done to him scant minutes before. Richmond stopped in his tracks and did his best to clear his eyes of the grit, but it was no use. He couldn't open his eyes, and even if he could, he'd still be unable to see.

Ryan sprung up to his feet, ran around to Richmond's side and rammed his heel into the sec man's knee. Richmond's leg bent backward, toppling him to the ground like a felled tree, and forcing him to drop one of his knives and use a free hand to try to clear the dirt from his eyes.

Ryan reached into his back pocket and pulled out the brass knuckles he'd been given earlier in the day. He hadn't planned on using the weapon, but since Richmond had set the tone for the fight, he had no problem slipping the heavy metal rings over the knuckles of his right hand.

Reaching back and cocking his arm, Ryan threw his fist forward, catching the downed sec man in the back of the head. The brass rings broke through Richmond's skull, allowing Ryan's knuckles to put a fist-sized hole in the man's head.

He was chilled instantly.

But Ryan wanted to make sure and threw four more punches before climbing off the body. He rose to the sounds of a rousing cheer.

Grundwold chose that moment to ring the bell, allowing everyone, including the crowd, a chance to rest, and giving the mutant Hambly an even chance of recovering from his wounds.

Ryan picked up his panga, then sat to catch his breath. He checked the pant leg that had been cut open and found the skin beneath unbroken.

"Are you hurt?" Mildred asked, handing Ryan a bottle of water.

Ryan upended the bottle and gulped down the water.

"I don't like the odds in this next round," Brody muttered.

"What do you mean?" Mildred asked. "There's only four of them." She cracked a smile for Ryan and winked at Brody. "I know what you're saying. I don't trust the four of them to fight fair."

"Who's been fighting fairly?" Ryan asked.

Mildred let out a small disgusted laugh, then excused herself. "Sorry to run, but I've got a dying mutie the baron wants mended. Good luck."

"Thanks," Ryan said, passing the water bottle to Brody.

Mildred took a few steps, then suddenly turned back. "Almost forgot. Krysty sends her love."

Ryan looked up at the stage and saw Krysty sitting there at the baron's side. The afternoon sun shone brightly against her hair, turning it the color of crimson fire. She waved at Ryan then, giving him a thumbs-up and blowing him a gentle kiss that was hidden from the view of the baron.

Ryan felt revitalized and decided that despite what Brody had said, the odds in the next round suited him just fine.

Chapter Twenty-Six

"How are you enjoying the contest, my pretty?"
Baron Fox asked Krysty.

The titian-haired beauty looked away from her lover
and said, "It's very, very bloody...and violent."

"Indeed it is. And exciting."

Krysty shrugged. "I suppose it is, if you like that
sort of thing...chilling people for no reason."

"Do you find it exciting?" the baron asked.

"I've seen plenty of men chilled in my life. Some
deserved it, some didn't, but it's almost always a waste
of life."

That seemed to excite the baron further. "I bet you
have seen plenty of dead men, even chilled a few of
them yourself, hey?"

"A few."

"Oh, you must tell me about them sometime...in
precise detail."

"If you like."

The baron raised his hand, summoning both sec
chief Grundwold and Norman Bauer to his side. He
spoke discreetly in each man's ear, and they left
quickly to carry out their orders.

In minutes, Norman Bauer returned with a young

red-haired girl with a full figure and pretty face. The look on her face was a mixture of excitement and fear.

The baron looked over the girl. "Excellent!" he said. Then he leaned back and pulled open his bathrobe to expose himself. Without a moment's hesitation the girl knelt between the baron's open legs and took him into her mouth.

"Better," the baron muttered. "Much better."

GRUNWOLD APPROACHED Ryan, a hard, angry look in his eye. "The baron wants no surprises this time around. No more extra weapons."

Ryan looked up at the baron on the stage and saw the girl knelt between his legs, her head moving up and down in a slow and regular rhythm. "The baron wants a lot of things."

"And he gets what he wants."

"That so?" Ryan said.

"Yes, always. And now he wants you to take off the rest of your clothes," the sec chief stated.

"What?" Brody shouted.

Ryan just looked at the sec chief, wondering how such a competent sec man could become the baron's whipping boy.

The sec chief sighed. "All of you. Mog and his men, too."

"What if we refuse?" Ryan asked.

Grundwold looked up at one of the towers overlooking the circle and signaled one of the men.

The crackle of blasterfire erupted suddenly, and Ryan could hear the rounds whizzing into the ground by his feet, throwing up small clouds of dust on impact. The sec man firing from the tower drew a line in the sand neatly between Ryan and the sec chief, delivering the sec chief's message loud and clear.

Ryan began undoing his belt.

"I knew you'd see it the baron's way."

The one-eyed man stared at the sec chief. "Does the baron always get what he wants from his sec slaves, too?"

Grundwold seemed confused by Ryan's words, but slowly their meaning became understood. "If you two are lucky enough to make it out of this circle, I'll see to it that you wished you hadn't said that."

Ryan stood his ground, speaking through slightly clenched teeth. "When I get out of this circle, you'll be wishing I hadn't, too."

Again the sec chief looked at Ryan strangely, not understanding the meaning of his words.

"Sec chief Grundwold!" the baron called out. "Is everything ready?"

Grundwold's body snapped straight, as if it had just been whipped across the back. "Yes, Baron."

"Then let's get on with it."

The sec chief stared hard into Ryan's eye. "To the victor go the spoils."

"Absolutely," Ryan said.

"And losers like you get fed to the muties."

Ryan ignored the comment and turned to retrieve his panga. When he was upright again, the sec chief was gone, climbing back onto the stage. "Are you ready?" he asked the men in the circle.

"Yes!" roared the crowd.

"Fight!"

Ryan and Brody moved forward.

Foghat charged at Ryan, while Dorfman, Billingsley and Mog surrounded Brody.

Their intention was clear. The sword-wielding Foghat had separated Ryan from Brody so the other three could easily do away with Brody. But instead of trying to chill Ryan, Foghat was just keeping Ryan away from the others.

It was the man's first and only mistake.

Ryan circled the outside of the ring until he came upon the extra weapons that had been left on the ground by the combatants. There was a rusty sword, a length of chain and a short-bladed knife. Ryan picked up the knife and, doing his best to remember Jak Lauren's instructions, threw it in Foghat's direction.

The knife was unbalanced and fluttered through the air instead of flying true. It also missed the target by more than a foot, but no matter. Foghat leaned far to the right to avoid the flying knife, and Ryan used the opportunity to swing his panga at his off-balance opponent. He caught Foghat on the arm, cutting cleanly through the flesh and tendons of the elbow, exposing the polished white bone beneath.

Foghat let out a cry of pain and grabbed at his arm to keep it in one piece. He was able to hold his arm together but couldn't staunch the flow of blood.

Ryan, feeling sorry for the man, kicked him from behind. He stumbled forward, tripped over the chain outlining the circle, and hit the ground hard with his shoulder.

Foghat screamed again, this time silencing the crowd.

Ryan turned into the circle and hurried to Brody's side.

"How are you doing?"

"I could use some help," Brody said breathlessly.

"At least the odds are in our favor now," Ryan said.

"But there's three of them."

"Exactly," Ryan said.

"Are you gonna talk or fight, One-eye?" Mog said in his booming deep bass voice.

"In a hurry to get chilled, Monster?"

"That's Mog," Mog said, his whole upper body quivering with anger.

Billingsley moved forward with his pike, tangling as he had before with Brody. But instead of their confrontation stalling into a stalemate, Mog came lumbering forward, swinging his chain wildly in front of him.

Brody pulled back, as did Ryan. They took several awkward steps backward until they came upon the chain ringing the circle, almost tripping over it.

They were in a dangerous spot with their backs against the chain. Mog and his two men could easily pin them down, tire them out, then chill them at their leisure. Ryan knew he had to level the field of battle.

The next time Billingsley charged forward with his pike, Ryan swung his panga across the shaft, cutting the hard wooden pole neatly in two. Billingsley suddenly found himself holding little more than a mop handle. Brody took advantage of the moment, lunging forward with his pike and piercing Billingsley's belly.

Billingsley let out a bloodcurdling scream of agony and clutched Brody's pike, but Brody didn't relent. He began to swing the pike from side to side as if he were waving a flag on the end of it. The hole in Billingsley's gut grew bigger, spilling more blood and entrails into the circle.

Mog grabbed the pike and pulled on it before Brody had a chance to let go, drawing him forward.

Dorfman, the one who'd chosen a knife similar to Ryan's panga, moved forward in an attempt to chill Brody, but Ryan headed him off, throwing a shoulder into the man's chest, which knocked the wind from his lungs with a whoosh and threw him onto his back.

Meanwhile, Brody had stumbled and had fallen face first into the dirt.

Mog raised his massive right arm, holding the chain high above his head for a moment, readying to bring it crashing down on his opponent's prone body.

Brody rolled right, trying to get away, but wasn't quick enough. The chain came down on his right leg, slicing through flesh and shattering the bone just below the knee.

Now it was Brody's turn to scream.

But instead of striking again and going in for the kill, Mog stood over the writhing Brody, as if he were admiring his handiwork.

Ryan took the moment to go after Dorfman, who

was still gasping to catch his breath. Ryan stood over the downed man, the bloody panga clenched tightly in his right hand. He raised it over his head to cut the man in two, but as quickly as a mutie ant, Dorfman crawled on all fours to the edge of the circle and under the chain.

Ryan turned to see Brody doing his best to keep Mog at bay with his pike, but it was a losing battle. The giant of a man was toying with Brody, kicking at his right foot, just to hear the wounded man scream.

"The next kick will be your last," Ryan said.

Mog stopped what he was doing and turned to look at Ryan. "So it's down to you and me, One-eye."

Brody tried to stand then, using the pike as a sort of crutch, but the added pain of his ruined leg was too much for him to bear. He let out another agonized scream, then fell back to the ground, this time lying still and motionless.

A few seconds passed as sec chief Grundwold waited to see if Mog would try to chill Brody. When he didn't, the sec chief rang the bell, signaling another break.

Sec men moved in to pull Brody from the circle.

"You be careful with him," Ryan said, turning to look for Mildred. He found her at the edge of the circle closest to the main building. "Fix him up," he told her.

Mildred just nodded in Ryan's direction, too busy directing the sec men carrying Foghat to answer him.

Knowing Brody would be in good hands, Ryan looked over at the mountain of a man named Mog. He knew he wouldn't take him up on it, but Ryan thought he should give the man the chance. "If you step out of the circle now, Mog, you might live to see another day."

Mog laughed, and the ground seemed to shake beneath him. "You're good, One-eye, but not good enough. I'm going to enjoy chilling you."

Ryan shook his head. "No, the pleasure's gonna be all mine."

Chapter Twenty-Seven

"This way," Mildred said, leading the way for the sec men carrying the badly bleeding Foghat.

The slave groaned in pain with each step the sec men took. His cries were growing weaker and weaker as the man's lifeblood dribbled out of the huge rent in his arm.

Mildred opened the door to the nursery. "Put him on that table in the middle of the room!" Foghat needed her immediate attention. When Brody arrived, he could be given a painkiller from the generous medical stores and be made to wait until she'd finished with Foghat. "And when the other one is brought in here, put him on the table by the wall."

The sec men carried Foghat across the room and eased him onto what was normally a delivery table. There were all sorts of medical instruments and supplies in the nursery, more than was generally necessary for the delivery of babies.

Mildred hoped it would be enough to save the man's life.

She began by checking the man's pulse. It was weak, but he still had one. She'd managed to staunch the flow of blood from his arm with a tight tourniquet, but didn't want to cut off the arm's blood supply for too long.

"Can I help you, dear?" the old woman who usually worked in the nursery said.

"Get his shirt off and clean up his arm," Mildred ordered, rifling through the medicine cabinet, hoping to find a vial of morphine. Luckily there was some.

One of the sec chief's lieutenants had followed the men carrying Foghat into the nursery and was now watching Mildred with a look of disbelief on his face. "What are you doing?" he asked.

"Trying to save this man's life."

"Why?"

"For old times' sake."

"What?"

Mildred paused for the briefest of moments. "Let's just say I'm doing this because I can."

"You're wasting time, and using up medicine on a slave. Just amputate the arm and send him on his way."

"No!" Mildred said forcefully

"But he's just a slave."

Mildred paused again, looking at the problem as the sec man would. "How much good to the baron is a one-armed slave? What do one-armed slaves go for at auction these days?"

The sec man fell silent.

"You don't tell me how to do my job, and I won't tell you how to do yours. All right?"

The sec man took several steps backward.

"Come on, dear," the old woman said, taking hold

of the sec man's sleeve and moving him away from Mildred. "We'll be a while in here, and it won't be pretty. We'll let you know when we're done."

Reluctantly the sec man left the room, standing out in the hall on the other side of the open doorway.

Mildred got to work on the wounded slave.

Foghat was falling asleep from the morphine, but before he went unconscious, he managed to look up at her, smiled and said, "Thanks."

"Don't thank me yet."

"I know you'll save my arm," he said before the morphine finally put him under.

Mildred sighed. "I wish I was as confident as he is."

JAK GRABBED the barrel of the .50 caliber and helped J.B. lift it into place on the back of the transport wag they would be using to free Ryan, Krysty and Mildred.

The Armorer had fit two of the P-39's blasters with makeshift pivots and was mounting them on the front-left and rear-right positions of the wag's open cargo area.

The two eased the blaster into position, and J.B. locked it in place with a single horizontal bolt and a cotter pin.

"Short bursts," Jak said. "Two, three seconds, not more."

"That's right. Anything longer and you're wasting ammo." J.B. took hold of the blaster handles he'd made from a bale of heavy-gauge steel wire he'd found on one of the loading docks and tested the movement of the gun. To his delight, it swung easily in both directions. "Should give a good range of fire. Pretty much a complete circle."

"Test in morning?" Jak asked.

J.B. nodded. "I'm sure the .50 calibers will fire without a glitch, but I'm not so sure about the cannon."

"Although I'm more than two centuries old, I never thought I would live long enough to see the day when John Barrymore Dix was unsure about anything to do with weaponry." Doc had wandered up to the wag and was standing by the rear wheels, looking up at J.B. and Jak with a delightful grin on his face.

"Mebbe Mildred right," Jak said.

"About what?" J.B. asked.

"Your dream."

J.B. was silent. Being reminded about his dream sent a chill down his spine. The .50-caliber design had been tried and tested for years. The cannon was another matter entirely, since it had probably had a few reliability problems during its lifetime, even when it was new. He'd done everything he could to make sure it was working properly, but there was still a chance it could fail when they needed it most.

But while the Armorer had some reservations about the cannon, Dr. Theophilus Algernon Tanner had none whatsoever.

"Of course the cannon will fire, John Barrymore. Not only will it fire, but it will fire magnificently...stupendously. It will cut a swath of destruction through the farm, unleashing a little bit of hellfire from its angry maw with each deadly round.''

Doc had his swordstick raised in the air and although they were underground, he seemed to be standing in the path of some strange breeze that blew back his white hair and made him look like a wild-eyed doomsayer atop a mountain.

''Thunder will roll, the earth will shake and barons and sec men will cower in fear at the mere sight of this infernal blaster.'' There was a strange shine in Doc's eyes, and his body was beginning to shake and tremble uncontrollably.

Jak signaled to Clarissa to come to Doc's aid. She came running, and when she reached Doc's side, she took his arm and led him to a nearby pile of crates where he could sit and rest, while whatever it was that was affecting him ran its course.

''He'll be all right,'' J.B. said.

''Not worried Doc,'' Jak replied. ''Worried Ryan and others.''

''If I know Ryan Cawdor, he's probably sitting back and enjoying his time on that farm. Who knows, after we break in, he might not even want to leave.''

The two men laughed.

Chapter Twenty-Eight

Ryan moved into the middle of the circle.

Mog stood facing him, his body somewhat grimy, but not nearly as bloody as Ryan's. "Just you and me, One-eye! Just like I figured."

Ryan had suspected it might come down to the two of them, but he wasn't about to give the mountain of a man any compliments. "Really. I thought you'd be chilled a long time ago."

"Mog always wins. And I'm going to feel good between Red's legs."

Ryan looked up at Krysty.

She was leaning to the side, trying to distance herself from the baron, who was now fully occupied with the woman servicing him. Her head continued to move up and down between his legs, but he now had firm hold of her hair, forcefully guiding her head in the movement and rhythms he wanted. The girl looked limp and lifeless now, as if she were either unconscious or dead.

Baron Fox either hadn't noticed or didn't care.

Ryan looked back over at Mog.

Mog flashed Ryan a gap-toothed smile. "If she's used to having you, One-eye, then she'll be thrilled to have a real man for a change." Mog reached down between his legs and scooped up his genitals in his hand. Ryan had paid little attention before, but now that the man was making a point of putting them on display, he couldn't help but notice how big they were. Like the parts of the rest of his body, Mog's penis and testicles were enormous, and it was no wonder he enjoyed the status of the farm's alpha male.

But while such equipment made for an impressive sight, it did nothing to give him an advantage within the circle. If anything, he was at a bit of a disadvantage having his equipment swinging freely, and vulnerable to attack. Ryan was seriously considering exploiting this advantage, since his panga was the right weapon for the job.

"She'd never have you, stupe," Ryan said. "I either chill you in the circle, or she'll chill you the moment you two are alone."

Mog looked up at Krysty, considering Ryan's words.

At that moment Grundwold entered the circle and approached the two combatants. "If one of you wants to leave the circle now, you can do it, no shame. It's been a good show."

"Nobody's walking out of the circle, Grundwold," Mog said. "Let's get it going."

"My thoughts exactly," Ryan agreed.

Grundwold nodded and left the circle, climbing onto the stage and calling out, "Fight!"

Ryan was caught momentarily off guard by Mog, who threw a pike at Ryan as if it were a spear, the second after the sec chief gave the call to fight. The long weapon glanced off Ryan's body, but not before the pointed tip broke the flesh on his right shoulder and blood began to flow freely down his arm.

Ryan countered by picking up the pike and throwing it out of the circle.

The crowd cheered.

Then Ryan gathered the rest of the weapons in the circle and threw them all out, as well.

The crowd roared in delight.

Now all that was left was Ryan's panga, which he picked up and moved just outside the circle, as well, next to the pile of his clothes.

"You think you can chill me with your bare hands, One-eye?" Mog laughed.

"No," Ryan said, running toward Mog and leaping into the air. He hit the giant in the chest with the balls of both feet. There was a loud whoosh as the air came out of Mog's chest.

After delivering the kick, Ryan fell heavily to the ground, landing hard on his side.

Mog stumbled backward a few steps, tripped over his own feet and landed heavily on his ass.

There was laughter from the crowd.

"Shut up!" he roared. "All of you."

The laughter died down, but not completely.

Ryan circled the big man, looking for another weakness. He was big and powerful, likely able to crush Ryan's ribs with a bear hug or able to suffocate him. Ryan had been lucky to knock him over by hitting him so high up and knew that the next blow would have to be different, since Mog would never fall victim to the same attack twice.

"You move fast, One-eye. But is it fast enough?"

Ryan didn't waste his breath answering.

He had moved to the right, looking to take Mog down once more. He darted in close and tried to sweep his right leg around to take out one of the big man's giant tree-trunk legs. He struck him in the calf with his foot, but the leg didn't give way.

Mog reached down and managed to catch Ryan's leg in his hands.

Ryan desperately tried to scramble away out of his reach, but Mog was able to reel him in, and in seconds he had his huge arms around Ryan's body and was pulling him ever closer.

The one-eyed man gasped for breath as Mog began to squeeze the life out of him. Ryan struggled to free himself, but his efforts only used up more air and tightened the grip the giant had on his body.

Mog continued to squeeze.

Something snapped in Ryan's torso, and a lance of pain shot through his chest. And then the world seemed to be getting dark around the edges.

He thought of Krysty and Dean first, almost simultaneously, and after that came thoughts of J.B. and Doc and Jak, and then images of the chilling he'd done over the years. Trader came next, as if the man were waiting for him somewhere up the road. Lush green fields, a home that was his and a family...Krysty and Dean out on the porch of their home, looking for him. Looking, looking, looking.

Ryan managed to get his right arm free. That freed up space for a breath, and to wriggle his left arm from the giant's viselike grip. Now with both hands free, Ryan jabbed a finger into one of Mog's eyes. The big man turned away quickly, though, and instead of his eye, Ryan found himself trying to poke a hole through the hard bone of Mog's skull.

The crowd was beginning to shout "Mog! Mog! Mog!"

Ryan took another breath, perhaps his last, then reared back with both hands and boxed Mog's ears as hard as he could.

Immediately the man's grip loosened.

Ryan gulped at the sweet, sweet air as it rushed into his open mouth and down into his needy lungs.

But Mog didn't let go.

So Ryan boxed his ears again.

Mog stumbled, then finally released Ryan, putting his hands to his ears as if it might do something to ease the ringing pain.

When Ryan hit the ground, another bolt of pain slashed through his body. He rose slowly, his eye always on the big man.

Mog was still stumbling, trying to keep his balance when all the balancing mechanisms inside his head had been scrambled. But as the seconds passed, the giant was recovering, shaking off the pain and noise inside his head, and readying himself to fight again.

Ryan knew he couldn't get in close to the man and survive. His only chance was lightning-fast attacks, darting in and striking a blow, then moving back just as quickly to a safe distance.

And with such a tactic, Ryan had to choose a target that was most vulnerable so his efforts would have the greatest effect. With that in mind, Ryan looked at Mog's dangling penis and testicles and knew exactly what he had to do.

Without another moment's hesitation, Ryan stepped forward and launched a kick into the soft flesh between the big man's legs. There was a satisfying smack of flesh on flesh, and then Ryan could feel his foot come up against the man's pelvic bone.

After the kick was delivered, Ryan pulled back, only to see Mog double over in pain. Vomit and drool leaked out of the side of his mouth, and he seemed to be struggling to catch his breath.

This was Ryan's chance to finish off the big man. But his earlier idea of removing the weapons from the ring had been slightly premature. Without a knife or sword, he'd be hard-pressed to chill the giant with just his bare hands. Mog had enough strength to brush Ryan aside if he tried to smash his head on the ground or tried to strangle him with a choke hold.

He needed a weapon.

Even a chain would be of some help.

Ryan looked to the edge of the circle and had an idea. He'd thrown all of the weapons out of the circle, so they couldn't be used against him, but what about the circle itself?

Ryan stepped up to one of the posts that staked out the perimeter of the circle and undid the chain connected to it. Then he went two posts over and undid the chain there, leaving a single post with chains on either side of it.

He pulled the post out of the ground, turned the pointed end toward Mog and charged across the circle.

Mog's eyes opened wide. He was still in pain, and still unable to stand upright. He turned to the right and brushed aside Ryan's thrust with his left hand.

The crowd was cheering on Mog. He had been their champion for a long, long time, and he was showing he had the strength and ability to take a beating and survive the circle. Ryan realized that if he didn't deliver the final blow soon, the big man would have had time enough to recover from his injuries.

When that happened, he'd be like a bear awakened from a deep sleep, fireblast mad and looking for payback.

Ryan turned the post around and held it by the pointed end, leaving the blunt end with the chains exposed. Then he spun the post over his head so centrifugal force would extend the chains to their full length. The post was four feet long, and the chains measured another six, giving Ryan a reach of more than ten feet. But more importantly, the chains were whipping around at lightning speed and when they struck something soft—like the back of Mog's legs—it would feel like a hammer blow.

So Ryan swung the post close to the ground and caught the stumbling Mog around the ankles. The chain cut through the big man's Achilles tendon, then swept him completely off his feet. Blood began to spurt from the wound as the length of chain wrapped itself around his leg, binding him like a slave in heavy leg irons.

Ryan jerked the post back and forth, twisting and turning Mog's leg in a number of unnatural directions. The big man screamed, and the deep bass howl of pain silenced the spectators as they wondered if their champion might fall, or even worse, be chilled, at the hands of the outlander.

Ryan unwound the chain, leaving behind an angry red wound and a ruined foot that seemed to hang from his leg by a string.

"Leave the ring and I won't chill you," Ryan said.

"Fuck you, One-eye!"

Ryan raised the post over his head and threw the pointed end to the ground between Mog's legs, tearing apart the man's scrotum.

Blood spurted up from the wound.

Ryan could feel the giant's scream in the pit of his stomach.

"Last chance to live," Ryan said.

"Fuck you!"

Ryan pulled the post from the ground and brought it down again, harder this time, piercing Mog's throat and smashing apart his neck.

The dying man gurgled a few wet and bloody words, then fell silent.

The crowd for the most part was left stunned, except for Ryan's crew, who had bet heavily on the one-eyed man and won.

Ryan looked up at Krysty, who was smiling, as

much in relief as joy. "Well done, lover," she said, mouthing the words slowly so Ryan could understand.

Ryan nodded at Krysty, then slowly headed to where his clothes lay in a heap. His ribs were on fire, and the cut on his arm stung from the sweat and dirt that was running into the wound. He needed to get dressed as quickly as possible to have some place to hide his panga if he wanted to leave the circle with it in his possession. When he put on his shirt, he made sure the big blade was concealed within it. Then when he slipped into his pants, he was able to slide the long knife into the rear of his waistband. It wasn't the best place for the knife, but hopefully it would be hidden well enough to get it past the sec men.

By the time he was fully dressed, the sec chief had come down from the stage and had entered the circle, holding Krysty's arm and leading her like a horse.

Up on the stage, the baron raised his hand and addressed the crowd. "You've done well, one-eye," he proclaimed. "You've defeated our champion, and provided us with some of the best entertainment we've had in months."

"I don't chill people for sport," Ryan muttered.

"Can it, one-eye," Grundwold advised Ryan under his breath. "You cross the baron now and you'll be full of blaster holes before you take a step. Keep your mouth shut and you get to spend the night with pretty little red here."

Ryan looked at Krysty, saw her smile, and steeled himself from saying or doing any more.

"And now," the baron said, "as the winner of our little contest, you shall have a prize like no other."

"To the victor goes the spoils!" the crowd cried out.

"A rutting mate of exquisite beauty. You will create offspring of exceptional quality and when you do, all will be taken care of, and you will yet again be rewarded for your service to your baron."

The crowd rose to their feet and began chanting. "Baron Fox relieves the burden! Baron Fox relieves the burden!"

Ryan thought of Dean, about having to turn him over to a complete stranger as some sort of prize, or product made in a factory or mill, and his blood began to boil.

Krysty, sensing Ryan's anger beginning to build, cautioned him. "Easy, lover," she said to Ryan as Sec Chief Grundwold presented her to Ryan as his prize. "This is not the time for it."

Ryan nodded. Krysty, of course, was right.

"We can chill the baron tomorrow," she whispered in his ear. "Tonight is for us."

She kissed him then, her tongue darting into his mouth and probing deeply. Ryan returned the kiss, holding Krysty in his arms as tightly as his aching ribs allowed.

The crowd roared in approval.

Even the baron seemed pleased.

Chapter Twenty-Nine

Night had fallen.

The underground garage remained illuminated by a few naked bulbs and smelled of cooked fish, machine oil and sweating bodies.

J.B. had finished arming the wag. It had .50-caliber blasters at the northwest and southeast corners of its cargo bed. Instead of fixing the 37 mm cannon to the side of the wag as he'd intended, the Armorer had to bolt it onto the hood of the wag. But in order to allow the huge blaster enough room, the wag's windshield and rear window had to be removed, which allowed the breech of the cannon to sit in the cargo area where it could be reloaded with shells.

Jak and Dean would man the fifties while Doc's job would be loading the cannon. That left J.B. the job of driving the wag, and, more importantly, aiming the cannon. Clarissa would ride up front bearing smaller arms. It would be her task to protect J.B. from any threat from close range. The Armorer would have his Uzi within reach, but his attention would be focused on driving and positioning the cannon.

"I must say, John Barrymore, that this time you have outdone even yourself. You've turned this wag into an awesome fighting vehicle, and you are to be commended.''

"Feeling better, Doc?''

"Yes, I am. The comforting ministrations of the young woman, Clarissa, did much to calm my nerves and rejuvenate my spirits. In a way I was reminded of my dear Emily. Why, it was almost worth catching cold just to have her make a fuss over me."

The time traveler was beginning to ramble.

J.B. grabbed his arm and gave it a firm shake. "Doc!"

Doc stopped talking and his body shuddered slightly, as if he'd just been awakened from a dream. "Yes," he said sharply.

"Get some rest. Mildred, Krysty and Ryan, they're waiting for us. We leave at first light."

"Yes, of course. Some rest might do me some good."

MILDRED SAT on the cot she'd set up in the nursery and let out a long sigh.

She had sewn up Foghat's arm as best she could, set it in a splint so he wouldn't tear the stitches and given him something for the pain. Then she'd fixed up Brody's leg and wheeled him over so he could spend some quiet time with Jasmine. After that, she'd watched over both of them for a few hours to make sure infection or any other complications didn't set in.

Now with the lights in the nursery turned down and her charges asleep for the night, Mildred lay down and rested for the first time all day.

The moment her head hit the pillow she was asleep, and dreaming of her days as an young intern.

THE FIRE ON THE BEACH had been put out for the night, and guards were posted on the edge of the marauders' camp. In the morning they would travel north to the falls. In the evening they would take up positions around a farm there. And during the night they would break into the complex and take men and women to breed with to insure the survival of Reichel ville.

Some of them wouldn't be making the journey home, and the mood in the camp was somber.

"Rhonda!" sec chief Ganley whispered when he saw the young woman approaching. He'd been lying on his back, staring up at the stars unable to sleep. "Unable to sleep, too?" he asked her.

Rhonda nodded.

"Scared?"

Again she nodded.

"Me, too."

She looked surprised.

"Do you want to talk about it?" the sec chief asked.

"No."

"Then what do you want?"

"For you to hold me."

The sec chief took her in his arms, their shared body heat keeping them warm through the night.

THE BIG CLAWFOOT BATHTUB in Krysty's room was full of hot, steaming water. Ryan lay back in the tub, his arms stretched out over the sides, his body's energy depleted and close to exhaustion. Krysty ran a soapy sponge across Ryan's chest, cleaning away the afternoon's blood and grime.

Ryan's ribs still ached, but now that he'd had some time to rest, the pain had ebbed to a level he could tolerate. The cut on his shoulder had also cleaned up well, the wound having looked far worse than it really was.

Krysty squeezed the sponge and let the water flow over Ryan's broad, muscular shoulders, then she guided it down his chest and over his stomach toward the water.

Ryan flinched the moment the sponge traced a line over his aching ribs.

"Sore, lover?"

"A bit tender is all, but I'll manage."

Krysty kept her hand under the water, but let go of the sponge and let it float to the surface.

Ryan could feel her fingers caressing him between his legs. He quickly responded by growing hard.

"I thought you were tired, lover."

"I am."

"But not too tired?"

"Never too tired for that," Ryan said.

"I can see that. Or should I say, I can feel it."

Ryan reached up and cupped one of Krysty's full breasts. She moved closer to him, bringing the nipple close to his mouth. Ryan responded by taking it between his lips and sucking until it condensed into a rosy nub of flesh.

"Oh, lover," Krysty whispered, continuing to stroke Ryan beneath the water.

"To the victor go the spoils," Ryan said.

Krysty joined him in the tub.

They made love long into the night.

Chapter Thirty

J.B. had roused the group before the sun rose, and they spent the first hour of the day just getting the wag started. After having sat in the garage for several months, the wag's battery had run down and was without power. So instead of using the wag's starter motor, the group had to push the wag while J.B. used the clutch to put the vehicle in gear. After a half hour of trying, it seemed the engine was never going to start, but then it coughed once.

Spurred on by that success, they tried again and again, cough turning into sputter and then finally into a shaky rumble.

And then the engine roared to life.

J.B. wasted no time getting everyone on the wag and moving. The exhaust fumes had a foul smell to them, and the less they had to breathe them in the better.

The group pulled the wag out of the underground garage just as dawn broke over the horizon. The sky was a dazzling shade of orange, and the cloud cover that had been hanging over them the past two days was now all but gone.

They left the garage and soon turned onto Niagara Falls Boulevard. With an open road in good condition in front of him, J.B. opened up the throttle and the rumbling noise from the engine smoothed out into a loud but regular hum.

They drove several blocks along the boulevard until they found the remains of a building that suited their needs. J.B. stopped the wag about a city block from a deserted and crumbling bank building on Pine Avenue, keeping the engine running in the hopes that it would recharge the wag's battery. The east wall of the bank building was made of bricks and painted white, and would provide an excellent test target for the 37 mm cannon.

J.B. judged the distance to be about one hundred yards, well within the range of the cannon and the .50 calibers, but a tough distance to cover with small-arms fire, especially from remades like those used by the farm's sec men.

''Put a round in!'' J.B. ordered.

In the back of the wag, Doc loaded one of the better shells into the cannon's breech. They had decided to try the shells in the order of the ones in best condition first, because if the cannon didn't fire the best-quality shells, it probably wouldn't fire at all.

''Ready!''

J.B. paused a moment, knowing that the cannon barrel could just as easily blow apart as fire the shell. At least if the barrel exploded, he'd be chilled instantly.

J.B. pulled the cord he'd fashioned into a makeshift trigger, and the cannon boomed.

The cannon's recoil pushed the wag back about two feet, despite J.B.'s firm pressure on the brake pedal.

There was a brief moment of silence, and then the cannon shell struck the side of the building, punching a wag-tire-sized hole in the brickwork ten feet off the ground and almost directly in front of the wag.

"Hot pipe!" Dean exclaimed.

"Hot pipe, indeed," Doc echoed.

"Well, at least we know the cannon works," J.B. said, a broad grin on his face. "Now we've got to get it to the farm so we can use it on some live targets."

"Excuse me, John Barrymore," Doc said, kneeling so he could talk to J.B. through the open window at the back of the wag's cab. "But I am not sure that the bridge we crossed the other day is stable enough to support the weight of this wag."

J.B. nodded in agreement. "And the other one we saw didn't look too sturdy, either."

"So close and yet so far," Doc muttered.

"There's another bridge," Clarissa said. "South of here."

"How far?" J.B. asked, shifting the wag into gear.

"Ten or fifteen miles. It crosses the river upstream at Buffalo."

"What's the bridge like there?"

"It's pretty rusty," she said, "but it's complete. You'd be able to drive the wag over it no problem."

That settled it for J.B. The fuel they had in the wag was old, but they had a tankful of it and they wouldn't be needing more than a quarter of a tank to drive the thirty-mile round trip to the farm. Sure, it would take longer, but they'd have to wait until dark once they arrived anyway, and it was better to spend some time traveling the better route than risk breaking an axle or puncturing a tire trying to cross the ruined remains of the Rainbow and Whirlpool bridges.

"All right, that's the way we'll take." J.B. let out the clutch and the wag lurched forward. "What's the name of this bridge, anyway?"

"It's called the Peace Bridge."

Jak smiled.

Doc laughed out loud.

SEC CHIEF GANLEY instructed a team to cover the boats with weeds and tree branches so they'd be hidden while they were away. He had considered leaving behind two men to guard them, but quickly dismissed the idea, knowing they'd need all hands to help with the raid.

They headed north on foot, moving quickly through overgrown forests and across the weed-choked flatlands. He got the feeling that the entire area had been farmland during predark times, but nothing had grown there since the nukecaust, except for weeds and muties.

About an hour into their hike, the sec chief heard it.

"What is it?" someone behind him called out.

The sec chief raised his right arm and clenched his hand in a fist. The raiders scattered, disappearing into the underbrush as if they'd never been there on the path.

Ganley could hear the rumble of an engine growing louder. Judging by the sound, it was running well and whoever was driving was in a hurry, with no worries about fuel. The sec chief crept forward, saw the road crossing his path up ahead and crawled through the weeds toward the strip of weedy pavement.

Carefully he looked down the road to the east.

A wag was approaching. It was manned by a large crew and was armed with a couple of machine blasters and a monstrous blaster up front.

Ganley quickly dived back under cover and remained still until the wag passed. He kept down for some time after, feeling safe enough to move only after the sound of the wag's motor had faded into the distance.

"What was it?" asked one of the raiders.

"Just a patrol."

"They have motorized patrols?"

"Were they armed?"

"I don't know if that was a patrol belonging to the farm we're planning to raid, or if it was just some baron's war wag passing through. Either way, we're in some bad country here and we might be getting into something we're not really prepared for."

Silence.

"Anybody who wants to turn around and go back to the boat, I won't stop you. And there will be no bad feelings when we return."

Ganley waited for someone to speak.

No one did.

"C'mon, Chief," Rhonda called from the back of the group. "We're losing daylight here."

"You all feel the same way?"

There were mumbles and words said by everyone, but the general consensus was a resounding yes.

"All right, then. Let's get moving."

Chapter Thirty-One

When Ryan awoke early the next morning, Krysty was still sleeping comfortably in his arms.

"What is it, lover?" she said.

"Time for work."

"But you won," Krysty said. "You don't have to work in the orchards for a week if you don't want to."

"Don't want to," Ryan said. "Have to."

"Why?"

"One of us has to be out in the orchards to look out for J.B. and the others. He's had time to get organized and come up with a plan. If he's got one, he might want to give us a message about when and where he's going to hit the farm. Someone needs to be out in the field to receive his message."

"What if you don't hear from him today?"

"Then we'll start making our own plans to get out of here."

"Good," Krysty said. "I'm starting to have some bad feelings about this place."

"Anything specific?"

"Not really. But I am worried about you, lover. You might be in danger somehow."

"I've been up to my knees in it since I got here."

"No, this is something else. Different."

"Thanks for the warning."

Krysty was silent a moment, then said, "What do you want me to do while you're out in the orchards?" she asked, sitting on the edge of the bed and getting dressed.

"Talk to Mildred. Find out more about where our blasters are being stored and see if we can get them out without anyone noticing. See if you can talk to some of the slaves and let them know something might be happening soon and that they should be ready." He paused a moment, thinking. "And mebbe the two of you could come up with a plan for a diversion. We'll need one whether we break out of here ourselves or J.B. comes to get us."

"Anything else, lover?" Krysty asked, her hands on her hips and a smile on her face.

Ryan looked at her a moment, then crawled slowly back onto the bed, where he made love to her one more time before starting the day.

BARON FOX HAD HAD trouble sleeping all through the night. He'd called for a nonbreeder before getting into bed, but the usual sense of peace and tranquillity he enjoyed after a good rutting had eluded him.

Even now, hours later, he was still too tense to rest and his mind was far from being at peace.

There was something on his mind.

It was the outlander with one eye.

He'd been magnificent in the circle, chilling his opponents with as much cunning as brute strength. He'd chilled Mog as easily as he might a dog. It had been a good show, but there was still something wrong about the one-eye, something not right.

Mog had been a monster, but he could always be easily controlled. A few breeders and he was happy, producing offspring that netted top jack. But this one, he was a rogue, a renegade, a rebel. He wasn't the type to be happy just working and rutting his life away on the farm.

He was wild.

Untamable.

And he was an outlander. Soon he'd be looking at the fence surrounding the farm as a prison wall, and he'd want out. Worse still was the possibility that he would spend his time on the farm convincing the other slaves to rebel. The slaves outnumbered the sec force ten to one, and any organized rebellion stood a good chance of succeeding.

And if that happened, Baron Fox knew he'd be chilled for sure, but only after a very long and painful torture session.

All it would take is the right man.

And that man was the one-eyed outlander. The baron was sure of it.

Earlier in the night, when the baron had first tried to get some rest, he'd drifted into a light sleep and dreamed of the door to his chambers bursting inward and the one-eyed outlander charging inside, blaster in hand, cutting him to ribbons with a burst of automatic fire.

That dream, a brief picture of his own hellish demise, had started the baron wondering about the outlander and whether it was wise to keep him on the farm, even if it was only long enough to ship him out and sell him at auction.

Each day would give him time to talk to the others and put thoughts of rebellion, escape and freedom into their little minds.

The baron shook his head. There was no doubt in his mind. He couldn't allow that to happen.

The one-eyed outlander had to be chilled.

The sooner the better.

"Number One!" the baron called out.

The door to the baron's chamber opened immediately, and Norman Bauer stood there in the doorway with the ledger in his hand, as if he'd been waiting on the other side to be summoned.

"The one-eyed outlander," the baron said.

"The champion of the circle?"

"Yeah, that's the one. I want him chilled."

"When?"

The baron considered it. "Immediately. Make an example of him."

Bauer seemed to hesitate, as if he didn't understand the nature of the baron's wishes.

"Problem?" the baron asked, noticing Bauer's unease.

"It's not my place to ask, Baron," Bauer said with a slight bow of his head. "But why?"

"You're right, it's not your place to ask," the baron said sternly. But then he shrugged. "I just have a bad feeling about him. That's all."

Bauer nodded. "I'll see that he's chilled."

Chapter Thirty-Two

Ryan tried to join the ranks of the slaves unnoticed, but his very presence attracted attention. The slaves either wanted to congratulate him on his victory over Mog, thank him for chilling the two sec men or else wanted to know if he was available for rutting that night.

Even the sec men seemed to be pointing at him and whispering among themselves.

Ryan didn't like the looks of that. Usually the sec men were uninterested in the daily comings and goings of the slaves, but now every eye seemed to be on him, watching his every move. The attention could be explained away by his victory in the circle, but they seemed to turn away every time he looked in a sec man's direction.

Strange behavior, even for sec men.

He could only hope that they had a sort of grudging respect for him, and not thoughts of revenge.

Ryan moved along the line, getting his breakfast. He'd had better morning meals, but he'd also had worse. This morning's offering included a mound of tan mush that smelled like oatmeal, a bowl of fruit salad, slices of toast and a choice of juice-flavored water or coffee sub. Ryan took his tray and tried to find a spot in the corner where there wouldn't be so many eyes upon him.

But he couldn't hide from the crowd of slaves.

"Great job yesterday, Ryan," said a young man from his crew. "We all won a lot of jack because of you, and we just wanted you to know how grateful we all are."

"No problem," Ryan said, wishing the man would go away.

"And in appreciation, we want you to have Simka here as your own personal slave for as long as you like. She can get you food, bathe you, and she's a good rutter with both men and women."

"Thanks, but no thanks."

The girl, Simka, looked disappointed.

"You're too good to be a slave," he told her. "My slave or anybody else's slave, including the baron. You deserve to be free."

She smiled at that.

"Make some other man happy," Ryan said, gently pushing her and the man escorting her away. He began eating his food, trying to look very much as if he didn't want to be bothered.

But after just three spoons of oatmeal, another slave slid into the seat next to him.

"You're the one-eye, right?"

Ryan said nothing, but turned so the blond-haired teenager next to him could see his patch.

"Okay, I guess you are, then."

Ryan took another spoon of oatmeal.

"Just want to tell you to be careful today."

It sounded like a genuine warning.

Ryan continued eating. "Why?" he asked, staring straight ahead.

"I work in the sec men's lounge serving meals. They were all quiet this morning, like something was going down. I wanted to know what it was, so when I finished my shift I hid in one of the empty lockers." The youth paused to take a quick glance around. "I heard one of the sec men say the baron wants you chilled."

Ryan wanted to know the reason why, but knew it didn't matter and made no difference to the sec men why the baron wanted him dead. "When?" he asked.

"Today sometime. Probably out in the orchards. Just be careful."

It occurred to Ryan that this might be some sort of trap being set by a group of slaves who'd been friendly to Mog. "Why are you telling me this?"

"You were good in the circle yesterday, and you chilled Richmond and Salazar. I hated those two sec bastards and was glad to see that they got what they deserved. With those two gone, slaves won't be gettin' chilled for sport anymore. Way I see it, we all owe you somethin' for that."

Ryan understood. "Thanks."

The man started to get up to leave, but Ryan caught the sleeve of his shirt and pulled him back down.

"Spread the word that something's going to be happening soon. Something big."

The youth turned to look at Ryan and for the first time he saw the jagged razor cut that went under the youth's right eye, across the bridge of his nose and down his left cheek. "You gonna try breakin' out?"

"No," Ryan said. "More like somebody will be breaking in."

"When?"

"Don't know. Soon."

The blond-haired teen with the scar nodded.

Ryan couldn't help staring at the man's scar. It was red and fresh and reminded him of his own scar.

"Nice, huh? That's Salazar's handiwork. And while he did it, Richmond watched...and laughed."

"Thanks for the warning," Ryan said.

"Likewise."

Ryan finished eating his breakfast, and, seeing he was done, other slaves offered him food off their trays. Ryan took them up on their offer, not knowing when he might have another chance to eat a hot meal.

J.B. PULLED THE WAG off the road at the top of a rise that overlooked the farm. He guided the big vehicle behind a stand of trees and cut the ignition. The wag's engine rumbled for a few more strokes, then came to a sputtering, choking stop. He wanted to try the battery to see if their short trip north had recharged it, but decided he'd find that out later when he really needed to restart the engine. No sense wasting power. Besides, if the engine didn't turn over, they could always roll it down the hill and start the wag that way.

"Got time before dark," Jak said, looking at his wrist chron.

"Better to be early than late," J.B. answered.

Dean hopped off the back of the wag. "What'll we do till the sun goes down?"

J.B. looked at Clarissa. "You find your mutie friends and let them know what's going down tonight. And let them know that once we get inside, they can have all the food they can eat."

Clarissa nodded and headed off.

"Jak and Dean," J.B. summoned.

The albino teenager and the boy stepped in front of J.B.

"We'll need to get a message to Ryan, Mildred or Krysty about our plans. Walk the perimeter of the farm and see if you can spot one of them and pass along the word. If I know Ryan, he'll be expecting you."

Jak and Dean turned and headed down the road toward the farm.

Alone with J.B., Doc cleared his throat. "And what might you be requiring of me, John Barrymore?"

"You're going to help me, Doc. The wag's still running rough, and there's a few more things I need to do to make sure the blasters and the cannon don't jam when we need them most."

Doc nodded. "While I am not well versed in the mechanics of such infernal devices as this wag and those blasters, I'll endeavor to be the best assistant armorer my limited abilities allow."

"And I'll need you to keep your blaster ready, in case any stray muties wander by."

"Or if need be," Doc continued, hardly missing a beat, "I will gladly assume the duties of sentinel, guarding against any intruders who might wish to thwart us in our quest to free the noble Ryan of Cawdor...."

J.B. merely looked at Doc for several seconds, then said, "Bring me the toolbox."

Doc looked up, as if yanked out of a daze. "The toolbox, of course."

The two men set to work.

RYAN COULD SEE the sec men moving into position, blocking off the exits. Several armed with longblasters were also walking the upper level that ringed the cafeteria.

He knew he didn't have much time.

"You," he said, calling over to a bearded man in his thirties. "Come here."

"You want to talk to me?"

"Yeah, you." Ryan nodded. "Come here."

GRUNWOLD WANTED to grab the outlander as soon as possible, but they couldn't move in on him just yet. If they singled him out in the cafeteria, that would arouse the suspicion of the other slaves. The man was, after all, their new champion, and there was no reason for him to be taken away and chilled. Doing it now would incite a riot, and that was to be avoided at all costs.

But if they waited too long, the outlander might get out into the orchards where capturing him would be much more difficult. Once a breeder named Clarissa had hidden out in the orchards for two days before sneaking into the barn and stealing their best wag right out from under their noses. This outlander was far more resourceful and dangerous than the female breeder had been, and if he got loose within the compound Grundwold might lose several sec men before he was caught.

The sec chief kept his eye on the outlander while he gave the signal to his sec men to tighten up the circle around him. If all went well, they'd wait until the slaves had finished with breakfast and were on their way out to the orchards. Sec men would escort the one-eyed man out a door leading back into the main building, and once the door was closed they'd chill him with a single bullet to his brain.

After that it would be up to the baron to explain to the slaves why their hero was suddenly dead, something Grundwold was interested in hearing himself.

Just then a fight broke out in one corner of the cafeteria.

"I'm rutting with her tonight!" someone yelled.

"She's mine," came the response. "I claimed her first."

Fights between slaves over rutting with breeders wasn't unusual, but the timing of this one seemed peculiar to Grundwold. These things usually took place at the end of the day when slaves began pairing up for the night. Another thing that wasn't right was how many other slaves seemed to have an interest in the outcome. At most a fight involved four men, but this one seemed to involve the entire side of the cafeteria. Men and breeders were piling onto one another, trying to strike their blows against the two that had started the fight.

The cafeteria was rapidly becoming a sea of jumbled bodies. The noise was growing louder, and the fight was beginning to move toward the doors.

Grunwold signaled for his men on the cafeteria floor to intervene.

Sec men moved in to break it up, but despite pulling bodies out of the fray, more were joining in. Several slaves were pushed away, falling through the exit doors that led outside. In moments streams of slaves were spilling out into the orchards, and the sec men on the floor still hadn't gotten a handle on the fight.

The sec chief quickly scanned the cafeteria, looking for the one-eyed outlander. When the fight broke out, he'd been content to finish his breakfast as the fight stormed around him.

But now he was gone.

"Son of a gaudy slut!" the sec chief shouted.

The fight below was still going on.

Grunwold unslung his longblaster, pointed it into the middle of the jumble of bodies and pulled the trigger.

The crack of the blaster's fire stopped the fighting.

Slaves moved back from the center of the scrap, leaving the young man who'd been caught by Grundwold's bullet to fall to the floor in a bloody mess, half of his head blown off and splattered against the faces and bodies of those around him.

"The one-eyed outlander!" Grunwold yelled.

"Where'd he go?" a sec man asked.

The sec chief, seething in anger over the loss of the

outlander, leveled his longblaster on the sec man who'd asked the question. He even toyed with the idea of pulling the trigger, but he put the weapon down, knowing he'd need every man on his force to find the man who surely had known they had intended to chill him. "He's gone out the door, you triple-stupe bastard!"

The sec man looked out at the orchards just beyond the open door.

"Don't just stand there," Grundwold fumed. "Go after him. All of you! And electrify the fence, no intervals."

The sec chief took a deep breath then, knowing it was going to be a very long day.

Fillinger came up beside Grundwold and looked down over the half-empty cafeteria. "What will we do with the other slaves?"

Grundwold slung his longblaster over his shoulder and turned to the sec man. "Get them all into their cabins and lock them down, then get every available man out in the orchards looking for the one-eye. Do whatever you have to do to make sure he'll be chilled on sight."

Fillinger looked confused. "It sounds like you're putting me in charge."

"I am, for now."

"What are you going to be doing?"

"Someone has to tell the baron what's happened."

Fillinger looked grave. There was a chance he would never see the sec chief again. "Good luck."

"Just find the son of a gaudy slut and chill him for me."

"Yes, sir."

MILDRED HEARD the rumble of boots outside the nursery and stuck her head out the door to find out what was going on.

A pair of sec men was coming down the stairs in a big hurry.

"What's the matter?" she asked.

"Your friend the one-eye killed a couple of sec men during the night, and now he's making a break for it," the lead sec man said as he unlocked the door to the armory.

Mildred didn't believe it. It didn't sound like Ryan to do something like that without letting her or Krysty know about it first. "He's no friend of mine. We just traveled together. I'm happy enough here. You sure he chilled them?"

The sec man nodded. "Fillinger told me." He started selecting longblasters from one of the racks inside the weapons room, handing one of them to the sec man behind him.

"Where's the coldheart now?" Mildred asked, trying to befriend the sec man with the hopes of catching him with his guard down.

"He's out in the orchards." The sec man put one longblaster back on the rack and selected another.

As he did, Mildred pulled a length of adhesive tape from the roll on her belt and stuck it over the bolt that locked the door to the armory. "Well, good luck finding him," she said.

"Plenty of jack for the one who chills him," he

said, closing the armory door and locking it behind him.

"I bet you're gonna be the man to do it." Mildred smiled, giving him the thumbs-up.

"Thanks," the sec man said and was gone.

"Don't mention it," she muttered, opening the door to the armory and slipping inside.

ONCE RYAN WAS out of the main building, he was on the run. There seemed to be plenty of commotion going on behind him, and with any luck the sec men in the cafeteria would have their hands full breaking up the fight.

When he heard a crack of blasterfire come from inside the building, Ryan knew that someone had been chilled, giving up their life so he could have the chance to slip away. Ryan swore that someone would pay.

Stretched out before him were acres and acres of orchards and gardens. There were countless rows of trees that all looked the same and provided enough leaves to create hundreds of hiding places above the ground. But the sec men would methodically check each tree until he was found.

It was better to hide closer to the main building and the complex's cabins and barn. There were just as many places to hide. And so, instead of running into the orchards, Ryan doubled back toward the complex, climbed the ladder to the farm's water tower and slipped inside.

Later on he would climb out of the tower and head

for one of the slave cabins. They'd certainly be checked that morning, which would make them a safe place to hide in the afternoon. From there he might be able to get in touch with Mildred or Krysty, and figure out a plan of escape or learn if there'd been any word from J.B.

That was the plan for later in the day.

For now, all he could do was wait.

Chapter Thirty-Three

"Say that again," the baron demanded.

"We were watching him in the cafeteria," sec chief Grundwold said, "and waiting for the best time to take him because we didn't want to make a scene so close to his victory over Mog."

"And then...?"

"And then a fight broke out over one of the breeders. In the confusion the one-eyed outlander got out of the building."

The baron was circling the sec chief now, like an animal going in for the kill. "Say that last part again."

Grundwold cleared his throat. "In the confusion, the outlander got away."

"You let him get away."

Grundwold said nothing.

"You let him get away," the baron repeated.

"Yes," Grundwold said, his shoulders slumping with the words.

"So now an already dangerous man has even more reason to rally the slaves against us. He's already their hero, but now he's a symbol of their own imprisonment."

Again Grundwold said nothing.

"Isn't that right?" The baron pressed home the point.

"He won't get away."

"Isn't that right?" the baron repeated, not letting the sec chief steer the conversation away from the subject of his own failing.

Grundwold lowered his head. "That's correct, Baron."

"If you were in my position, what would you do with such gross incompetence?"

Grundwold knew exactly what he'd do to a sec man who screwed up. He would demote him several ranks and give him the most menial job until he was aching to prove his worth again. But of course, that wasn't even close to the way the baron would handle such things. As a result, Grundwold said nothing, knowing it was a question he couldn't possibly answer correctly.

"You can be sure I wouldn't send you to clean toilets," the baron said. "That might be your style, but it's not mine. You see, I happen to need a sec chief at the moment, more than I've ever needed one before. But I need a competent one."

"Yes, Baron."

"I believe you are a competent sec chief, Grundwold, so I'm going to give you another chance to find the one-eyed outlander."

"Thank you, Baron."

"But not before I impose a suitable punishment."

Grundwold closed his eyes, knowing that suitable

punishment from the baron could be anything from a slap on the wrist to the removal of a limb.

"On your knees, Grundwold," the baron ordered. Then he turned to Norman Bauer. "My special crop, please, Number One."

Norman Bauer, who had been standing by impassively, went to a cupboard high up on one of the walls in the office and took out the baron's "special crop." It was an electric cattle prod, thicker than his usual leather crop, and was fitted with rechargeable batteries. It could administer a powerful and painful electric shock with a single touch.

Baron Fox circled the kneeling Grundwold, then touched the prod to his shoulder.

Grundwold's body jumped as the room was suddenly bathed in the warm glow of electric blue. He groaned in pain as he tried to remain upright on his knees.

"Repeat after me... 'I *will* catch the outlander.'"

"'I will catch the outlander,'" Grundwold grunted.

Baron Fox touched the prod to Grundwold's hip.

Grundwold's torso jerked sideways as all the muscles on his right side contracted.

Then, as Grundwold lay on the ground struggling to catch his breath, the baron touched the prod to his thigh and watched the sec chief's leg twitch and convulse with electricity.

The sec chief screamed in pain.

The office smelled of ozone and burning flesh.

"Say it again," the baron said. "Louder this time, and with conviction."

Grundwold's words were lost in a scream.

THE MAIN BUILDING was quiet, except for someone screaming in pain in a distant part of the building. At this time of day there would be people and sec men walking the halls outside her room, and there would be sounds of the workday beginning outside.

But there was none of that this morning.

Krysty opened the door and found that there wasn't a sec man in the hallway. The building seemed abandoned, and she sensed it had something to do with Ryan. He was somehow in mortal danger, but was at least safe for the moment.

She stepped into the hallway, closed the door to her room and set out to find Mildred. If something was going terribly wrong, they'd have a better chance of surviving if they were together.

WHEN CLARISSA REACHED the entrance to the part of the hydro-electric tunnel she called home, there were still several muties waiting outside. They seemed happy to see her, and even happier still when she opened up a bag of leftover fish and uneaten scraps for them.

"Gather the tribe," she told them as they ate.

"Series?" one of the muties asked.

He'd meant to say "serious," but it had come out wrong. Of course it was serious, but what was the best way to explain it to the triple-stupe brain-damaged muties so they would understand. "Yes," she said in the end. "Triple-big serious."

The muties seemed to respond well to her words,

but she decided they needed to be even more excited about what was going to happen.

"Tonight. All you can eat."

That did the trick.

The muties cleaned up the fish scraps, then scrambled away to gather the tribe.

"I DON'T SEE ANYBODY out working the orchards," Dean said as he crouched amid a tumble of weeds. "All I see is sec men walking up and down the rows between the trees like they're looking for something."

"Someone," Jak said.

Dean looked at Jak. "You think someone escaped?"

Jak nodded. "Ryan."

"But if no one's out working, how will we get a message to my dad, Krysty or Mildred?"

"Don't know. Mebbe give signal."

"What kind of signal."

The albino shook his head. "Don't know yet."

SEC CHIEF GANLEY brought the raiders to a rest atop a rise north of the ruins of the city that had been labeled Clifton Hill. From here they were able to see the waterfalls, what had once been Niagara Falls and, more importantly, the thriving farm complex. Behind the perimeter of a wire mesh fence was the wealth of breeding men and women that Reichel ville desperately needed to survive.

"Is that the place?" someone behind the sec chief asked wearily. They had been carrying fish to offer in trade for hours over the rough terrain, and many were close to the point of exhaustion.

"Yes, it is," Ganley answered.

"It's fenced in, and there are sec men on patrol everywhere."

It seemed madness now to think they could trade their meager fish for slaves, but that had been their plan from the start and Ganley was determined to try trading first. If he succeeded, they might be able to trade for breeders on a regular basis, and if he failed, then they would return to try to take what they couldn't get in trade.

"I'll need two to come with me," Ganley said. "The rest of you can rest here until dark."

Rhonda was the first to step forward, followed by several men.

The sec chief put a hand on Rhonda's shoulder. "No women. They'd take you as a slave in a second. Besides, I need you here to lead the raid if I don't return."

Rhonda looked disappointed, but understood.

"Franz and Ruznicki," he said.

The two men stepped forward and picked up the fish they'd be offering in trade.

Ganley turned to the rest of the raiders. "If we're not back by dark... We hope we won't meet you on the last train heading west."

And then they were gone.

Chapter Thirty-Four

Emon Kauderer walked the fence to the west and north of the main building. Along with the other sec men in his squad, he'd been walking the orchards all morning, searching them tree by tree for the one-eyed outlander. But as thorough as their search had been, there'd been no sign of him. It was if he'd simply vanished into the misty morning air.

Grundwold was feeling the heat from the baron over it, too, and Kauderer hoped they found the outlander soon. If they didn't, then the sec chief would be chilled, enslaved or sold off at auction, and who knew which one of the sec men would take over. One thing was for sure, anyone who desperately wanted the job wouldn't be right for it; anyone good enough for the position knew enough about the baron not to want it. For a moment Kauderer thought of putting his name in for consideration, but then thought of the fate of Grundwold hanging on the search for this one man, and thought it better just to be an ordinary sec man for a little while longer. The jack wasn't all that much, but the food was good. It wasn't all that tough a job, and he could rut as often as he liked with the skags in the sec men's lounge. It wasn't a bad life, all things considered.

Suddenly Kauderer felt a sharp burning pain in his right leg. He looked down and saw a piece of metal embedded in the muscle of his thigh.

Shouting in pain, he dropped his blaster and tore open his pant leg to get a good look at his wound. A leaf-bladed knife protruded from his flesh.

Where in the rad-blasted Deathlands had it come from? Kauderer wondered. No one was in sight. Maybe he'd been caught flat-footed by the one-eyed outlander, sneaking up on him from a stand of trees, stabbing him in the leg and retreating again, as invisible as the wind.

The blood was running freely down his leg now, and he was beginning to feel weak.

Fillinger came up behind him and grabbed Kauderer's shoulders to steady him. "What's wrong?"

"Been stabbed."

"Where?" Fillinger asked. "By who?"

"In the leg…by the outlander."

"We better get you to the nursery. The healer there's pretty good with wounds. She'll fix you up."

Fillinger summoned a few nearby sec men to take Kauderer away. Then he moved a couple of squads from the east side of the farm to the west.

They'd be sure to find the outlander now.

DEAN LAY CLOSE to the ground next to Jak about twenty yards from the fence surrounding the farm. "How can you be sure they'll know that's the sign?"

"Knife," the albino teenager said. "Know leaf blade."

"I still can't believe you got the knife through the fence, and hit the sec man in the leg."

Jak nodded. "Good throw."

"But the gap in the fencing couldn't have been more than six inches across."

"Was enough."

They remained behind long enough to see the sec man being taken away, then started back to the wag so they could make a report to J.B.

"MILDRED?" Krysty called out, entering the nursery.

The woman was nowhere to be seen.

Krysty went back out into the hall and noticed the door across the hallway was open. It was the door to the armory.

She approached the door cautiously, sensing something was amiss.

Then the door suddenly sprung open and Krysty found herself at the wrong end of a Czech-built ZKR .38-caliber target pistol aimed directly at her head by one Mildred Wyeth.

"Hello, friend!" Krysty said.

Without a word, Mildred pulled Krysty into the armory and loaded her up with the several boxes of ammunition. "Bring them into the nursery."

"What about our weapons?" Krysty asked.

Mildred removed the tape covering the lock on the door, then closed and locked the door to the armory behind her. "I've already got all our blasters back."

"Where are they?"

"Safe in the nursery, until we need them."

Just then there was a commotion on the stairs. Two

sec men were carrying another who was bleeding badly from a wound on his leg.

Krysty dumped the ammo boxes into an empty bassinet and covered them with a blanket.

"Bring him to the table over there," Mildred instructed.

They carried the wounded man, now unconscious, and lifted him on the table. "He was stabbed by the one-eyed outlander," the sec man on the right of the wounded man said. "You better be able to save him."

Mildred ignored the threat and set to work, motioning for Krysty to stay in order to give her a hand.

When the sec man protested, she said, "She knows how to prepare field dressings and clean wounds. Your friend can live with her helping me, or take his chances with me working alone."

The sec man reluctantly nodded, and took a step back.

Mildred cut away what was left of the man's pant leg and gasped audibly at what she saw.

"That bad?" the sec man asked.

"No," she answered. "He'll be fine."

The sec man left the nursery a moment to inform the other sec men milling about in the hall.

Krysty tied off the man's leg with a tourniquet, and Mildred gently pulled out the leaf-bladed throwing knife. "Well," she said, "either Ryan has done the impossible and finally learned how to throw one of these knives, or a certain teenage albino has just sent us his card."

RYAN SHIVERED in the cold water of the tower.

He'd been hidden for hours, listening to sec men

come and go around him, most of them eager to chill him and collect the big jack being offered by the baron.

But for all their efforts, they hadn't once tried looking in the water tower. There had been a few close calls, with sec men hanging around the base of the tower awaiting new orders, but Ryan had remained still, making no sound, and eventually the sec men were sent to some far corner of the farm.

And then, twenty minutes earlier, there'd been some action. Judging by what he'd heard, Ryan figured that a sec man had been wounded on patrol. They were crediting Ryan with the deed, but that only made him smile. Ryan knew that it meant his friends were at work, either on the inside creating a diversion or on the outside preparing to break them out.

It had been quiet around the base of the water tower for the past ten minutes, and if Ryan was going to get out of the tower before dark, now was the time to do it. After the sec man had been wounded, the bulk of the sec force had hurried to the western fence looking for him, leaving only a shadow force around the main complex. If he could make it to the slaves' quarters unnoticed, then he could spend the rest of the day there in warmth and comfort waiting for dark.

Ryan lifted himself up to the top of the water tank and took a look over the rim. In the distance he could see the sec men patrolling the fence and searching the trees. There were a few sec men closer in, but they were headed west to join the search with the others.

Ryan turned to scan the eastern stretch of the farm and spotted a pair of sec men walking the fence, looking more as if they were patrolling rather than searching. One last quick look around and Ryan was convinced that it was time to move.

He lifted himself over the top of the tower and climbed down the ladder to the ground. His clothes had left a wet trail down the side of the tower and on the ground beneath his feet, but with any luck the midday sun would dry any tracks he left behind.

The slaves' quarters were about fifty yards away, across a stretch of fine, tan-brown dirt. To the left were patches of grass and weeds that would cover his trail but would add another twenty-five yards to the distance he had to travel.

He decided it was better to hide his tracks.

But instead of running, Ryan walked slowly, almost casually, as if he, too, were looking for the one-eyed outlander. Hopefully, if anyone saw him from a distance, he would look like just another sec man out on patrol.

He was halfway to the closest cabin when he heard voices shouting loudly.

"Do you see him?"

"I think so!"

Ryan wanted to run or dive for cover, but he was out in the open. He heard no more voices, and he thought that he'd be hearing blasterfire at any moment, but no one fired a shot.

He took another look and saw two sec men standing

near the main building. They were pointing at something out past the main gate.

"That's a mutie, you triple-stupe bastard!" one of the sec men said.

"It could have been the one-eye."

"Yeah, and I'm Baron Fox."

Ryan picked up the pace slightly and reached the cabin without further incident. He put his hand on the doorknob and turned it. It was unlocked. Without another moment's hesitation he opened the door and slipped inside.

"Who the—?" a man said.

"Don't stop now, baby!" a woman urged.

Ryan stood motionless inside the doorway as a man and a woman halted their rutting and lifted their heads to see who had just joined them.

"Afternoon," Ryan said.

The woman smiled. "It's the outlander."

"Hey, they're looking all over the place for you," the man said.

Ryan reached over his right shoulder to touch the hilt of his panga just in case these slaves thought about turning him in. "I thought I would hide here for a while. Till dark."

The woman's facial expression turned coy, and she ran a hand over one of her full and heavy breasts. "You're welcome to join us if you like."

"No, thanks," Ryan said. "I'll just wait till dark."

"We heard something might be happening tonight. Something big," the man questioned. "Is that right?"

Ryan was glad to hear it. Krysty and Mildred had

done a good job of spreading the word. "You heard right."

"Well, you're welcome to stay," the man said. "The sec men have already been here twice today."

Ryan nodded. "Thank you."

"Maybe we should help him," the woman said.

"After."

"All right."

Then the couple turned and looked at him.

"Don't let me interrupt you," Ryan said.

They got back to rutting.

Ryan took a look around the cabin and found that it was little more than a single room with a bed set against one wall and wash and toilet facilities against the other. He picked out a comfortable spot near the door and sat on the floor. Then he tried to rub out the cold ache the water had left in his legs, but his joints and muscles were still stiff and would need more time to recover.

Luckily, several hours remained before darkness fell, and judging by the way the couple was going at it on the bed, they would be busy for the next little while, giving him enough time to rest and recover.

Chapter Thirty-Five

"Traders at the gate," the sec man said.

The baron stood at the north window of his office watching the sec chief and his men search the orchards. "Where are they from?"

"Someplace called Reichel ville. It's on the south shore of Erie Lake."

"Are they armed?"

"Yes."

"With what?"

"Remades and handmades."

"Are there any breeders among them?"

"No."

"What have they brought to trade?"

"Fish."

The baron wrinkled his nose at the thought of fish, but knew that it wouldn't hurt to supplement his slaves' diet with an alternate source of protein. "Are the fish fresh?"

"No, baron. Preserved with salt. Some are smoked."

"And what do they want in exchange for their fish?"

The sec man hesitated.

"Speak up, I can't hear you."

The sec man cleared his throat. "A breeder."

Baron Fox laughed heartily. "A breeder, for salted fish?"

"Yes, Baron."

"Number One," the baron said to Norman Bauer. "Trade them some fruit and vegetables and send them on their way."

Norman nodded and left the baron's office.

The baron turned to the lone sec man left in the office. "Find sec chief Grundwold and tell him I want an update."

WHEN THE COUPLE had finished rutting, the woman got up from the bed and walked naked across the room to the wash facilities, where she towel dried the sweat from her body and combed her hair. The man lay back on the bed and watched her.

"So," she said, approaching Ryan, "what's happening tonight?"

Ryan wondered if they could be trusted, but realized that if they were loyal to the baron they would have turned him in hours ago. "Some people will be coming to get me and my friends."

"What people?"

"Other outlanders."

"An escape?" the man asked from the bed.

"Yeah."

"Can we come with you?" he said, sitting up.

"I won't be taking anyone with me, but you'll be free to leave if you have the chance."

He looked up at the woman standing in front of

Ryan, and it was obvious that they had something more in common than just rutting.

"What can I do to help you?" she asked.

"I need you to let my friends know where I am."

"Sure. Where are your friends now?"

"One's a healer working in the nursery. The other is the redhead, and she's staying in the visitors' quarters."

The woman nodded. "I can get to the nursery easy."

"What's your name?" Ryan asked.

"Debby. He's Maurice."

"All right, then, Debby, here's what you need to tell her when you get there," Ryan said.

A BREAKER HAD CUT OFF the electricity flowing through the main gate. Norman Bauer had stepped through the open gate to negotiate the trade, and it was still open.

"We don't trade breeders for anything but blasters," he said, the ledger open in his hands. "From the looks of the remades you're carrying, you don't have anything we want. Not for a breeder, anyway."

"We're from a small fishing ville," sec chief Ganley said. "All we have to trade is fish, and we need new breeders to keep the ville alive."

"Not my problem," Bauer said. "You want to trade fish, we can give you some fresh fruit and vegetables for them."

Ganley nodded. "If we bring blasters to trade next time, might we trade for breeders then?"

Bauer was impressed. Obviously this was a man who understood the nature of trade. Established trade partners got better deals than new ones. "Your chances of taking a breeder back to your ville would be better, yes."

"Then we'll take your fruit and vegetables now, and return another time for a breeder."

The two men shook hands, exchanged goods and went their separate ways. The fish went straight to the cafeteria, where it would be included in the next meal. Most of the fruit, however, was dumped by the raiders while on the way back to camp, since it was too heavy to carry such a distance when they'd be needing all their strength and energy for the raid later that night.

The raiders were sorry to see the sec chief come back empty-handed.

But the muties along the way were happy for the fruit, and now thought of the raiders as friends.

DEBBY RETURNED to her cabin an hour later.

"Did you find Mildred or Krysty?" Ryan asked.

"I found both of them in the nursery," she said, handing a few fresh fruit to Ryan. "Thought you might be hungry."

"How were you able to get there and back without arousing suspicion?" Maurice asked.

"I told the sec men along the way I was having women's problems. They didn't seem too interested in hearing the details and let me through to the nursery."

Ryan took a bite of an apple. "Did Mildred and Krysty tell you anything?"

"They sure did. Mildred said to tell you they were healing a sec man who the one-eyed outlander cut with a leaf-bladed throwing knife." She said the last four words very carefully so as to not make a mistake.

Ryan was confused for a moment, then understood that Jak was somewhere close by.

"And Krysty wanted me to give you something."

"What?" Ryan asked.

"This." She pulled Ryan's SIG-Sauer from beneath her dress, and two full clips from the deep cleavage between her breasts. "She said you'd know what to do with it."

Ryan took the blaster in his hand, quickly checked it over to see that it was in good working order and then stuffed the clips into his pockets.

"And I guess she was right," the woman said.

"Did she say anything else?" Ryan asked.

"Yes. She said, 'See you after dark, lover.'"

Chapter Thirty-Six

J.B. sat on the hood of the wag, wiping down his Uzi. The .50 calibers and the cannon were in as good a working order as he could manage. The wag was running better now, too, but it was clear that one or more of its eight cylinders was dead, and there was no guarantee it would be running long enough to get them all out of the farm complex.

They'd get in on the back of the wag, but getting out might just have to be done on foot.

Just then Doc called out to him. "I believe Jak and young Dean are returning from their recce."

"Are they alone?" J.B. asked.

"Afraid not. Jak seems to have picked up a wild hare or some sort of squirrel."

J.B. jumped down off the wag to meet the two youths.

"There's something happening on the farm," Dean said excitedly. "There's sec men all over, but Jak sent a message to Dad. Man, what a message—"

The information was coming too fast, and with too much noise for J.B.'s liking.

He waved his right hand at the boy to cut off his words and turned to Jak. "What happened?"

"Slaves all inside. Outside looks someone escape.

Mebbe Ryan, mebbe not. Sec men on triple red. Stuck sec man in leg with knife. Send message to Mildred. No mistake. Tonight be ready.''

J.B. nodded.

"I could have told you all that," Dean said, visibly disappointed.

"I know, but I wanted the facts first."

Doc interjected. "Quite often, young Mr. Cawdor, someone's life will depend on the rapid exchange of information. Although we have got plenty of time to go before sundown, it is still a good rule to obey."

"All right," Dean said, dejected. "I'll make a note of it for next time."

J.B. put a hand on the boy's shoulder. "C'mon, you can tell me all about it while Jak puts those squirrels on the spit."

Dean's face lit up in excitement. "Well, there was only a six-inch gap in the fence and…''

"FRUIT?" RHONDA ASKED, holding an apple in her hand.

"Said they don't trade breeders for food," Ganley said.

"But you told us that they send wag trains to the eastern villes all the time, trading breeders for all kinds of supplies. Not just blasters."

"They do. I've seen them do it." The sec chief shook his head. "Felt to me like their trader was busy with some other problem right now and just wanted to get rid of us, quick as he could."

"I got that impression, too," Franz said.

Ruznicki nodded. "Me, too."

"So," Rhonda said, "what do we do now?"

"We wait for dark," Ganley said, pulling a peach out of the bag of fruit they'd brought back to the camp. "And then we take from them what they wouldn't give us in trade."

CLARISSA RETURNED to the wag late in the afternoon. She was being trailed by a few muties, but they were hanging well back and seemed more concerned with the farm than following her.

"Muties are ready?"

"They can't wait to get inside," Clarissa said. "But there's something else you need to know about."

"What's that?" J.B. asked.

"Traders at the farm today."

"We saw them," J.B. said. "Did their business and went away."

Clarissa shook her head. "Not quite. There's more to the group than the ones trading. They're camped to the south of the farm."

"What want?" Jak asked.

"Not fruit—that's for sure. They dumped half of what they traded for on their way back to their camp."

"That is strange," Doc commented.

"The muties loved it," Clarissa said. "They've circled their camp waiting for more."

Jak looked at J.B. "Call off tonight?"

J.B. was silent a moment, noting that the sun was low in the western sky and less than an hour from sliding below the horizon. "No. There's no time," he said. "Ryan, Mildred and Krysty are expecting us tonight."

"What about the traders?" Clarissa asked.

"If they wanted more than fruit, my guess is that when our blasters light up the dark, they'll be on our side."

THE SUN WAS ALMOST GONE from the day and the sky was streaked in a rainbow of fiery reds, glowing oranges and searing yellows. Flashes of greenish-blues cut between the hues like portals to another time.

It was a beautiful sight, one few had the time to admire.

For Grundwold, the setting sun meant he had failed. The one-eyed outlander was still hidden somewhere on the farm, and his chances of escaping the complex outright would improve with every minute of darkness.

"Should I call back the sec men to guard the main building through the night?" Fillinger asked.

Grundwold considered it, but knew he couldn't tell the baron that the outlander was still on the loose. And as long as he kept searching, he hadn't failed. "No more than a dozen men," Grundwold ordered. "Turn on the lights and leave the rest of them out there in the orchards."

"But they'll be easy targets to chill for a single man in the dark," Fillinger stated.

The sec chief realized he was putting his men at risk, but there was no other choice; the search had to continue. "If one of them gets chilled, then at least we'll know where the one-eye is."

Fillinger was silent a moment, then said, "What about the baron. He'll want a report."

"Find Norman Bauer," Grundwold said. "Tell him to send two breeders to the baron's quarters. That should keep him busy for a while."

Fillinger nodded, then turned to carry out the sec chief's orders.

"Now," Grundwold muttered. "Let's go find the outlander."

THERE WAS a single knock on the door before it opened.

Ryan had been sitting on the edge of the bed and only had time to dive to the floor between the bed and the wall. His SIG-Sauer was in his hand and ready to fire, but he resisted the temptation to rise up with his blaster blazing. He'd be able to take out the first sec men, but there would be more coming through the door without another way out of the cabin.

"What is it?" Maurice asked. "You've already been through here twice today."

Ryan slid under the bed and looked out from beneath it through a slit in the overhanging sheets.

The sec man had ignored Maurice's comment and was looking at Debby, who was still lying on the bed. "You," he said to her. "Let's go!"

"Go where?" she asked, dutifully getting up from the bed and putting on a bathrobe. "What have I done?"

"Nothing wrong," said the sec man. "You're going to see the baron."

Debby looked over at Maurice with a pained expression, then at the bed where Ryan had been only second before. "Is it a celebration? Did they find the one-eye?"

"Not yet."

"Then why is the baron calling for me?"

"Not the baron, sec chief Grundwold," the sec man said. "He wants the baron kept busy while we continue the search."

"Oh, my pleasure," Debby cooed, in what Ryan knew were words solely for the sec man's benefit. She was in love with Maurice and he was in love with her, but they could never admit it. Not yet, anyway.

"Let's go."

At the door she stopped, turned back to face Maurice and said, "If you get busy tonight, please don't forget about me. Don't leave me behind."

"Never," Maurice said.

Chapter Thirty-Seven

Baron Fox was lying back on his round, oversize bed, looking through another stack of predark hard-core skin mags. This one was called *Dominas* and featured naked and provocatively dressed breeders subjugating men in a variety of different ways.

The baron turned the page and there were two women, one dressed in red, the other dressed in black, standing on a naked man. Each of the women wore spike-heeled shoes and the heels were pressing into the man's flesh, threatening to break the skin at any moment. In photo after photo they moved slightly so that their deadly shoes pressed against the man's arms, throat and face. In the last photo, the woman in black had taken her shoes off and was smothering the man with her stocking-covered feet. The man seemed to be turning red from lack of oxygen, but like in all the other photos, he had an enormous erection.

Here were breeders acting as he would, as the baron. The men in the photos were the slaves, happy to be humiliated, punished, physically injured, by the wickedly evil breeders.

The baron wondered if he might be able to experience such a thrill. It was unlikely, since he was the baron and if he let himself be dominated by any of his breeders, it would be looked upon as a sign of weakness. He'd been able to keep Grundwold in line, but if the man detected a weakness, he could use it to his advantage.

Perhaps, the baron thought, he could subject himself to such breeders, and then chill them, so that they would take what they knew of the baron to the grave with them. It was certainly a possibility, one that would prevent Grundwold from learning that his baron could be controlled under the right circumstances.

Just then there was a knock on the door.

"Enter," the baron said. He'd been expecting Norman Bauer, but was surprised to see a sec man enter.

"What is it?"

"Breeders, Baron," the sec man said nervously.

"I never asked for any breeders," the baron said, putting the skin mag aside for now and rising from his bed.

The sec man let the two breeders enter the baron's quarters. They were attractive, perhaps on the heavy side, but good breeders. Good rutters, too, the baron admitted, as the larger one had visited him before. "Sec chief Grundwold sent them, sir."

"What?"

"He knows you've had a stressful day and could use some breeders to unwind."

"He said that?" the baron asked, the anger rising within him.

The sec man, obviously frightened of the baron, simply nodded.

"He hasn't caught the one-eyed outlander yet, has he?"

The sec man shook his head.

"Triple-stupe fucker," the baron shouted. "And he thinks I'll just forget about his incompetence by sending me a couple of breeders."

The sec man stood still and silent.

The two breeders were trembling in fear.

"I was hoping he'd show a little imagination in his search, but he's just as triple-stupe as the rest of you." The baron went over to a dresser and pulled open the top drawer. In one fluid motion his hand slid inside and came out with a blued steel 9 mm Luger blaster. He turned to the sec man. "Find the sec chief and tell him to meet me in the nursery."

"Yes, Baron."

"And find that redheaded gaudy slut of an outlander and bring her to the nursery, too."

The sec man ran off to carry out the baron's orders.

"If the sec chief can't find the one-eye, then maybe we can use his friends to draw him out."

The two breeders remained.

"You two wait for me here," the baron said. "I'll be back."

THE SUN WAS GONE from the sky.

The raiders had just finished building a pair of wooden ladders that would help them get over the fence and into the compound.

"All ready?" Ganley asked.

"Ready," the raiders answered in a jumble of voices scattered over several seconds.

"Then let's move."

J.B. TAPPED HIS FINGER on the key, waiting for word to come from the back of the wag that everything was secure and the rest of the group was ready to move.

When Jak and Dean were in position behind the .50 calibers, Doc was in the wag's bed overseeing the cannon shells and Clarissa was riding shotgun with J.B.'s Uzi at the ready, J.B. grabbed hold of the wag's key and turned it.

The starter motor turned over weakly, the engine sputtered and then stopped.

"Want us to push?" Clarissa asked.

"Not yet," J.B. answered. He turned the key again and the starter let out a series of slow protesting groans. The engine sputtered once more, but this time it suddenly roared to life.

J.B. beamed proudly as the work he'd done on the engine over the course of the day had paid off. The engine was running more smoothly than it had in the morning, and he was confident it would keep running for as long as he needed it to.

"Hang on!" he said, then put the wag into gear.

The wag lurched forward.

J.B. drove slowly in darkness, not wanting to try the wag's lights. If they worked, it would help with the driving, but it would make the wag a good target for the farm's sec men. As it was, all they had to shoot at was a sound in the darkness and such things were hard to hit at the best of times.

Their plan was simple.

They would use the 37 mm cannon to take out the farm's electric supply. That would shut off the lights, shut down the electric fence and generally create chaos within the complex.

Then they'd use the weight of the wag to break through the front gate.

Once inside the complex, Clarissa and Jak would head into the main building to look for Ryan, Krysty and Mildred. J.B. would select strategic targets for the 37 mm cannon, such as sec towers, wags and emergency electricity and lighting while Dean and Doc would use the .50 calibers to keep the sec force under cover.

Depending on how the wag stood up, J.B. would stay with the wag they had, or they'd try to take one of the baron's wags from inside the barn.

While all this was going on, Ryan, Krysty and Mildred would be working their way out from the inside of the complex, splitting the sec force, chilling sec men and distracting other sec men from the front gate.

Add to that the muties, who would be streaming in through the gate and over the fence, taking out sec men and eating them raw, and the slaves themselves who would have been warned about what was coming and would be all too eager to escape or chill their former masters.

Organized chaos, J.B. thought. He'd have preferred to sneak in with a precision strike, but the electric

fence made that too difficult, and they had the firepower to go in with blasters blazing. So why not go
with their strengths?

And it was all going to start going down in less
than five minutes.

THE DOOR to the nursery burst open and Baron Fox
strode in, a blaster in one hand and an electric cattle
prod in the other.

"Grundwold," the baron shouted.

The sec chief stepped forward. "Yes, Baron."

"You're no longer sec chief."

Grundwold's mouth opened to utter words of protest.

But the baron didn't give him a chance to respond.
He raised his Luger and shot the man in the shoulder,
sending him flying backward against a supply cabinet.

"Anyone else have anything to say about Grundwold's demotion?" the baron demanded.

No one said a word.

Mildred moved toward the sec chief to see if he'd
been fatally shot.

"Leave him!" the baron ordered, then turned. "Fillinger!"

"Yes, Baron."

"You're my new sec chief now."

"Yes, Baron!"

"Take this fire-headed gaudy slut outside and have
her walk the grounds in the lights of a wag. Put two
sec men on her, a blaster trained on each side of her
head. Tell the one-eye either he comes out of hiding,

or we'll blow her pretty little head clean off her shoulders.''

"Yes, Baron!" he said with obvious glee.

Mildred moved closer to the bassinet that held her blaster.

"C'mon, Red, let's go for a walk," the baron said.

Krysty remained where she was. Mildred inched still closer to the bassinet.

"I said let's move."

Suddenly a loud boom thundered from somewhere outside. Several glass containers in the nursery shook. Babies were awakened from their sleep and began to cry.

The noise was followed by several seconds of silence.

"Find out what that was!" the baron ordered.

Sec men began running up the stairs.

A second loud boom sounded, and then all the lights went out. The entire building was shrouded in inky darkness.

Chapter Thirty-Eight

J.B.'s first shot had missed the tall wooden pole that held the power lines bringing electricity into the complex. He adjusted the wag slightly, moved in closer and the second blast from the cannon cut the pole down better than any ax ever could.

The pole had toppled slowly, and it took several seconds for the lines to snap and the lights to go out inside the complex. There would likely be reserve or emergency lighting coming on at any moment, but J.B. didn't wait around to find out for sure. He threw the wag into gear, circled back around toward the front gate and was now speeding toward the chain-link fence.

"Hang on and cover up!" he cried.

He expected spotlights to catch the wag as they headed toward the main gate, but the complex was still in darkness. Maybe there was no emergency lighting after all.

The fence was in front of them.

"Three, two, one!" J.B. counted down.

The front of the wag struck the fence. The vehicle slowed, and for a moment it seemed as if they might be stopped dead in their tracks, but the steel gave way and they burst through the gate with plenty of speed.

J.B. also expected to be under fire at this point, but the sudden plunge into darkness had caused confusion among the ranks of sec men. Many searching the orchards were now caught in the dark.

As they charged across the courtyard, a sec man came out from around the corner of the main building. Dean saw him first, cutting the man down with a sweep of the .50 caliber.

"Shorter bursts," J.B. shouted to Dean.

"Sorry."

J.B. slowed the wag rather than stopping it, deciding a moving target was much harder to hit than one that was standing still. "Go," he told Clarissa.

She jumped out of the wag, followed by Jak.

A moment later they were gone.

J.B. turned the wag in the direction of one of the sec towers overlooking the courtyard and main gate. "Doc?" he said.

"Ready when you are, Captain," Doc answered.

J.B. pulled the trigger. The cannon let out a loud thud. The air around the wag smelled of cordite. Then the sec tower was suddenly without one of its legs.

It slowly began to fall—toward the wag.

"Uh, might I suggest that we move our vehicle to avoid an unhappy circumstance," Doc said.

J.B. didn't answer. He was too busy trying to get the wag out of the way of the falling tower.

WHEN THE EMERGENCY lights came on, the baron was gone.

And so was Krysty.

But there was little time to dwell on that with so many sec men in the room.

In the dark, Mildred had retrieved her ZKR target pistol, and when the lights kicked in she was ready. She fired two shots at the sec men at the door to the nursery, hitting the first in the head, blowing a chunk of skull off the top of it. She caught the second in the throat, and he fell to the floor clutching at his neck in a futile attempt to staunch the flow of blood.

Grundwold was still moaning in pain on the floor, trying to get to his feet despite the wound to his shoulder. Mildred lowered her blaster and put a round into his heart before he had a chance to get onto his knees.

"What's going on in here?" asked the old woman, who up until now had been taking care of the newborns in another part of the nursery.

"Liberation," Mildred said. "We're getting out."

"These people don't know anything about freedom," the old woman told her. "I remember it, but most don't know any other kind of life. In fact, some even like it here."

"Well, maybe now at least they'll have a choice."

The old woman shrugged. "I suppose. Good luck to you. I've got children to tend to."

Mildred reached down and took the Persuader 500 pistol-grip longblaster from the holster of the dead former sec chief. "Here," she said. "It might come in handy."

The old woman took the blaster and hefted it in her hand. "It might at that."

Then she picked up Krysty's Smith & Wesson from its hiding place and tucked it into the waistband of her jeans. Obviously Krysty had been taken hostage by the baron and his new sec chief.

The two men might as well have signed their death warrants.

WHEN THE FIRST BOOM sounded, Ryan thought it might mean that J.B. was near. When there was a second boom and the lights went out, he was sure of it.

"That's it," he told Maurice. "Time to move."

The two men left the cabin and headed for the main building.

SEC CHIEF GANLEY had been first over the fence at the onset of darkness and was now helping others climb down from the wooden ladder.

In the distance, something boomed like a cannon for the second time.

The sound startled one of the raiders who was at the top of the outside ladder and crossing over to the one on the inside of the complex. The man faltered and was forced to reach out with his hand and grab at the fence. He screamed loud and shrill in anticipation of the electricity that was about to flow through his body.

But nothing happened.

"The fence is down," Ganley called out, realizing they'd just been given a lucky break. "Everyone over as quick as you can."

Minutes later the raiders were roaming the orchard freely, hunting for breeders.

HUNGRY MUTIES POURED IN through the broken front gate like water through a sluice.

And when they realized the power was out, they began climbing over the fence, too, surging into the complex from all sides.

In the eerily dim glow of the emergency lights, sec men raised their blasters at the charging muties, but hesitated when they saw how many of the hunger-mad creatures they were up against.

Some sec men fired; others ran, as far as the front gate and beyond.

Most ended up as meals for the starving mutants.

The lucky ones were chilled quickly.

The unlucky ones were eaten alive.

Chapter Thirty-Nine

Ryan left the cabin and, along with Maurice, ran to the main building. The sec men in the area didn't seem all too concerned with their progress as the thud of a large-bore weapon and the crackle of heavy-caliber machine blasters had them all scrambling for cover.

As Ryan turned the corner on the building, a familiar flash of white caught his eye.

"Jak!" he shouted.

The spot of white reappeared in the blown-out hole where the front doors used to be. Jak waited for Ryan and when they met, the two shook hands.

"Good see you," Jak said.

"Likewise." Ryan nodded.

Clarissa came up behind Jak. Maurice was standing by Ryan's side.

"This Clarissa. Friend of muties. Helping us."

"Maurice," Ryan said, gesturing with his head in the slave's direction. "Friend of mine."

"There's the one-eye," someone shouted.

Blasterfire suddenly began slamming into the wall behind them. They all dived for cover, scraping and cutting their hands on the shards of glass scattered around the building. Ryan found himself pinned behind a column supporting the building's second floor.

Jak and Clarissa had also gained cover, but Maurice had been caught by the sec men's blasters. His body jerked as he was torn apart by rounds coming from somewhere high up and out of sight. He stood for several seconds, then finally fell to the ground a bloody mess.

"He was going to take me to the nursery," Ryan said. "That's where Krysty and Mildred are."

"I can take you there," Clarissa said.

Ryan wanted to move, but they were still being pinned down by sec men on the roof of a nearby building.

But just below the sound of blasterfire came the grinding of a wag engine, low at first, but growing louder by the second. Without warning there was a boom that shook the ground, followed by a small explosion.

Men screamed, debris filled the air and the rain of blasterfire abruptly came to an end.

"Lead the way!" Ryan told Clarissa.

The three of them entered the building.

RYAN, JAK AND Clarissa hurried down the steps, taking them two at a time. They all had their blasters at the ready, expecting a sec man to turn the corner on them at the bottom of the stairs and they'd have nowhere to turn.

But they made it down without incident.

"Left or right?" Jak asked.

"Right," Clarissa answered.

A crack of a blaster echoed from down the hall, and all three took cover against the wall of the stairwell.

After several seconds of silence, a second shot rang out, followed by a groan and the sound of a falling body.

J.B. was best at recognizing the sounds various blasters made and could sometimes even identify the type of ammo being used, but even Ryan knew enough to identify the sharp crack of a .38-caliber Czech-built ZKR. It was possible that a sec man was now using Mildred's target pistol, but the spacing of the single shots and their accuracy told Ryan all he needed to know.

"Mildred," he called out in the direction the shot had come.

"Who wants to know?" came the response.

"Me, Ryan."

She turned the corner, blaster raised in case it was some sort of trick, and smiled. "It's good to see you, Ryan, and I have to admit, I would have even been happy if it were Doc instead of you."

"I'll have to tell him."

"He'll never believe you."

Ryan was done with small talk. "Where's Krysty?"

"The baron took her hostage when the lights went out," Mildred reported.

Ryan turned to Clarissa. "Where would he have gone with her?"

"Depends what he wanted to do with her."

Ryan thought about it for a second. "To get away?"

"Then he'd go to the barn and try for a wag."

"Then we head back outside."

Ryan and Mildred began moving back up the stairs, but Jak and Clarissa remained where they were.

"What's wrong?" Ryan asked.

"Sister prisoner in basement," Jak explained. "Promised rescue for help."

Ryan understood. "All right. You go with her, Jak. Mildred comes with me. If you're not outside in twenty minutes, we'll come back in looking for you."

"Won't have to," Jak said. "Not be there."

Without another word the two pairs went their separate ways, Ryan and Mildred heading up, Jak and Clarissa heading down.

JUST OUTSIDE the nursery, Baron Fox escorted the two breeders from his office along the hallway. He'd given instructions to the new sec chief to use the redheaded beauty to convince the one-eyed outlander to leave the farm without destroying it completely. If it worked, wonderful, but even if it didn't, he'd be safe and in a position to reclaim the farm in no time.

When he reached the dungeon, he found a sec man standing guard there.

"Make sure no one comes down this hallway," the baron ordered. "No slaves, muties, outlanders... Not even any sec men. Understood?"

"Yes, Baron!"

Baron Fox pushed the breeders past.

Farther down the hall and around a corner, the sec man heard a heavy door open, then close, and then the sound of a heavy mechanism locking into place.

And then only silence.

Chapter Forty

The slaves opened the doors to their cabins.

It was happening.

The one-eyed outlander had spread the word that there would be something happening that night, a chance for escape, for freedom, and now it was happening.

There were dead sec men everywhere, falling like ripe fruit at the end of the season. Blasterfire cut them down like axes, and their remades were being scooped up by slaves, the new masters of the farm.

Muties were running through the complex, eating everything in sight, especially uniformed sec men.

It was total chaos, and the slaves were never happier.

Marguerite, a black-haired breeder who had given the baron six offspring in four years, could hardly believe her eyes. Slaves ran from cabin to cabin, some carrying blasters, some with tree branches, all with wild-eyed excitement in their eyes.

"Come look, Joshua," she said, stepping out of her cabin. "They're chilling a sec man over there, doing him with his own blaster."

Joshua, the man Marguerite had been rutting with the past six nights, stepped out of the cabin and joined her outside. About twenty-five yards away, four slaves were kicking and beating a sec man who'd been caught out in the orchards alone. They had shot him in the belly with his remade and were now taking great pleasure in torturing him before letting him die.

"This means we're free," Joshua shouted.

Marguerite shook her head and looked away. She was an older woman, well into her thirties, and had been a slave so long she feared her own freedom. Everything had been provided for her in the past, and she'd become comfortable with that. Being free meant fending for herself, feeding herself and finding her own way in life. The thought of it terrified her.

"We can leave here," Joshua said. "Together. We could go to one of the eastern villes, maybe another barony. Whatever we do, we'll be doing it together."

Joshua's words gave Marguerite confidence, reason to hope.

Just then an arrow caught Joshua in the throat. Great gouts of blood began to pour from the gaping wound, and the fire that had been in his eyes just a moment before began to dim.

Marguerite turned in time to have her face covered in a fine red mist, and her body streaked by the blood that was leaving Joshua's body like oil from a can.

"What, where?" she asked in confusion.

Joshua fell to the ground.

"Who wants this one?" sec chief Ganley said.

A dozen raiders stood behind him armed with a mix of blasters, bows and pikes.

"I'll take her," a young man said, barely out of his teens.

"What's going on?" Marguerite asked. "Who are you?"

Ganley ignored her questions and pressed on, the rest of the raiders, save one, following him.

"My name's Matthew," he said. "I've come from Reichel ville, a fishing village on Erie Lake not far from here."

"What do you want?"

"You," he said. "We've come for breeders, new blood for our dying ville."

"I can give you offspring," Marguerite said.

"Good," Matthew said, leading her into the orchards and the staging area they had set up on the other side of the fence. "I hope you can help me raise them, too."

Marguerite was confused. "I'm not going to be a slave?"

"No, not a slave. You're going to be my wife."

JAK AND CLARISSA passed the nursery and rounded the corner to the dungeon, then stopped and backtracked around the corner again.

A sec man stood guard in front of the door that led to the dungeon. He was armed with a 12-gauge pump-action blaster, and he looked determined not to let anyone get by him.

"Must chill," Jak said in a whisper.

Clarissa put her hand on Jak's arm. "No, we need him alive."

"Why?"

"My sister and the others are chained to the dungeon wall. We'll need keys to unlock and set them free."

Jak nodded, then reached inside his coat for one of the leaf-bladed throwing knifes he kept hidden on his person. He balanced the knife in his throwing hand, mentally counted to three, then rolled past the corner into the hallway and came up onto his knees to make the throw. The knife sailed straight and true, catching the sec man in the right bicep and involuntarily forcing open his right hand. The blaster fell to the floor with a heavy clang, and Jak got to his feet, his huge Colt Python leveled at the sec man's chest.

The sec man grabbed at his wounded arm with his left hand and tried to kneel to pick up his longblaster.

"No," Jak said.

"Give us the keys for the dungeon," Clarissa yelled as she came up behind Jak, "and he won't chill you."

"Fuck you, you snow-headed mutie freak!"

Jak squeezed the trigger and blew off part of the sec man's right foot.

"Where are the keys?" Clarissa demanded.

The sec man was too busy writhing on the floor and screaming in pain to answer.

Jak pushed the barrel of the Python against the man's genitals.

"Tell me where the keys are," Clarissa said softly.

The sec man stared at Jak's big blaster in horror. "There's a master key in my right pocket." He fished inside his pants with a trembling hand and produced a key on a Lucite fob that had a picture of the falls on it in all its predark glory.

Clarissa took the key from him. "Thanks."

Jak raised the Python to the sec man's head. "Lose lot blood," he said to Clarissa. "Die anyway."

She nodded.

Jak looked at the sec man. "Not mutie."

Then he pulled the trigger.

RYAN AND MILDRED were back outside the front doors to the main building looking for Krysty and her captor.

The courtyard was in shambles and utter chaos. The bloody remains of several sec men were strewed across the ground, several of them in the very circle Ryan had fought the day before. Muties ran through the compound, eating fruit, brandishing weapons and generally making up for years of hunger and near starvation.

There were sec men still in the complex, but they all seemed to be trying to escape out the front gate, like rats jumping off a sinking ship. It was obvious to them all they'd lost the battle, and now they were just saving themselves.

"Where are we going to find Krysty in all this?" Mildred asked.

Ryan scanned the complex. "I know from experience," he said. "There are a hundred places to hide out in."

"She could be anywhere."

And then Ryan saw something, a familiar flash of titian hair, and he knew that their search was over.

"You can stop looking," Ryan said, pointing. "She's found us. There."

Mildred followed the line made by Ryan's finger. "That's the baron's new sec chief. Name's Fillinger."

Fillinger stood on the roof of the main building with Krysty in front of him. Her hands were bound behind her back, and he had a large blued blaster pressed to the side of her head.

"One-eye!" the sec chief called.

Ryan looked up but said nothing.

"I got something you want."

Ryan said nothing to the man on the roof, but just under his breath he muttered to Mildred, "He's too far for me to try with the SIG-Sauer."

Mildred gauged the distance, wind, the slight movements of the target and shook her head. "He's got Krysty too close. If I'm a fraction off, she's on the last train west."

"I want to make a deal," the sec chief shouted.

The last thing Ryan wanted was to make a trade or strike some deal for the lives of his friends. Trading blasters and goods for food and shelter was one thing, but trading humans for those same items was just plain wrong. But this wasn't just any human the sec chief was holding hostage; it was Krysty. His friend and lover. He'd listen to the man's offer, and try to figure out some other solution in the meantime. "I'm listening."

"You leave now and take your friends with you—the fish traders, the muties, all of them."

There were a few moments of silence. So far the deal wasn't sounding very good. ''And?'' Ryan asked.

''And Red won't be chilled.''

''That's not much of a deal,'' Ryan said.

''Best one you get, One-eye.''

''Let her go and we'll leave.''

The sec chief shook his head. ''The baron wants her. We need to rebuild the breeding stock, and she's just what we need.''

''You sure you can't take him?'' Ryan muttered.

Mildred made a second assessment. ''Sorry, Ryan.''

''If you don't let her go, there won't be a piece of this farm left standing by the time I'm through with it.''

''I'll take that chance,'' Fillinger said.

''What are we going to do, Ryan?'' Mildred asked.

''I don't know.''

THE REICHEL VILLE raiders had made it all the way through the orchards and had taken a dozen slaves with them—nine of them women. The entire operation had gone easier than they'd expected, and they were about to leave with eight more than they arrived with.

The ville would survive and flourish.

As Rhonda led a party of six toward the large group of buildings at the far end of the complex, she was looking for something to give sec chief Ganley. He'd been a selfless leader to the raiders, and they had all expressed their wish to thank him in some way. A mate of his own would be a excellent show of gratitude, but what sort of woman would suit him?

They turned the corner on the cabins housing the men and women living on the farm, and Rhonda caught sight of a sec man standing on the roof of the biggest building on the farm. There was a woman with him, a woman with the most amazing red hair. He seemed to be shouting down at someone on the other side of the building.

"Dwayne," she said.

"Yeah," came the response from a middle-aged man as he came up behind her.

"That first night we camped out on the south shore of the lake, what did the sec chief say when we asked him what he'd like in a mate?"

Dwayne thought about it a moment. "Uh, he said she'd have to be healthy, and that he always liked red hair. Red hair, or dark skin, one or the other."

"Look up there." She gestured with a flick of her head.

"That's red, all right."

"Take two others up onto the roof. When we take the sec man out, you bring the redhead down to the staging area. We'll cover your back along the way."

"Right."

"As soon as we're on the other side of the fence, we're outta here."

"WELL, ONE-EYE!" sec chief Fillinger said. "I don't see you leaving."

"Can't leave her behind," Ryan said.

"Sorry to hear that."

"You chill her, there won't be a farm left to re-build."

"It's already gone to shit."

"Let her go!" Ryan shouted, then turned to Mildred and whispered. "Take your best shot."

Mildred raised her target pistol slowly, knowing that once the sec chief saw the blaster she'd only have a split second to take the shot.

But then the sec chief's body suddenly jerked to the right. The man let go of Krysty and stumbled to keep his balance.

With several feet of darkness between the sec chief and Krysty, Mildred had no trouble marking the target. She raised her ZKR and fired off two rounds, catching the sec chief first in the chest and then in the head.

But he didn't fall.

Instead he turned away from Krysty and in the dim glow of the auxiliary lights, the arrow that had pierced his neck and shattered his throat became visible to the friends on the ground.

"Let's get up there and grab Krysty," Ryan said, already running toward the main building.

Mildred followed him, five steps behind all the way through the building and finally up the ladder that brought them to the roof.

But when they got there, all they found was a dead sec chief.

Krysty was gone.

Chapter Forty-One

J.B., Doc and Dean had taken up a position outside the barn where they'd been told the baron kept a LAV and a few transport wags. They had considered storming the barn and capturing one of the wags, but a dozen or more sec men had already gone inside and following them in would have brought on a firefight.

So instead they parked the wag about a hundred yards from the barn doors with the cannon loaded and the .50 calibers aimed at the open door.

"How many shells left, Doc?" J.B. asked.

"Six," Doc answered. "Of differing quality from good to questionable."

"How about the fifties?"

"Six feet of belt on the back," Dean reported. "Four and a half on the front."

A noise came from the inside of the barn.

"Hear that?" J.B. asked.

"If I am not mistaken," Doc said, "that's the rattle and thrum of a diesel engine, most likely made in the predark city of Detroit, or perhaps one of the smaller villes such as Flint or Pontiac."

"Diesel, all right. Get ready."

Doc and Dean manned the fifties. J.B. tightened his grip on the cannon's trigger.

All at once the door to the barn was filled by a black

LAV. It had four large wheels, a small compartment for a crew and a single blaster mounted on a pivot at the top of a conically shaped turret. It weapon was smaller than the 37 mm, and it was also pointed in the wrong direction.

J.B. held back on firing until the LAV approached his line of fire. Leading the target by about a yard, he pulled the trigger and the front wheels of the vehicle were blown off their mounts. The LAV foundered, falling forward like a horse that just had its front legs pulled out from under it. The blaster began to swivel in their direction, but the LAV had come to a stop directly in J.B.'s line of fire. Still, the Armorer turned the wheel of the wag to the left and backed it up about two feet, bringing the LAV's turret directly in line with the cannon's barrel.

"Doc, is it loaded?"

In the back of the wag, Doc was busily making sure that the gun was loaded and wouldn't jam on the next round.

"Doc?"

"Do not wait for me, John Barrymore."

J.B. pulled the trigger and the cannon thudded again, this time hitting the LAV's turret and shattering its blaster into a pile of hot steel.

The top of the LAV popped open and sec men began to scramble out. Dean peppered them with .50-caliber fire, chilling two and sending the other running unarmed and empty-handed out of the complex.

"Hot pipe!" Dean exclaimed.

THE DUNGEON was little more than a damp, dark and musty basement. It housed water heaters, and electric heaters to keep the farm buildings warm through the winter, as well as filters and a few tables with seedlings being cultivated under banks of fluorescent lights.

And six women were chained to the cinder-block wall behind them. All appeared to be in their third trimester and ready to give birth at any time.

But unlike the well-kept plants being cultivated under the lights, these women had been abandoned in the dark. Jak found a light switch that turned on a single bulb in an old ceiling fixture, and the women cringed under the dim light of the low-wattage light. The floor was cold and wet, stinking of feces and urine, and crawling with bugs that seemed to roam over the women's bodies with a purpose—as if the living beings were simply part of the terrain.

Not surprising, the bodies of the women were covered with sores and scabs. Their flesh was pale white and pasty in texture, like the skin Jak had seen on hundreds of muties over the years.

And then there were their eyes...

They were full of fear, terrified that they'd be beaten, raped or otherwise abused. If the baron had brought women down to this place to break their spirit and obliterate their will to resist him, he had succeeded magnificently.

These women were waiting to die as much as they were waiting to give birth.

"Which one your sister?" Jak asked.

Clarissa stared at the six women with a confused

look on her face. "I'm not sure," she said, sounding afraid and just a little bit desperate.

Jak wasn't surprised. These women barely looked human.

"Melanie?"

Jak didn't wait for one of them to answer. He began unlocking all the women.

"Is that you, Clarissa?" the second woman from the end called out.

"What's going on?" another woman asked.

"What has happened?"

"Who are you?"

Clarissa lifted her sister off the damp and dirty floor. Her sister, Melanie, was unable to stand straight after months of crouching on the cold hard floor, but Clarissa bent to put her arms around her.

"You came back," Melanie said.

"I never left." Clarissa was near tears.

"What?"

"I stayed outside the farm, waiting for the chance to rescue you."

"Who is he?" Melanie asked. By now the other five women were on their shaky feet, as well, and they all seemed to want to know the answer to that question, too.

"This is Jak Lauren," Clarissa explained, drying her sister's eyes.

Jak gave them a slight wave.

"He and his friends have freed the slaves."

"Free?" one of the women asked.

Jak nodded. He pointed to the stairs leading out of the dungeon and then out of the building. "This way."

THE MORNING SUN WAS just beginning to peek over the eastern horizon. It felt warm and comforting after a long, dark night full of chilling.

In the growing light, Ryan and Mildred ran to the back of the building and could see several people running into the orchard, heading for the far corner of the fence.

Most of them were out of range by now, but a few stragglers were still within their reach.

"Can you take him down without killing him?" Ryan asked Mildred.

Mildred took her shooter's stance and followed the running man's route closely. And then she fired a shot.

The man stumbled, pitched forward, and then rolled up against an apple tree.

He didn't get up.

Mildred and Ryan ran to catch up to him.

When they arrived, the man was backed up against the stump. Mildred's shot had torn up his left calf and broke a bone or two, but the wound wasn't fatal.

"Who are you people?" Ryan asked. "Where do you come from?"

The man didn't seem interested in answering.

Mildred pointed her ZKR at the man's head, but that didn't seem to make any difference.

"We're not sec men," Ryan said. "We've been fighting on the same side, against the baron."

That seemed to catch the man's interest, but Ryan

didn't have time to slowly win him over. He reared back and hit him square in the jaw with the back of his SIG-Sauer. "Your party captured one of our group. I want her back."

The man was slow to answer, so Ryan prepared to give him another blow.

"Wait," he said.

"I'm waiting."

"We're from Reichel ville. We needed breeders, new blood for the survival of the ville."

"Where is Reichel ville?"

"On Erie Lake. We've camped on the north shore of the lake, at Fort Erie. That's where the others are headed now."

"How long ago?"

"A few minutes, maybe more. I don't know. I got separated. They left without me."

Ryan looked up at Mildred. "I'm going after them."

"We could all go together," Mildred offered.

"No time," Ryan said. "We have to go now."

"Then I'm going with you, but we need to let the others know where we've gone."

Ryan looked at the wounded raider. "I need you to do something for me."

"A favor?" the man asked, through swollen lips.

"Yes. I need you to let the others know where we've gone."

"What if I do?"

"Then you can tell them that Ryan Cawdor said

they have to take you with them, to meet up with the others from your ville.''

"How do I know they'll do that?''

"If you give them my name, they'll do it.''

Mildred nodded.

"All right.''

Ryan and Mildred were gone without another word.

WHEN JAK and the women reached the top of the stairs and stepped through the door leading out of the dungeon, the freed women took cautious steps into the hallway, as if they didn't believe they'd actually been emancipated.

"You're free to go,'' Clarissa explained.

"Where's the baron?'' her sister asked.

"Missing right now,'' Clarissa said.

"We can't be free if he's still alive.''

"We're going to look for him.''

"Chill when find,'' Jak added.

"I know where he's hiding,'' Clarissa's sister, Melanie, said. "There's a bunker at the end of this hallway. I heard someone go down that way a few hours ago. It has to be him.''

"Take me there,'' Jak said.

The other women suddenly began moving in the other direction, not wanting any part of the baron, not even to see him get chilled.

"Follow me,'' Melanie said.

Chapter Forty-Two

Ryan and Mildred jumped the fence and were on the raiders' trail, but weren't any closer to rescuing Krysty.

Every mile or so, a straggler would fall behind the main group, fire several shots in their general direction and then disappear into the underbrush. The guerrilla tactics didn't give Ryan and Mildred the time or chance to fight, but were slowing their progress enough to let the group, and Krysty, slip farther and farther away.

Currently they were pinned down behind an outcrop between two stands of trees. The trail wound to the left slightly, and the shots were coming from somewhere to the right.

Ryan took his brass naval telescope from his coat and scanned the terrain in front of him, but he couldn't pick the shooter out of the shadows.

"We know his general area," Mildred stated. "Let me see if I can come around from behind and flush him out."

"Have to hurry," Ryan said.

Mildred started to move, but Ryan held her back.

"No, I'm going," he said. "You stay here and try to keep him pinned down."

Mildred nodded.

Ryan left without another word.

He moved quickly through the trees and waist-high weeds, making sure to keep some cover between himself and the direction the shots had come from, while always on the lookout for movement in the surrounding underbrush.

Ryan raised the SIG-Sauer as he neared the spot where he judged the shots to be coming from.

Mildred had been firing, as well, throwing a well-spaced sequence of rounds at the shooter to keep him from moving off.

When Mildred had fired her last shot and had to reload, Ryan focused on the forest before him, looking for any movement.

As he'd expected, the shooter used the respite to return fire in Mildred's direction, and the blast from the muzzle of his weapon allowed Ryan to spot him. It was a young man, a kid really, not much older than Jak. It was a shame to chill the teenager, but Ryan had no choice. The shooter was keeping him from rescuing Krysty and had to be eliminated.

Ryan squeezed off two shots from the SIG-Sauer, the first shot hitting the shooter in the shoulder, the second putting a tiny black spot in his left ear and blowing out a huge hole on the right side of his head.

After several minutes of blasterfire, the area was filled with an odd silence. Mildred came over the top of the outcrop and approached Ryan in a more direct route than the one he'd taken to get to the shooter.

"We've lost a few minutes," Ryan said.

"Then let's not lose any more."

They turned and ran along the trail. Ryan wasn't as good a tracker as Jak, but there seemed to be enough freshly trampled grass and weeds to indicate that the raiders had been through here recently.

He hoped he was right.

"THIS DOOR LEADS into the bunker," Melanie said.

Clarissa checked it. "Locked."

"Stand back," Jak told them.

As the women complied, the albino teenager raised the guard's pump-action blaster and leveled it on the door's locking mechanism.

The first shot mangled the door's handle.

Jak pumped another round into the blaster's chamber and fired again. This time the lock was pushed inward, twisting it inside the door and away from the frame. Jak lowered the blaster and gave the door a push with his finger.

It opened.

He shouldered the longblaster and led the two women inside, his Colt Python at the ready.

Stairs led down to a second, much heavier, door. They tried this one, and it was unlocked.

Opening the door slowly, and silently, they stepped into a dimly lit room.

The baron was in the room at the bottom of the stairs, lying on a satin-covered bed, in the company of two women. He was bound to the bed with lengths of nylon around his ankles and wrists. One of the women was sucking the baron's cock while the other one was straddling his head.

Against one of the concrete walls was a wine rack that held upward of one hundred bottles of different wines. There was a refrigerator, walk-in freezer, stove, water stores and washroom facilities. A few blasters hung from racks on the walls, but the baron wasn't going to make any of those anytime soon.

Someone turned on a light, and the two women looked up in surprise. The baron looked surprised, too, and tried for the Luger on the table next to the bed. His hand got close, but with his right arm tied to one of the bedposts, it was well out of reach.

Jak raised the Python, making sure the baron's head was in his sights.

"Don't chill him!" Melanie said, walking over the table next to the bed and picking up the Luger. "I want to do it."

Jak looked at Clarissa. She nodded, and Jak lowered the Python and holstered it.

"Get away from the bed and I'll let you live," Melanie told the two women.

The two women scrambled off the bed.

The baron said nothing.

Melanie pointed the Luger at the baron's head. "Didn't expect to find yourself in this situation, did you, Baron Fox?"

The baron shook his head.

"At my mercy." Melanie paused and traced a line on Fox's body with the barrel of the Luger, starting from his right temple and moving down past his neck, over his chest and abdomen, and finally ending up between his legs.

His erection was still there.

"You find this exciting, don't you, you sick fuck!"

The baron said nothing.

"I bet you'd love for me to shove this gun up your ass and fuck you with it, wouldn't you?"

The baron only smiled.

"I knew it," Melanie said coyly. "But not yet."

The baron's eyes closed as if the anticipation was too much to bear.

"First I want you to suck on it." She raised the blaster and brought the barrel to his mouth. "Kiss it."

The baron kissed the end of the blaster.

"Now lick it."

The baron did what he'd been told, seeming to enjoy what he was doing.

"Now put your mouth over it and suck on it."

The baron opened his mouth, and Melanie pulled the trigger.

Gore and gray matter splattered on the wall behind the bed.

The two women who had been rutting with the baron minutes before screamed.

Melanie turned to Clarissa and Jak. "I'm done. Let's get out of here."

RYAN AND MILDRED came to a rise in the terrain that gave them a good overview of the land in front of them. In the distance they could see a large body of water, which had to be Erie Lake, and which was obviously where the raiders were heading.

But the lake was still several miles away, and they hadn't caught sight of the raiders for a long while.

"Where do you think they could have gone to?" Mildred asked.

"There," Ryan answered, pointing to the southwest. He drew his extended finger back and made a fist. "Fireblast!"

He could see the members of the group clearly as they crossed a weed-infested, two-lane roadway. There were at least two dozen in the party, and in the center of them all was the unmistakable red hair of Krysty Wroth.

"We're farther away from them now than when we started," Mildred stated.

Ryan nodded. "The straggler we chilled was a good man. He led us down a different trail to give them the chance to get away."

"We'll catch them," Mildred said.

"If it's the last thing we do," Ryan vowed.

THE JOB OF CLEARING sec men from the courtyard and securing it had been completed. J.B. had two shells of questionable quality left for the 37 mm cannon, and each .50 caliber had less than a dozen rounds. They still had plenty of ammo for their blasters, but it looked as if the firefights were over for now.

J.B. had pulled the wag back to the main gate so they could cover any of the approaches and make sure anyone trying to get out wouldn't be cut down by any sec men still in the complex. They had been waiting at the gate for almost a half hour, but there was no sign of Ryan and Mildred, or Jak and Clarissa.

"It might not be my place to suggest such a thing," Doc began, "but considering that none of our friendly forces have made their presence known to us, perhaps we should make a search of the grounds."

"We could do it in a wag," Dean suggested.

"I've thought of that," J.B. said, "but I just know that as soon as I move from here they'll show up."

As if on cue, Jak, Clarissa and three women stepped through the front doors of the main building.

"Ah, right on time," Doc said.

As the group approached, J.B. kept his eyes fixed on the building. "Where's Mildred and Ryan?"

"Went after Krysty," Jak said. "Not back yet?"

J.B. shook his head. "All right, hop on back, we'll search the grounds for them."

Jak helped Clarissa and Melanie onto the wag. The two women who had been in the baron's bunker wanted on, too, but Jak shook his head.

Just then a weak voice could be heard saying a familiar name.

"Ryan!" the voice said. "Ryan Cawdor!"

J.B. turned to look at Clarissa. "Do you know this man?"

"No," she stated. "Never seen him before."

Dean was the first off the wag, his blaster drawn and pointed precisely at the center of the man's forehead.

"Where is he?" Dean shouted. "Where's my father?"

"Ryan, Ryan Cawdor."

Dean looked as if he was getting angry, thrusting the blaster hard against the man's face.

J.B. got out of the wag and ran around to where the man was standing. "How do you know the name Ryan Cawdor?"

"He shot me with his blaster," the man said, "and told me to give you a message."

"What's the message?"

The man fell to one knee. "Said you would take me with you when I told you."

J.B. looked at the others on the wag, then nodded. "All right, what's the message?"

"I was a member of a raiding party from Reichel ville. We came for breeders and one of the ones we took was the redhead. Ryan Cawdor and Mildred went after them."

"Where are they headed?"

"We came here on foot, but our boats landed at Fort Erie, on the north shore of the lake."

"How long since they went?"

"Hour, mebbe more."

"We can meet them there," Clarissa said.

J.B. stood up. "What do you mean?"

"We drove through Fort Erie on our way here," she said. "We can get there in the wag and beat Ryan and the raiders to the shore. We can be waiting for them when they arrive."

J.B. considered it.

''Do you think this jumble of bolts and metal is fit to make the journey?'' Doc asked.

J.B. looked at the wag. It had taken some hits, was leaking radiator fluid and the brakes were gone. The engine was running rough, too, but they had enough fuel and everything else seemed to still be in working order.

''Yeah,'' he announced. ''We can make it.''

''Hot pipe!'' Dean said, leading a cheer from the rest of the friends.

''Doc and Jak, get this guy onto the wag!''

''We should take them, too,'' Clarissa suggested. ''The women will come in handy.''

J.B. was silent a moment, thinking. ''Good idea.''

Jak and Doc put the raider on the back of the wag, then helped the two women on, as well.

''After you, ladies,'' Doc said, bowing his head.

The two women smiled and looked at each other. '' *'Ladies,'* he said,'' one of them echoed Doc's words.

Jak and Doc climbed up onto the back of the crowded wag.

''Hang on, everyone,'' J.B. shouted. ''It's going to be a bumpy ride.''

He put the wag in gear, and they were off.

Chapter Forty-Three

Ryan and Mildred had made up their lost ground. They were directly behind the group now, and could begin picking off members of the party the next time they stopped for rest.

And that would be coming soon, since the air had become filled with the smell and feel of a large body of water close by. They had to be within a mile of Erie Lake, and if Ryan and Mildred were going to make a try for Krysty, they'd have to do it soon.

If the raiders made it to their boats, who knew when Ryan might see her again?

"Maybe we should head straight for the shore and wait for them there," Mildred suggested. "I can take them out one at a time as they come out of the woods."

"That wouldn't stop them from hurting Krysty," Ryan countered. "We'll wait for them in their boats. If they don't turn over Krysty, we'll fill them with holes."

"The boats, or the raiders?"

"Both."

"Now, that's a plan," Mildred quipped.

Just then a twig snapped somewhere to their left. It sounded like a patrol, or perhaps a straggler had doubled back again to give the rest of them a better chance to reach their boats.

Ryan moved cautiously in the direction the sound had come from.

Mildred took his right flank, the ZKR out in front of her.

There was a second movement. The leaves on the branches of a sickly looking tree just ahead trembled as if something had passed beneath them.

And then another branch flicked unnaturally, this time closer to the two of them.

They dropped to their knees and readied for a fire-fight.

"Dad?"

The voice was familiar.

"Millie?"

Ryan looked at Mildred.

"It sounds like Dean," she whispered.

"A trick?"

"I doubt it."

"Dean!" Ryan said.

"Over here."

They made their way over to where they thought the voice was coming from, but still kept their weapons ready.

And then they came to a slight clearing and Dean was indeed there, looking well. Doc was also there, and Jak was just returning from a recce in the other direction.

"How did you get here?" Ryan asked.

"Wag," the boy said. "Only way to travel."

"Ah, my dear Ryan, and dearest Mildred, how good to see you," Doc said.

"I hate to admit it," Mildred responded, "but I'm glad to see you, too, you old bag of wind."

"Is Krysty with you?" Ryan asked. There would be plenty of time for proper greetings later.

"No," Jak answered. "Still waiting for raiders."

"Then let's get moving."

SEC CHIEF GANLEY USHERED the raiders past, counting heads as they went. There were thirty-one now, significantly more than the number that left Reichel ville a couple of days before, but of those thirty-one, ten were new blood. Not bad considering where those ten had come from, and what they'd had to do to get them.

Now it was just a simple matter of getting into their boats and paddling across the lake to the southern shore. Once they were there, they could spend a day or two recovering from their trip and getting to know the new members of the ville...especially the redhead.

Ganley would never have taken a breeder for himself, but it was testimony to the amount of respect his raiders had for him that several of them went out of their way to acquire this gift. She was beautiful—gorgeous was probably a more apt description—and she was strong willed, feisty and in excellent physical shape. Unlike the other freed slaves, the redhead didn't seem to be so enthusiastic about living in Reichel ville, but she'd come around. Once they reached the south shore, the sec chief would have the time to charm her.

She would learn to appreciate him, especially when

she saw the reception he'd get on their return to Reichel ville. Once they left camp on the south shore it would be just a single day's journey to the ville, where there would be a hero's welcome for the victorious sec chief and his band of fearless raiders.

It was all so close to him, he could taste the sweetness of the triumph on his tongue.

The boats were less than a hundred yards away.

Past that, open water.

Just then, blasterfire cut a line in the sandy shore in front of the raiders. Fountains of dirt rose up from the ground, sending them all running and jumping for cover.

The burst lasted just a few seconds.

It was followed by silence.

Then came a voice.

"You have something we want!"

Ganley looked around, wondering what it could be.

RYAN LET THE WORDS linger in the air for a few moments, then repeated them. "You have something we want!"

"What is it?" came the reply.

"The woman with the long red hair. She's one of us, and you're not going to Reichel or any other ville until you hand her over."

"Fuck you!" a voice said, different from the first.

"We captured her like the others. She's coming with us," another voice said.

Ryan was losing his patience, but he didn't want to give the task of trading for Krysty's life to anyone else. "We have two women here who want to join your group. We'll turn them over to you for one of ours."

There was silence for a long time.

"If you don't agree to this trade, we have a cannon pointed directly at your two boats. If I don't hear the word 'yes' from you in the next five seconds, the weapon'll make sure none of you'll be going home."

"One!"

"An offer they can't refuse," Mildred muttered under her breath.

"Two!"

A moment of silence.

"Three!"

"Yes! Yes!" shouted several people in the group.

Doc helped the two women and the raider down from the back of the wag.

And then Krysty appeared out of the bushes.

"Go!" Ryan told the two women and the raider.

They passed Krysty along the way.

A man stepped out onto the beach. He looked to be the raiders' leader. "We'll be on our way now."

Ryan nodded.

The rest of the raiders hurried past the man to the water. The two women were welcomed into the group and then directed toward the waiting boats.

Krysty ran toward her friends, falling into Ryan's arms, where she held on to him for a very long time.

Epilogue

They kept the cannon trained on the boats until they were out of range, and then out of sight.

The companions offered to take Clarissa and Melanie to a ville on the east coast, but they wanted to go back to the farm, where they thought they might have a chance to make something of their lives, especially now that Baron Fox was gone.

"I've got my sister back now, thanks to you," Clarissa said, riding in the back of the wag, "and I think I can look after her just as well on the farm as I can anywhere else. There's food and shelter there, medical facilities, electricity, clean water...and a lot of my friends will still be there."

"It will be a different place now," Mildred said, "but I think you'll be able to make it."

"Good fighter, smart leader," Jak said.

"You could stay with us, Jak," Clarissa suggested shyly, smiling.

The albino teenager considered the offer, then shook his head. "Had wife, child once. No more for me." He looked at the others in the wag. "Stay with friends."

"I understand," Clarissa said. "Anyway, I'll have a niece or nephew to take care of in a little while."

"I wouldn't be surprised if you have one of each to contend with," Mildred said with a smile. "Girl, you are ready to pop!"

They all laughed at that.

Overhearing the friendly banter, Krysty leaned closer to Ryan and put her head on his shoulder. "Strange, huh?"

"What is?" Ryan asked.

"Life."

"What's strange about it?"

"Well, even here in the Deathlands, where death and destruction are a part of the everyday routine, life still finds a way to carry on."

THEY SAID THEIR GOODBYES and turned the wag around. A little less than half a tank of fuel remained. It wasn't enough to get them anywhere significant, but it could at least get them someplace safe to spend the night.

They could all use a little rest before moving on to the nearest redoubt.

The Falls ville was a good bet. If nothing else, they could take the time to admire the falls. Although a mere trickle compared to what it had been in predark days, the flow of water was still pretty impressive.

J.B. shifted the wag into gear and headed out.

WHEN THE WAG was gone from the farm complex and he was sure the outlanders wouldn't be returning, Norman Bauer stepped out of the shadows of the woods across the road from the front gate.

He climbed onto the road and stood there waiting with his ledger under his arm until three sec men came out of the woods to join him.

He looked up at the sign that read Fox Farm. It had been riddled by blasterfire and the second *F* was about to fall from its perch.

He'd be changing it anyway.

Bauer ville suited the place best anyway. After all, that was the name of the man who'd really been running the complex these past few years.

TAKE 'EM FREE
2 action-packed novels plus a mystery bonus

NO RISK
NO OBLIGATION TO BUY

James Axler
Outlanders®

TALON
AND FANG

Kane finds himself thrown twenty-five years into a parallel future, a world where the mysterious Imperator has seemingly restored civilization to America. In this alternate reality, only Kane and Grant have survived, and the spilled blood has left them estranged. Yet Kane is certain that somewhere in time lies a different path to tomorrow's reality—and his obsession may give humanity their last chance to battle past and future as a sinister madman controls the secret heart of the world.

In the Outlands, the shocking truth is humanity's last hope.